UNDER THE TRIPLE SUNS

By
STANTON A. COBLENTZ

ARMCHAIR FICTION
PO Box 4369, Medford, Oregon 97504

*For more information about Armchair Books and products, visit our
website at…*

www.armchairfiction.com

Or email us at…

armchairfiction@yahoo.com

WHEN MUTUALLY ASSURED DESTRUCTION DOESN'T WORK...

When the Cosmic Blight overwhelmed Earth there was only one thing Man could do—leave Earth or die! Atomic power had made space flight possible, but in view of the scarcity of spaceships, not more than one person in thousands could save themselves. As civilization disintegrated, men thought only of their own survival. Dave Harrowell, director of the Rand Astral Project, was no exception. His spaceship, Shooting Star, lay ready on its launching site. In a state of suspended animation, Harrowell, his wife, and a third unwelcome passenger—the man partly responsible for the Cosmic Blight—blasted off into space, heading toward faraway Alpha Centauri.

However, when the Shooting Star landed, it was far from the Alpha Centauri system. Harrowell and his companions had landed on a strange planet—a planet with three suns! Where they were, they could not tell. Not that it mattered, because Earth was lost to them forever…

CAST OF CHARACTERS

DAVE HARROWELL
Tired of the feud between warring factions on Earth, and wary of the same on Mars, this brilliant space engineer blasted off into the wilds of deep space to find a new home.

EUNICE HARROWELL
Dave's beautiful, intelligent assistant—and when she married him, she knew her honeymoon would be in another star system!

EARLE W. HENESSEY
Henessey was the Chairman of the Weapon Control Board. He fought fire with fire, and the whole world lost.

THE LIL-BRO
A cheerful, beautiful race of beings, native to the planet of the triple suns. Hobbies included singing, flying, and dancing on the wind!

THE UGWUGS
These cruel taskmasters were a nocturnal race of eight-legged brutes. They captured and enslaved the Lil-bro.

GO-GLABBO
This Lil-bro was the Knowing One of his tribe. He taught Dave their language, and thought the poor human was off his nut!

LO-KLANTHO
As leader of a Lil-bro tribe, it was up to him to decide whether his people would flee from their enemy, or stand their ground...

CHAPTER ONE

THE RED SUN GLOWED HIGH in the copper heavens. It was as wide as a dozen moons and of the color and brightness of smoldering embers; and it did not end sharply as a disk should, but terminated in a nebulous crimson fringe. It shed its rays like a dying fire over a great sweep of wooded, partly hilly country, terminated in the distance by saw-toothed mountains, and marked at closer range by the loop of a cascading river and the oval of a lake, and by a cluster of shimmering beehive structures that billowed and fluttered in the breeze.

After a time, above the serrate edges of the far-off ranges, a white illumination began to spread; and the mist-banks about the peaks, ruddy before, took on a sheet-like glare as a globe that seemed of a hand's width slowly swam into sight. Although much smaller than the red sun, it dominated the scene by its intense hot flame.

The white orb was about fifteen degrees above the horizon when another light began to emerge. Of an almost unbearable brilliance, it looked not much larger than a silver dollar; but its companions seemed almost pale beside its terrible sea-blue incandescence. Evidently the blue sun and the white belonged together, like the earth and the moon; and the three luminaries, along with a Saturn-like ringed fourth that had no fire of its own but glowed red, white or blue according to the influence of the moment, circled with a gradual movement from west to east.

The last sun had just risen when some of the beehive structures began to flap as if shaken from within. And dozens of two-legged creatures streamed from circular roof passages. Each was from three to four feet tall; each had two pairs of dragonfly-shaped diaphanous wings that caught the light of the three suns in all manner of jeweled red, white and blue reflections. All were unclothed, but none gave the effect of nakedness; their bodies

5

were covered with small metal-like scales, enameled emerald and ruby and gold, amber and purple and canary and white, ever flashing and gleaming, ever changing tint in the vari-colored light. Their heads were proportionately large, and were featured by two pairs of eyes: a huge flame-hued set in front, and smaller scintillating orbs behind. Aside from this, their appearance was rather like that of children, with their milky-pale faces, minute lips and tiny noses, and translucent soft yellow hair that cast back rainbow sparks and shimmers as it streamed behind them on their swift frolics.

It seemed that they lived only to play. Their flight was like the hummingbird's: back and forth, back and forth they flew, leaping and diving in air, pirouetting, somersaulting, chasing one another in mad spirals, now hovering high above the plain with furiously beating wings, now sweeping to rest in long graceful curves, and now, after scarcely a moment's pause, looping again skyward in their never-ending round of fun.

And as they flew they sang; and their songs were such as you might expect of angel hosts: an ecstatic chorus, pure, sweet, and serene, as if in thanks for the very bliss of living.

But before they had been long in air, their music was interrupted. One, who in sheer exuberance had soared above the others, let out a startled cry, and pointed skyward with one of the two arms that entered his shoulders just in front of the forward wings. And the others instantly stopped singing; and joined him in scanning the heavens.

To a man's vision, nothing would have been visible. But these creatures had no difficulty in making out the black object descending miles above them through the purplish atmosphere.

It was shaped like a chopped-off pencil, and was not falling directly. Rather, it was moving in long spirals, zigzagging back and forth as if following a planned route; and it left a faint glowing trail, which rapidly died out behind it. By degrees it became larger, and the watchers could see that it tapered in front to a sun-reflecting point; and that something was whirring behind it with exceedingly rapid rotations.

As it drew nearer, still sweeping back and forth in tremendous spirals, the watchers' chattering and babbling gave place to panicky squeaks and screams...until all at once they rushed shrieking back into the shelter of the beehive dwellings.

Five minutes later, after a final series of wide ponderous loops, a metal cylinder sixty yards long crashed through a thicket of trees and bushes, and buried its nose in the soft soil near the lake.

*   *   *

After a time, small heads began to peep out at the round roof openings, and flame-colored eyes stared with a steady scrutiny toward the strange object near the lake. Low musical voices rang out with a tinkling bell-like quality; then rose in pitch and excitement as one of the four-winged creatures—an actual giant, a full head taller than the others—stood out boldly upon the roof. He differed from the others not only in size: his face had not the carefree smoothness of his kindred, but was wrinkled and dented with deep creases; and his wings, instead of being gauzy and transparent, were opaque and pearly, with veinings of rich green and crimson that flashed brilliantly in the rays of the triple suns.

He let out a low call, a little like the cooing of a dove; then started away in a long circling flight, followed by five or six of his kind, who trailed after him single file in a wavy line.

Reaching a point just above the metal cylinder, he began swinging about it in swift spirals, now almost touching the object, now spurting high above it, and then swooping back like a bird of prey. These maneuvers were followed exactly by all the other creatures, whose eyes never left that strange visitant from the skies. They now saw that the mechanism, of a weather-stained gray alloy, was marked by a long even row of tiny round openings, which flashed back the sunlight in the manner of glass or quartz. At the front there was a large brilliant crystalline disk, a sort of giant eye; in the rear, a huge metal blade was still revolving slowly; and midway between these objects the side of the ship—for evidently it was a ship—had been torn by a tree, leaving an open gash several yards long.

It was about this point that the winged creatures hovered. Their leader at last came down only a few arms' lengths from the aperture; and walking gracefully on his two thin long legs, slowly approached the ship, while his comrades flitted back and forth just above with warning cries.

Their cries became shriller and more excited, with the stridency of fear, as the leader peeped into the broken compartment, confirming the amazing observation he had made from above. On the floor of the damaged compartment, three silent creatures lay!

They were beings such as no one had ever seen before on this planet of the three suns. They were half as large again as the natives; but they had no wings, not even two; and their skins were of a hideous pinkish brown complexion; and they were half blind, for they possessed no eyes on the backs of their heads; and their hair was ugly brown or black, and had no light within it; and their noses and mouths were so big they looked like magnified copies of real mouths and noses. Stranger still, they had no colored scales, but were cloud-gray and dust-hued over most of their bodies, as if their natural selves were covered by something that was not themselves, though it was hard to imagine why it was worn. They were lying so still that one could scarcely say if they were asleep or dead.

The bird-leader still stared at the strangers, while his fellows began crawling all about them, like wasps about a ripe pear. Their keen eyes saw that the newcomers were not all quite the same; perhaps they were even of different species. Two of them had hair that horridly grew all over their faces and far down their chins; while the third, who was a bit smaller, had no hair on its face but abundant golden-yellow locks on the head, and had a shapelier form than the others, with some sort of an immense round swelling in front, a little below the neck.

For several minutes the observers conferred in puzzled whispers. Then the leader, with a whirring of wings, spurted into the air, and dived into the ship. As he did so, he sneezed violently—the strange mustiness and the queer chemical odors offended his nostrils. And no sooner had he sneezed than something more startling occurred.

The smallest stranger—the one with the hairless face—stirred slightly. Her lips opened, and gave out a low groan.

Instantly, screams, of terror burst from the onlookers. With a wild fluttering of wings, most of them retreated, not to pause until safe inside the beehive houses.

But the leader, after joining the others in their panicky flight, doubled back on his course, and hovered uncertainly above the broken compartment.

It may be that the wind from his fast-beating wings acted as a restorative. For the stranger gave another groan, and stirred again. Her limbs twitched; she gasped; then rolled half over. And all at once her eyelids opened. And the bird-creature found himself staring into eyes such as he had never seen before: eyes of a cerulean blue.

At this he uttered a low surprised cry, which was echoed by the stranger. There was more bewilderment than fear in her voice as she looked up with popping incredulous eyes.

Then she drew one hand across her moon-shaped brow, as if to wipe the haze from her brain; and after that, with a staggering movement, lifted herself on her elbows. As she did so, she caught a glimpse of the sky, with the huge red sun and the smaller white and blue orbs. And a shriek came from her lips.

At this the bird-leader, frightened, went winging away.

And she, as if she had forgotten this queer being, turned suddenly to her companions, who lay before her like statues. She clutched at one of them, one with long slim limbs and jet-black hair; she clung to him fervently; shook him frantically.

"Dave! Dave!" she wailed, with a hysterical note. "Dave! Wake up!"

With shaking fingers, she snatched a vial from a wall-compartment, and pressed something to his lips.

A moment later he too began to stir; groaned; then opened a pair of puzzled dark-brown eyes, and stared at the girl in the manner of one awakening from a long sleep.

"Eunice!" he muttered, still in a daze; and reached out a hand to draw her close.

CHAPTER TWO

DAVE HARROWELL FELT AS if someone had slugged him with a lead pipe. Nothing seemed quite real as he blinked beneath the glaring red-tinged blue-white light.

"Euny, where—where are we?" he gasped, as he shielded his eyes with one hand from the painful illumination. "We—we—what's happened?"

"Easy now, dearest, try to adjust yourself," she soothed, pressing soft healing fingers across his brow, which was hurting abominably. "We—we—I think we've landed."

"Landed where?" he roared, rising on one elbow, and then falling back as the effort sent a stab of agony through his head.

"I—I don't know, dearest," the girl faltered. "We—we thought we might come down somewhere, you remember."

With a painful effort of recollection, he tried to clutch at something in the past, the infinitely remote past. But at first it was no use. So he just lay there panting, in an atmosphere that seemed somehow too warm, breathing in great breaths of invigorating air as greedily as a fever victim gulping down cool water—air that seemed thicker and heavier than it should have been, and that was permeated with strange sweetish odors as from unfamiliar flowers.

And as he lay there on the floor of the spaceship, the second man began to stir. He was a few years beyond Dave's apparent twenty-eight or twenty-nine, and was shorter in build, with a slim wiry body, a slim long head dominated by a high narrow brow, an abnormally long twisted ridge of a nose, and thin lips that even in repose had a slightly cynical curve. Now, as he slowly revived, his eyes opened in the narrowest of slits, a little like cat-eyes, revealing the quizzical gray-green depths, in which bewilderment and fear mingled with inquiry. In every way he contrasted with Harrowell, whose eyes were clear as a schoolgirl's, and whose features had a craggy ruggedness but at the same time a disarming candor and openness.

The older man groaned; rolled over on one side; coughed and gasped; then, in a stunned manner, muttered, "Where—where are we, Miss—"

"Mrs. Harrowell."

"Mrs. Harrowell. I beg your pardon."

The man groaned again. "That terrible big red light up there—I can't quite make out—"

"I can't, either. It looks like we've gone further than we intended. We've missed Alpha Centauri. I don't quite figure what part of the Galaxy—"

It was those words—"Galaxy" and "Alpha Centauri"—that supplied the missing links in Dave's mind; touched a button, as it were, that restored the whole vast breathtaking series of memories. Now suddenly he could see again, just as if they were happening only now, all the stormy, explosive events that had led to his being in this space-car, with this girl and this man, heaven alone could say in what remote corner of the universe.

In a single intense moment, he lived again through tumultuous years—the most tumultuous that the earth had ever known.

Dave's thoughts went back to his early youth, when the Cosmic Blight had not yet overwhelmed the world. In those halcyon days before the turn of the twenty-first century, he had thrilled to the knowledge that atomic power had at last made space flights possible; and that expeditions to the moon, Venus and Mars had already been accomplished. Then, with all the ardor of his budding manhood he had enrolled as a student at the Pillsbury Sky Institute, and at the end of a strenuous six years had graduated with honors as a space engineer. He had immediately been placed in charge of the Rand Astral Project—in those days space engineers were few, and youth was no hindrance to recommended graduates of the world's foremost Sky School. There, under government auspices, he had labored at his post in the San Gabriel Mountains of California, toiling and planning to perfect the first ship to range beyond the Solar System.

His problem at first had seemed insuperable. The distances were so vast that even at the speed of light—a speed attainable in theory only—it would take about nine years for a round-trip to Alpha Centauri, the nearest "fixed star," while most of our other "close neighbors" would require several times as long. Actually, even if a speed a quarter of that of light could be reached—a velocity of more than forty-five thousand miles a second—it would require a man's normal "three score years and ten" to bring him to the star Sirius and back (Sirius, at 8,8 light-years, being almost next door to us in space).

Even if anyone could make such a journey, starting as a babe and returning as a graybeard, few would remain sane during the monotonous, confined years of space travel. So Dave had reasoned; and it was little wonder therefore that the problem had appeared beyond solution. Nevertheless, there was a solution—and one that came to him all in a startling flash.

If a man could pass the years of travel in a state of suspended animation, he might be able to reach his destination in full vigor, unimpaired either physically or psychically. Theoretically, he might travel for centuries as easily as for years!

At any previous time in history, this conclusion would not have been helpful. But it happened that the renowned physiologist Dr. Alonzo Salvador of San Martin University, had recently announced the discovery of a paralyzing drug, Morphedric Acid, whereby the vital processes might be interrupted for years or scores of years, after which the subject might be restored to full activity and consciousness in the manner of one awakening from a night's sleep. This could be accomplished by the injection of the Acid, which halted breathing, the heartbeat and all other bodily activities, yet left the cells in a state of unimpaired preservation. The method involved the sealing of the individual in an airtight compartment; the amount of the drug would control the term of the suspended animation, which might last as much as eighty or ninety years, though if air was admitted into the compartment at any time, the slumberer would automatically revive.

To adapt Morphedric Acid to space travel would, in Dave's judgment, be comparatively simple. The voyagers, after flying to a point well beyond the earth's atmosphere and setting the controls upon the desired course, would in any case have little or nothing to do until they approached their destination. Therefore, if they would inject themselves with the Acid in an airtight chamber, they would sleep away the long interval of the trip; and might awaken in any desired number of years. True, there would be risks involved—after all, what space explorer can escape risks? There was the possibility of collision with a meteor; there was the hazard of going too far off course and never reaching the goal; there was the menace of deadly radiations, which, however, were held off by a special ray-resisting asbestos-composite screen; and there was the peril that Morphedric Acid—which still had not been put to every test that Dr. Salvador thought desirable—would not work altogether as predicted. Beyond this, there was just the chance that the fliers would reach their goal too soon, and come crashing down in a fiery blast.

Dave thought, however that he had mostly overcome the latter difficulty by a double provision: first, the Brace Wheelan vacuum compartments and propeller that made the vessel capable of flying as an ordinary airship upon striking a planet's atmosphere; and, secondly, an automatic system of reverse engine controls. As soon as they drew near any body of strong gravitational pull, the engines would swing into reverse, slowing the ship down so that it would make a leisurely descent in a series of long, wide-swinging curves. Of course, if it happened to alight upon some world with a lethal atmosphere, or upon the fiery surface of a sun—But Dave shrugged these possibilities aside as among the inevitable dangers.

And so, in the course of his work at the Rand Astral Project, he had equipped a vessel for a flight between the suns. A sixty-yard metal cylinder, driven by the latest Pellington-Wyatt atomic engines, the *Shooting Star* was capable of carrying two or at most three passengers through the fearful outer void. Dave had looked forward to being one of the passengers; and he had hoped that his fellow passenger—the only one—would be his young technical assistant, Eunice Sancourt. He and Eunice, ardently in love, were to be married in June of the year before the century's last. And shortly after their marriage they were to ascend on their space-flight, to which the girl also looked forward enthusiastically.

And then, on the thirtieth of May, 1999, the War of the Cosmic Blight broke out, transforming Dave's plans and Eunice's as it did those of three billion other persons.

The conflict had been long expected. For more than half a century the world's nations had gradually been drifting into two great alliances, popularly known as the Reds and the Whites; and the struggle had been held off only while the leaders of the two groups were experimenting with various new weapons, rumored to be the most deadly ever known. Yet even the most lurid advance reports did not do justice to their actual powers.

Immediately upon the war's outbreak—it began with the rocket obliteration of a Mediterranean seaport—Dave had been automatically enlisted in the army of the Whites, along with all other able-bodied men between seventeen and fifty-two. However, since he was working at a "top priority" job, he was allowed to continue as head of the Rand Astral Project. But he was compelled to abandon all thought of interstellar travel, and concentrate upon "Defense Move C 35 X"—the fulfillment of an idea more than half a century old, involving the creation of an artificial satellite to revolve several hundred miles above the earth, too small to be much of a target for rocket fire, yet large enough to serve as a launching base for anti-Red missiles. As the establishment of this "island in space" was a prime objective of the White Military Command, Dave's activities were shrouded in thick secrecy. The authorities felt it necessary to rule against all employees not "strictly essential"; and among those excluded was Eunice—not that she was suspected of disloyalty, but merely that the inspectors were over-scrupulous to reduce the number of potential betrayers. She had been transferred to a government laboratory at Glendale, and her marriage to Dave had of necessity been postponed until "after the war."

In his niche in the San Gabriel Mountains, Dave learned little about the actual conflict. He did, indeed, now and then receive word of the destruction of a city by old-fashioned methods such as jet bombers and plutonium and hydrogen explosions; the year 2000 had not drawn to a close before he knew of the elimination of Paris, Moscow, Tokyo, Detroit, Buenos Aires and Hong Kong as centers of population, along with the annihilation of thousands of smaller towns and cities and the devastation of huge once-productive empires. Nevertheless, all this was only what had been expected. It was not until the dawn of 2001 that the real destroyer appeared.

Rumors had occasionally announced the discovery of a "cosmic weapon," but as the most rigid secrecy had been maintained, even scientists could only hazard wild guesses as to its nature. At the moment of its appearance, however, it was unspectacular enough. It was in the nature of a bomb, a little like the conventional explosives. When it burst, it seemed to give out little more than a sizzling white heat; not the least of its diabolical qualities was that its actual potency was due to invisible rays. From all that Dave could make out—and, like nearly everyone, he could only conjecture—the bomb-makers had confirmed the old suspicion that the cosmic rays were produced by atomic fission in the sun and stars. They had been able to duplicate those rays in their own atomic piles; and had confined the ray-producing substances in the bombs, which, upon exploding, showered forth their radioactive poison for an indefinite period. Without the full sheltering blanket of the atmosphere—if was this alone that had prevented the cosmic rays from exterminating human life—the beams would kill at hundreds of yards, would kill by a lingering, bone-withering, blood-drying process.

This, however, was not the worst. Since the new weapons were limited in range, it was not at first supposed that they would be nearly as devastating as the old-time atomic bombs. But the optimists were reckoning without the chain reaction. Every object, every spot of soil touched by the rays was contaminated; its atoms were subject to a little understood process of fission that engendered new rays of the same type; and these in turn produced others, in a never-ending succession. Once a single ray-bomb had been released, the effects were worse than those of Pandora's mythical box. The brood of troubles, having been uncorked, could never be checked! The lethal area would spread from the original focus in a slowly widening circle, consuming first acres each day but eventually whole square miles—square miles in which no man or beast could venture without facing certain death.

In the beginning, it appeared, no one had fully realized the facts. Amid the destruction of wartime, the Reds had used the weapon before making the proper tests; and the Whites, who had been developing the same instrument but knew little of its potentialities, hastily hurled their own ray-bombs lest they be caught at a disadvantage. This was due, Dave thought in bitter accusation, to the three-man secret Weapon Control Board, which dictatorially fixed White policy. Dave's only excuse for the leaders of both sides was that, "They knew not what they did"; their scientists had not properly warned them, or else they had not the imagination to take the warnings to heart. In any case tens of thousands of the bombs had been dropped by both factions before the world began to shake itself free of its hysteria sufficiently to realize what it had done to itself.

But when that moment of clear-seeing arrived, it was already too late. In America, Asia, Europe, Africa and Australia the blight was covering millions of square miles; borne on the tides, it had reached the islands of the Pacific and Indian Oceans; it had been reported from regions so remote as Greenland, Spitsbergen, and Antarctica. Great cities had been attacked, and their inhabitants had fled in long bedraggled streams; wide once-fertile valleys lay brown and deserted, every bush and grass blade shriveled; whole states and provinces were dotted with abandoned villages and silent mills, their furnaces cold before the destroyer. Of a common will, men forsook the war against one another to wage the fight against the enemy they themselves had let loose—but even the most hopeful could do little except to pray. Scientists were baffled; they did not know how to check the devourer in a single case. Within a year or two at most, they acknowledged, the earth would be a dead world; only in the depths of the sea, if even there, would life survive.

Consequently, the one hope for any man was to leave the earth—to emigrate to some other planet. But in view of the scarcity of space accommodations, not more than one person in several hundred thousands could hope to save himself. The Reds, according to rumor, were rescuing their high officials by means of a shuttle service to Mars, the only planet in the Solar System that astronomers judged capable of preserving the human race. (Venus was ruled out because its steamy atmosphere and super-tropical temperatures made it impossible for men to survive there without artificial refrigeration). It was said that most of the White space-cars were also flying to Mars, and that dangerous disputes as to land ownership were arising between the Reds and the Whites.

As the world gradually disintegrated, and men began to follow the law of "each for each," Dave's first concern was to save Eunice and himself. The spaceship *Shooting Star,* which had been built under his direction and whose secrets he alone understood, lay in wait at the launching platform of the Rand Project; it had been provided long before with compressed food, medicine and other supplies, including Morphedric Acid; and it awaited only Dave's word to launch it into space. But where should it go? Of course, it might be aimed at Mars; but Dave wished no further involvements in the feuds of the Reds and the

Whites; and, besides, he had always looked forward to the astral adventure. It was not hard to pick Alpha Centauri as his goal; it was the nearest of the stars, a mere four and a half light-years away; the brightest member of the group (it was really a triple star, with one widely separated member) was almost a duplicate of the sun; and possibly therefore it was surrounded by planets, at least one of which might resemble the earth. At a speed approaching one fifth that of light, the maximum attainable by the *Shooting Star,* it might be possible to make the flight in a little under twenty-five years.

Dave waited until there seemed not even a forlorn last chance that the world could save itself. And then he wondered whether he had waited too long. Radio dispatches had told of armed riots at many spaceports, in which frantic refugees had battled to crowd aboard departing Mars-bound ships. Thus far the spaceport of the Rand Project had been immune, since its very existence had been known only to high government officials; even its employees had not realized that the launching platform contained more than the dummy of a ship. Nevertheless, there was no telling just when the facts would leak out.

Therefore Dave had felt more than vaguely uneasy as he stepped into his coupe, and started down to Glendale for Eunice. The trip was a nightmare: every few miles he ran against a roadblock, with the telltale sign: "DETOUR: ROAD AHEAD PERILOUS." Well knowing just why the road was perilous (for the Cosmic Blight had not spared Southern California, any more than it had spared most regions), Dave would crawl along some back lane amid a stream of cars crowded with families and household possessions; and, after circling twenty miles, might find himself two miles nearer his destination. He noticed the disintegrated state of the countryside: the large number of open, abandoned houses; the looted stores and shops; the crops unharvested in the fields and orchards—fields and orchards sometimes already overspread by an ominous withering brown.

But somehow he did reach Glendale. Somehow he found Eunice, who clung to him tearfully, hysterically, as eager as he to escape into space. Somehow they managed to find a Justice of the Peace to perform the marriage ceremony; somehow they drove through the maze of detours and returned to the site of the Rand Project. No, thank heaven; the place was not invaded by a mad mob of would-be space voyagers. Nevertheless, he and Eunice were not to begin their flight without incident.

They had reached the landing platform, and stood before the little slit of a door that gave admittance to the gray cylindrical hulk of the spaceship. But before they could enter, before they could even fling the door open a figure stole toward them out of the shadows of a pile of packing cases. The form was that of a small. slim man; he had a high narrow brow, a long twisted nose that seemed vaguely familiar, and lips that curled in a sort of half-amused cynical enjoyment.

"Well, Harrowell!" he exclaimed, flinging out a small, carefully manicured hand. "I've been waiting for you!"

"For me?"

Dave drew back with an almost instinctive dislike; he could guess the intruder's purpose.

"Yes, for you, Harrowell. I realize you don't know me; but these are days when we can't stand on formalities. The fact is I'm faced with an urgent personal necessity—the need of saving my life. You can save it by taking me with you. That's why I'm here."

"Who the deuce are you?" gasped Dave.

"Me—well, in these days what matter who a man is?" The stranger shrugged, then went on with that faint irony which was as evident in his tones as in his looks. "If you have to give me a name, you can call me John Smith."

"I can call you that, knowing I might as well call you Christopher Columbus!" rasped Dave, who shrank before visions of an unwelcome third on his flight with Eunice.

"The spaceship—well, it's only built for two," he countered, weakly.

"Yes, for normal conditions. However, the plans of the Space Authority actually provide for an emergency capacity of three."

"What the heck do you know about the plans of the Space Authority?"

Disregarding this question, Smith went on, with a slightly amused, slightly sardonic note.

"You know, I hate dreadfully to inconvenience you people. If the official Mars transport hadn't been overcrowded, leaving me without a seat at the last moment—"There was something about the man's manner that awed Dave just a little. He clearly knew more than he admitted, clearly had inside information.

With a courteous wave of one hand, Smith turned to Eunice.

"Pardon, Miss, but I'll try not to be a burden to you. After all, it wouldn't be a pleasant thought to take away with you—that you might have saved a life, but didn't."

Eunice, who felt a faint repugnance, faltered. "But we—we don't know who you are."

"In times like these, Miss, isn't it enough that we're all human beings together?"

The stranger knew how to put just the right degree of persuasion into his voice. He was manifestly an educated man; and the gray-green light looking out from his little slits of eyes showed an alert intelligence. Besides, Dave reflected, it might be valuable to have another man at his side in the unknown adventures ahead. But the clinching argument, of course, was that they simply could not let the fellow stay behind to die when by a little effort they could save his life.

"Oh, all right," Dave heard himself conceding. "We're headed for the wilds of space, and I don't guarantee that any of us will come through alive. Hop aboard, Mr. Smith!"

CHAPTER THREE

HOW MANY YEARS AGO HAD that conversation taken place? Surely more than twenty-five, probably fifty, possibly seventy-five, eighty or ninety! As Eunice had remarked, they seemed to have missed Alpha Centauri altogether; an error of a fraction of one per cent in aiming would have taken them wide of their mark. But how could they have made even that much of an error? Perhaps the pull of some unknown dark body had drawn them off their course. Or perhaps, in the haste of their preparations, they had not allowed for such obvious details as the motion of the earth and the movement of the system of Alpha Centauri through space. It was just such elementary oversights that sometimes upset the most intricately laid plans!

Even so, they had gauged their Morphedric injections so that they would awaken in a little more than twenty-four years. And, clearly, they had not awakened within that time. Had they overdosed themselves? No! Dave remembered how carefully he had measured the amounts. But there had evidently been some factor they had overlooked. Probably it was that under the artificial flight conditions, with subnormal temperatures and pressures, the drug was much slower-acting than in the laboratory. In any case, they had remained asleep while they winged their way far past Alpha Centauri—how far, Dave could not even guess. All that he knew was that he could identify no near red-white-and-blue stellar system. Could it be that they had slept for centuries, traveling scores of light-years before being caught in a planet's gravitational pull? Possibly on earth—that is, if any men had been left on earth—this would now be the year 2500, or even 3000!

"Thank God," he heard himself saying, "for the retarding mechanism, which slowed us down automatically and brought us to a safe halt. Lucky, too, that the ship was damaged just enough to let in the air, oxygen being the best antidote for Morphedric Acid."

And then suddenly his thoughts turned to more human matters.

"How you feeling, dearest?" he asked, rising on one elbow and looking earnestly at Eunice, who was standing before him uncertainly.

"Oh, all right, Dave. Just like somebody's turned me topsy-turvy and run a threshing-machine through my head. But the head's gradually clearing. I'll be tiptop in a minute."

"Wish I could share your optimism, Miss—I mean, Mrs. Harrowell," said the second man, as, shading his eyes, he rose to a sitting posture. "I feel—well, I feel like someone's been trying to make mincemeat of me, and pretty much succeeded. That awful red light up there—I've never seen anything like it."

The red sun was, in fact, staring straight through the open side of the ship, as if wishing to spy upon the party with its monstrous crimson eye.

"Soon as we can pull ourselves together," proposed Dave, "I suggest trying to get out of here for a little exploring."

"Well, maybe—if we have to," sighed the other man. "Way I feel now, I'd rather play Rip Van Winkle."

Automatically he took out his watch, winding it from ancient habit.

"Afraid that won't do you much good up here," laughed Dave.

But at the same time he noted the initials on the fob.

"E. W. H.," he read, slowly. "Humph. Funny initials for John Smith."

Dave could see the sarcastic twinkle beneath the slits of the gray-green eyes.

"Well, folks, since you've guessed it, I might as well own the truth. After all, there's nothing like frankness among friends. John Smith, of course, was only a blind. Maybe, though, you've heard of Earle W. Henessey?"

Dave uttered a low dismayed gasp, Eunice's lips opened wide, and she started back in half-unconscious horror. This, then, was why there had been something vaguely familiar about the man! This was why he had known about the *Shooting Star,* even to the detail of its emergency capacity! Earle W. Henessey, of course, had been the central figure of the secret Weapon Control Board, Dave had often seen his picture in the papers; had seen him, too, on the television screen. And he loathed him with all the intensity of loathing that one reserved for the man who, more than any other among the Whites, had been responsible for releasing the fatal ray-bomb. True, he had had the excuse that the Reds had used it first; but if instead of replying in kind, he had given himself to finding an antidote, the Blight might have been checked before it had exterminated the human race. Knowing that this was the man who had shared his accommodations—his probable partner for the rest of his life— Dave shuddered like one who finds that he has been bedmate to a cobra.

Still with the same sarcastic glint in his eyes, Henessey let out a low whistle.

"Suppose we've got such things as cigarettes round here?"

Dave fumbled at a wall compartment. "There's a supply— not unlimited," he said, as he drew out a hermetically sealed pack and a carton of matches.

The match flamed with exceptional vigor, and the end of the cigarette glowed with unexpected brightness.

"I'll be—look at that!" Dave pointed out. "The oxygen content of the atmosphere must be pretty high—maybe fifty or even a hundred percent more than on earth."

As soon as he was puffing away, Henessey seemed much more composed.

"Well, folks, I see you're not exactly gratified by the company," he remarked, in an ironic drawl. "I had just a suspicion you wouldn't be, which was why I thought it best to be John Smith for a time. There's been a prejudice against me down on earth. That was the reason, if you want to know, why they wouldn't let me on any of the Mars transports, when other officials were slinking aboard like rats off a burning ship. But what have I done to make people so prejudiced? What have I done, let me ask you?"

"Well, after all, it's a few years late to go into that," countered Dave.

"But what have I done except my duty? I want you to get this straight, folks, because we're likely to be together quite a while, and might as well be pals. What would you have done if you'd had the last say and the Reds were using the ray-bombs?"

The other two remained silent.

"You can imagine what a row it would have kicked up if I'd let the Reds get away with a thing like that and couldn't answer in kind. Why, it would have been as much as my skin was worth. I can't tell you how I hated to let that fiendish bomb loose, particularly as our experiments were still in the half-baked stage. But if I'd held back, what would have happened? I'd have been kicked out feet first, and my successor would have used the bomb. So what would it have gained anyone? I can understand your feelings, though. You had to have a scapegoat. And I was very conveniently on the spot."

Seeing the earnestness of Henessey's plea, the burning seriousness that had replaced the satiric amusement in the gray-green eyes, Dave for the first time felt a touch of sympathy. After all, his position had been hard. Most other men—yes, even Dave himself—might have done no better than the Chairman of the Weapon Control Board.

"Well, I'm not setting myself up as a judge and jury," he conceded. "All that has happened so far away and long ago. We're on a new world now. So let the past be the past. Here, Henessey, shake! We've got to go on—together."

As the two men joined hands in a hearty clasp, the ex-official turned toward Eunice.

"Hope that goes for you too, Mrs. Harrowell."

The girl hesitated ever so briefly. "Yes, I—I'll try not to hold any prejudices. We've all got to take each other as human beings, and forget the past."

"Well, I'm glad to know, Ma'am, you're as sensible as you're pretty," he answered, waving one hand in a courtier's attempt at gallantry. "Say! Did you see that?"

For the barest fraction of a second a four-winged creature, with flaming eyes and pearly wings veined with green and crimson, hovered in the air just beyond the break in the vessel's side. But almost instantly it darted away again.

"Tell me, am I suffering from hallucinations? Or have we come to heaven—or hell?" demanded Henessey. And then, peering out of the aperture, "God Almighty! There's a whole flock of them!"

"I—I saw them before," stammered Eunice, as she joined the others in staring out. "But I—I thought maybe I was only dreaming."

"Maybe we're all only dreaming, Ma'am."

"Anyhow, let's get out and look around a bit," proposed Dave. "We won't go far; we'll have to make the ship our base. But better take a few knickknacks, just in case anyone gets hungry."

He unlocked a little vault, wherein food was preserved in airtight containers; and distributed a few biscuits and chocolate bars.

"Me—I'm going to take this trusty little 38," decided Henessey, as, opening his traveling case, he snapped out an automatic pistol and a clip of cartridges.

Eunice gave a low horrified gasp. "But you wouldn't use that!"

"On a strange planet, my dear lady, never can tell what you'll have to use."

"But those lovely flying creatures—they look so harmless."

"If they stay harmless, believe me I won't waste any shots."

"As for me," decided Dave, taking up a clasp-knife and a long slender steel cane, "I'll confine myself to these. The cane'll come in useful if we meet any snakes or other dangerous animals. But I agree with Eunice—those bird-things don't look menacing."

Without much difficulty, the three climbed out over the jagged edge of the broken compartment. To their surprise, they could move with unexampled agility, taking three steps with as much ease as a former two. At first, however, they had trouble to control their movements, being inclined to step higher and stride further than they had intended.

"Say, what's this?" whistled Henessey. "Am I regaining my lost youth?"

"Better than that," explained Dave. "It looks like gravity on this planet is a lot weaker than on earth—even though the atmosphere seems denser than on earth at sea level. That's why those big birds—if that's what they are—are able to fly so well."

"Lordy, but this glare is cruel!" protested Henessey, as he shielded his eyes from the triple suns. "If you'll excuse me, I'm going back for some goggles."

Within a few minutes, all three had equipped themselves with amber glasses, in addition to green visors, for the eyes of all had begun to water and smart after a brief exposure to the intense illumination: Fortunately, in equipping the spaceship, Dave had foreseen just this possibility.

For a short while the explorers pushed their way through the swath of broken trees and bushes that marked the spaceship's path. They had time only for casual observation but did note that many of the bushes had sword-shaped blue-green leaves longer than a man's arm, while some of the trees were featured by javelin-like thorny dead limbs, which bristled from their lower portions like field-guns, seemingly as hard as steel. Evidently it was one of these that had ripped the gash in the *Shooting Star.*

Just beyond the thickets, they entered a sloping meadow, crossed by small streams, and covered with a stringy grayish plant, whose flower-bells were transparent as glass, and shimmered like living rainbows according to the way in which they caught the light of the three suns. Upon the travelers' approach, these blossoms would close with a plop, and a brown spiny husk would envelop them, to be withdrawn after the disturbing footsteps had left.

Like the flower petals, the beehive structures in the distance glimmered with all the hues of the spectrum, while fluttering faintly in the breeze. Above the roofs suddenly a flight of four-winged creatures appeared, at least a score of them, circling swiftly toward the three strangers, while their dragonfly pinions flashed back the light in glittering red, white and blue. And as they whirled and swung above, they shrilled, cooed and babbled to one another in tones no more menacing than the cries of doves. One of them, swooping low, pointed to the earthlings' goggles and visors, and let out a roar suspiciously like laughter; another plunged down for the stub of a cigarette that Henessey had discarded, and after examining it in evident bewilderment, bore it away as a prize; still others motioned with shouts of amusement to the eyeless backs of the visitors' heads, the clothing of their arms and legs, their odd footwear, their wingless shoulders, and their beards, which seemed to strike them as particularly funny.

"Well," Dave remarked, "I guess they feel about like a lot of kids at a circus parade."

"Yes, and we're the five-legged calves or the performing kangaroos," laughed Eunice.

"Just the same," grimly added Henessey, tapping at the holster of his pistol, "I'm keeping careful guard on this."

At that moment the large pearly-winged bird-creature settled on the ground just before them. They saw the milky pale face, with the translucent flowing yellow hair that cast rainbow sparks; they noticed how the creature cocked its head in all directions, showing now the flame-colored front eyes, and now the smaller scintillating pair behind. They also observed how it was lifting its diminutive seven-fingered hands, and pointing—pointing toward the beehive structures, while a low musical tinkling came from between its lips.

"By George," interpreted Dave, "it's inviting us to its home!"

CHAPTER FOUR

"HOW DO YOU KNOW IT isn't just a ruse? A trick to trap us?" asked Henessey, taking out his pistol.

"I don't see why!" argued Eunice. "Why should they want to trap us?"

"Well, I've found that an inch of caution is worth a yard of regrets," Henessey remarked, darkly.

"But on the face of things, what have we to fear?" reasoned Dave. "Those creatures haven't any fangs, claws or talons. They don't carry anything that even looks like a weapon. Isn't it just possible that things in this world are so peaceful that it doesn't enter their heads to be unfriendly?"

"Well, maybe, maybe. But I'd advise you to keep close hold on your cane—and your knife," counseled Henessey.

While Henessey dragged behind, muttering to himself, Dave and Eunice followed the four-winged leader, who flew excitedly overhead, calling to them in his melodious voice. As they drew near the beehive dwellings, half a dozen more of the winged creatures joined them, and began to wheel above with cries of pleasurable agitation. To Eunice and Dave, it seemed that the creatures were urging them on, impatient at their crawling pace.

At last they stood before one of the beehive structures.

It was large, larger than they had thought; and would have covered a quarter of the average city block. Its sides were of some silken material, with a glossy sheen that changed color with every shift of the wind, now opalescent as a seashell, now rosy, now lavender, now sky-blue, now streaked with shifting veins of emerald, topaz, amethyst, sapphire, and palest lemon and lilac. It was still billowing in the breeze, but seemed hardly more substantial than a cloud.

The leader, pirouetting near an opening fifty yards above, seemed half to expect his visitors to climb and enter. But suddenly, as if realizing that they were cripples who could not fly, he plunged down and pulled a little flap near the ground, opening a space barely large enough to admit them. And meanwhile he uttered a series of quick chirping cries, which seemed to say, "Enter! Enter!"

"Not for me!" grumbled Henessey.

But Dave, touching the wall, found that it was soft as satin. It was held in place, as he saw upon glancing inside, upon a cleverly woven wicker framework, proving the inhabitants to be not unskilled with their hands.

"As a trap, this couldn't hold us one minute!" he answered Henessey's objections. "Come on, Eunice! I'm going to have a peek in here!"

The light within was dim but sufficient, having passed through the semi-translucent walls as through a veil. The whole interior, which had a fragrance as of new mown grass, formed but a single chamber. And the whole at first, to Dave's unaccustomed eyes, appeared empty. But soon he made out a series of swinging perches, about a hundred feet above, on which fifteen or twenty of the flying creatures were resting. These immediately dashed down in a rustling, fluttering flock, and began darting about the newcomers with cries of glee. They were all quite small, some measuring hardly more than a foot— evidently the children of the hive! And like children—amiable, mischievous children, who do not know what it is to be afraid— they flitted all about the visitors and even settled on their heads and shoulders. One of them pecked curiously at Dave's goggles with his small talon-like hands; a second pulled the visor off his head; still others jerked at his shirt and jabbed playfully at his nose; and one fumbled at his shoestrings as if he could not imagine what these might be. And all meanwhile let out riotous cries, like ten-year-olds before the monkey cage at the zoo.

While the visitors were protesting these attentions, the leader and several other adults entered, and drove the youngsters off with, sharp, rebuking cries. At the same time, they began to point their minute noses upward, and to sniff peculiarly; and their milk-white faces were distorted with wry grimaces. They cast accusing glances at the newcomers; and then hurriedly opened dozens of little flaps throughout the building, admitting the air and light.

"Goodness!" exclaimed Eunice. "Do we smell that bad?"

"I guess it's just the human odor," decided Dave. "Something they're not used to."

And then, peering out through an open flap at Henessey, who had still refused to enter, "Come on in! Can't you see, we're not dead yet!"

"Just the same, I don't think it's a bad idea to have a guard posted out here," flashed back Henessey.

And he began pacing back and forth as if on sentry duty. "Well, what are we to do now?" asked Eunice, as she and Dave squatted together on the floor, which was covered with the same silken substance as the walls. "Do you know I'm getting hungry?"

"Maybe our hosts will bring us something to eat," surmised Dave.

But no… What they did was something much stranger.

After flapping about in all sorts of excited antics, the leader and his followers rushed away, to return after a minute with gourd-like vessels, filled with sparkling clear water. These they set down before their visitors, with ceremonious gestures.

"Glory!" exclaimed Dave. "They seem to be saying, 'Feast, good people, and be merry! '"

"Well, my throat's pretty dry. I could stand a drink," declared Eunice, as she lifted one of the containers to her lips… "It's not as cool as I'd like, but it's good enough water, all right."

Shrieks of mirth burst from the onlookers in such a chorus that the walls shook. Then one of them, as if wishing to demonstrate how to drink water:, fluttered above one of the gourd-like vessels, flicked out a long tongue a little like a hummingbird's, let it suck up a few drops, and flitted away.

"I can see," remarked Dave, with a rueful smile, "that we've got a few things to learn."

"What I'd like to know," reflected Eunice, "is why it doesn't seem to occur to them we might be hungry. Here, some chocolate?"

But what a commotion as she and Dave began to munch at a chocolate bar! It was not only the youth of the tribe that came rushing back with shouts and screams of merriment; the elders too all flocked about the guests, with shrill cries of astonishment, amusement and disgust. It was as if they had never seen anyone eat before!

Then suddenly Dave made a peculiar observation. "Do you know, Euny," he pointed out, as soon as the din had begun to die down, "there isn't one darned bit of food about the place—

which is queer if this is where the natives live. More than that, there isn't any sign of any former meal—no seeds, shells or crumbs of any kind, and no eating or cooking utensil. When you consider all that, along with their surprise at the chocolate—"

"And here's another thing," Eunice added. "When they open those wee mouths of theirs, I don't see any teeth."

"Neither do I. Maybe, of course, they take only liquid food. However, birds on earth don't have teeth. But another idea comes to me. It may sound fantastic, but scientifically it's not impossible. What if they don't require anything but air and water?"

"Gracious! How can that be?"

"Well, we know that's almost the case with plants on earth. By means of the green substance, the chlorophyll, they make carbohydrates out of air and water, with the aid of sunlight, though they must take nitrogen and other elements out of the soil. On this planet, the animals may have the food-manufacturing properties of plants. This may be because chemical reactions not known on earth are stimulated by the light of the three suns. Also, the atmosphere may have ingredients not found in our own air; its nitrogen may be capable of being assimilated directly. There's even the possibility of a different chemistry than among earth-animals. But the point I'm driving at is that no One on this world may have to eat. That would account for the surprise of those bird-creatures to see us gnawing at the chocolate."

"Well, if that's true," meditated Eunice, "think what a wonderful planet this would be! I've often noticed that nine tenths of man's troubles came from the need to fill his stomach. If no one had to fight for bread—if everything came as naturally as the air—then there wouldn't have to be any struggling or fighting. Everyone would be free, and natural—and secure!"

"Yes, and that may be why these bird-people receive us so graciously, and don't suspect any wrong. Maybe they've never known any wrong in all their lives."

"Well, folks, that's what you think," contributed Henessey, who had been listening in on the conversation from just outside the flap. "Then why is it that that big bird—the leader, I guess—has such a creased face, like someone with a lot of worrying to do?"

Neither Dave nor Eunice could suggest an answer.

CHAPTER FIVE

FOR SIX DAYS THE VISITORS remained among the bird-people—or so at least Henessey estimated, reporting that his watch had registered twelve full revolutions. Days in the earthly sense, however, did not exist, since one or more of the three suns were in the heavens more than four fifths of the time. The movement of these suns, from rising to rising, required about thirty-two hours; and the intervals of darkness lasted less than six hours. Even so, the darkness was far from complete; three dazzling planets, surpassing Venus at her most brilliant as seen from the earth, shone in various parts of the sky; and two moons were visible, one of the apparent size of an orange, and the other somewhat larger than our own moon. Both were near their full, and each had a deep band of red at one side, and a corresponding band of bluish white opposite, while a zone of blended red, white and blue intervened—due to the way in which these satellites reflected the rays of the three suns. In addition, the ringed dead sun, larger than either of the moons and colored exactly like them (even the rings were red, white and blue) shone in the eastern sky for an hour or two before setting.

"What I hope and pray," remarked Dave, when he first saw this weird sight, "is that we can have complete blackness, so as to get a better idea of the constellations."

But after the ringed sun had set, the sky was discolored with no more than the ghostliest red and blue, and thousands of stars were visible (though fewer than on a clear night on earth). At these the wanderers gazed long and earnestly.

"Lord help me, I used to think I knew some astronomy," Dave broke the silence. "But I'm a jumping ape if I can recognize one of those constellations."

"Nor I," admitted Eunice. "Of course dear we've travelled trillions of miles."

"Even so, I didn't think a few light-years would put everything so completely askew," pondered Dave. "There would be some dislocations, of course, but considering that many of the stars are hundreds, even thousands of light-years away—

"Then you don't know where our Own little earth happens to be?" asked Henessey.

"Haven't the haziest idea. Our sun may be one of those glistening dots up there, but to save my life I couldn't guess which. Looks like we've gone a whale of a ways further than we expected."

For a moment no one spoke. The stars, in their unfamiliar arrangements, peered down upon three small beings suddenly smitten with a sense of their loneliness, their utter homelessness, the sense of being lost beyond escape amid measureless immensities.

"Maybe we'll never know," sighed Eunice. "But maybe it doesn't matter, either. We'll just simply have to start a new life, and forget the old."

"Yes, start a new life, and forget the old," the others echoed.

It seemed that the bird-people were doing their best to launch the visitors on their new life. As the days passed, they did nothing to justify Henessey's suspicions; their leader, in fact, seemed to make it his chief business to take the newcomers on tours of inspection. Flying above them with the fluttering solicitude of a mother hen, and calling out in his tinkling musical voice, he took pride in showing them just how his people lived. He led them to the brooding-house, a beehive structure where jet-black eggs of the size and shape of small melons lay on high warm platforms. He took them to the nursery, where chirruping adult guardians watched over jelly-like waddling creatures who had not learned to fly: he introduced them to the Singing Meadows, where an instructress was training a score of youths in the art of speaking melodiously and of singing; and led them to the Dancing Airways, where those same youths were being taught the principles of harmonious movement. And after that, the guide escorted his charges to the fields and woods near the lake, where they saw the adults in typical occupations.

At least, they judged that these were typical occupations. Some, in great choruses, were singing with voices that Eunice compared to the chanting of angels. Others engaged in aerial dances that seemed to continue for hours. Still others spoke to small gatherings in tones not quite like song and yet so sweet-sounding that they might have been poetry. And others were dabbing great splashes of color upon a board-like material— making paintings of a kind, though the observers could not decide just what any of them represented.

"Strange thing," Henessey remarked, "I've never seen one of those folks doing a lick of real work."

"Maybe they can live without working," surmised Eunice.

"Well, if they don't have to get any food," Dave reasoned, "what is there to work for?"

"Clothes," suggested Eunice.

"But they don't wear any clothes."

"They must have worked to build their houses," Henessey concluded. "But maybe that was long ago, and they've sort of gotten out of the habit."

Truly, the life of the bird-people appeared as nearly carefree and ideal as could be imagined. And yet the visitors, during their second night on the planet, found cause to wonder.

According to their habit they were passing the few hours of darkness in the spaceship, which offered fairly comfortable if somewhat cramped accommodations. But they could not sleep; the spectacle of the night skies held them fascinated. They were absorbed in observing a red-and-blue comet rising in the west, when Eunice gave a low excited cry, and pointed toward the beehive houses. A crowd of swift flying things were flocking above them, and disappeared high in air. They were not proceeding with the swinging, playful movements usual among the bird-people; they streamed ahead in a straight, hurried line, like creatures that flee some peril.

"Good Lord! What under heaven are they scared of?" questioned Dave, with a low whistle.

"Well, I've always told you folks, I've suspected those birds from the first—"

"Oh, nonsense, Mr. Henessey," protested a girl's voice.

"Just because something has frightened them, it doesn't follow you've anything to suspect."

Until the sky was crimsoned by the red sun, the watchers remained at their station. And, just at sunrise, they saw the winged things returning in a long procession.

But nothing about them seemed changed a little later in the day. They flew as gaily, they sang as sweetly, they escorted the visitors as solicitously as ever; and never did the latter wish more fervently to know the native language, so as to ask about the night's event.

One possible clue, however, they did have—or was it a clue? On the soft soil near the lake, they noticed a series of large footprints, apparently newly made. A little bigger than a man's palm, these were featured by the indentations of seven hooked toes or claws. Judging from the depth to which the impressions had sunk, the creature was either very heavy, or had approached very slowly, in the manner of a carnivore stalking its prey.

"Looks to me like maybe those bird-folk had good reason to fly away," decided Dave.

Henessey cast a doubtful glance into a clump of purple-tasseled cane-like reeds near the water's edge; and then, as if to reassure himself, felt for his pistol.

"You can say what you want, I'm going to keep close watch over this," he muttered, "I wish, though, it was a good stout elephant rifle."

Eunice shuddered, and drew close to Dave as if for protection.

"The animal that made the tracks," she pointed out, "why, we don't know if it's any more dangerous than a cow."

"Maybe not," mumbled Henessey. "But we'd better keep in the open."

As the days passed, a more pressing problem filled their minds. Their supplies would not hold out indefinitely, even though the spaceship contained food enough for several months; and they not only foresaw the exhaustion of their store, but feared that meanwhile they would not remain healthy on food that lacked essential bulk and vitamins. Yet the bird-people still showed no sign of realizing their need. Hence they began foraging about on their own account.

They first experimented with a chrome-yellow egg-shaped nut, which looked as if it might be nutritious, and indeed was almost palatable, but after a time invariably produced nausea. Then they tried some sea-blue clustered fruits, shaped a little like peapods; but these, though sweet to the taste, were so astringent they could hardly be eaten. Their next attempt was with a big bulbous root a little like a turnip, but striped black and white like a zebra; and this might partly have solved their problem had two of the bird-people not chanced to be looking on. Both of them, flying above on flapping wings, protested with loud squawks when Dave uprooted the plant; and their cries rose to a pandemonium that brought out half the community when he sliced the root into three pieces with his knife and divided the remains among his companions and himself. Although it had an appetizing flavor a little like new-baked bread, none of them could get more than a bite, since the natives flew about them with such shrill objections that it was impossible to eat.

"Maybe it's some sort of sacred plant," Dave suggested.

"Maybe all plants on this world are considered sacred," Eunice added.

"Yes, and maybe the people are just plain nuts," Henessey grumbled, with a disgusted sniff.

But their next attempt was destined to be even more ill-fated. Early one morning, just as they were returning to the beehive community, they heard a rustling in a blue-green thicket; and a pair of flaming orange eyes looked out from amid the sinuous ribbons of leaves. With automatic swiftness, Henessey whipped out his pistol. There came a flash, a bang, a shriek that sounded strangely human; and a Crumpled form lay amid the shrubbery.

The victim proved to be an eight-legged, four-eyed thing about as large as a jackrabbit; covered with scales instead of fur, and with an exceedingly small toothless mouth. It was without claws or other means of self-defense, and looked harmless as a puppy.

With a triumphant shout, Henessey held up the carcass, which was dripping a substance that might have been blood, had it not been for its yellow-green color.

"Come on, folks! Let's build a fire! Now we can eat!"

As the wanderers carried matches, and as there was plenty of dead wood lying all about, as well as rock for a fireplace. It was not long before the flames were blazing beneath the spitted beast.

Its flesh, they found, was yellow-green like its blood; but was tender, and as delicious as roast chicken. Dave and Eunice had forgotten their faint scruples at taking the creature's life, and were chewing away hungrily, when all at once they became aware of a circle of onlookers. In their preoccupation with the meal, they had not observed that the bird-people had flown up, and now, perched on the rocks and tree trunks in a wide circle, were observing them like spectators in an amphitheater.

At first their silence seemed that of dazed horror. Their milky faces were contorted, like those of civilized men at a cannibal feast. They pointed toward the fire with startled gestures, as if they had never seen such a spectacle before; and they indicated the banqueters in a sort of dazed dismay. They sniffed the air meaningfully. Then their excitement broke forth in speech; and their leader and some others, with a whirring of wings, started toward the earthlings. Round and round they circled above the visitors' heads, behaving much as after the rape of the turnip-like plant, but with even louder, more vigorous squawks of protest.

"Lord save my soul!" grumbled Dave. "Looks like we're not expected to eat."

And he threw a half-eaten leg into the brush—which brought a cry of approval from above.

Eunice at once followed his example; and even Henessey, though he growled like a dog losing its bone, ended by abandoning the meal.

"Curse 'em all," he complained, "you'd think we'd been getting away with murder!"

"Well, maybe that's what it looks like to them," Eunice suggested. "Like murder."

"In that case folks, I think we'd better clear out. The atmosphere here is too rarefied for me to live."

"Afraid you're right," Dave coincided, as he solemnly stroked his bearded chin. "Seems sort of unreasonable, doesn't it? They won't give us anything to eat, and won't let us gather our own food. So it's get out, or be starved out. Since we've got to go, the sensible thing is to leave while we still have some food left."

"But where shall we go?" asked Eunice.

"You've got me there. Guess we'll just have to take our chances, I sort of hate to leave the spaceship, but we'd want to do some exploring anyway."

"I—I hate to leave those lovely bird-people," said Eunice.

"If we have luck, maybe we'll see them again. Tell me, either of you got any hunch which way to go?"

"Simplest thing," Henessey proposed, "would be just to follow the river downstream. It's sure to lead somewhere— maybe the sea, maybe cities of real honest-to-goodness people instead of half-crazy bird-things. If nobody has a better idea—"

"River way will suit me," agreed Dave.

"Me too," added Eunice.

Without a word, they turned back to the spaceship, to select the provisions for their journey. Yet a depression had fallen over Dave and Eunice. It was not only that they must leave their friends, the bird-people; somehow, by one of those weird intuitions which we all feel at times, they felt that the halcyon phase of their adventure was closing, and that something grimmer lay ahead.

CHAPTER SIX

WELL, FOLKS, WE look just like long-distance hikers."

"More like mountain climbers, if you ask me."

"Mountain climbers without climbing gear. Chances are we've got just about everything except what we need."

In the uncanny light of the red sun, the three adventurers stood before the spaceship, taking perhaps their last look at that familiar object. Each, including Eunice, was dressed in a khaki jacket and trousers; each wore a khaki-colored woolen shirt, a wide-visored cap of the same hue, and amber-tinted goggles; each had heavy tramping boots, with leggings laced halfway up the calves; and each had a knapsack strapped about his shoulders containing compressed food, medicines, matches, a water flask, a flashlight, and various other necessities. Each, in addition, was borne down by the burden of a sleeping bag; while Henessey still carried his pistol and Dave his steel cane, and all three were provided with clasp-knives.

"And now here's another thing," Dave proposed, after he had plunged back into the spaceship and drawn three shining little objects out of a storage chest. "Let's each take one of these police whistles. Hope to heaven we'll never need them, but they may be like a mercy from above if we ever get separated."

"Oh, but we mustn't get separated!" protested Eunice, as she wove one arm about Dave as if for protection. "We just can't let that happen. It would be—simply awful!"

"You bet it would!" agreed Dave, as he gave his wife an affectionate hug. "Believe me; we'll stick together like babes in the woods!"

Nevertheless, they all carefully took charge of their whistles.

"Thank God, gravity here is much less than on earth!" Dave enthused, as they started briskly out. "In spite of all I'm carrying, I feel only half loaded."

"Just you wait a bit, and you'll think you've got a truckload of lead!" foretold Henessey, mopping his brow. "Particularly considering how darned hot the weather here always is."

"It does seem a shame to be leaving," Eunice lamented. "What will those nice bird-people think of us? Why, we haven't even anyway of saying 'Thank you, good folks! Good luck to you! May we meet again! '"

"Oh, they'll understand soon enough," predicted Dave.

This prophecy, indeed, was promptly fulfilled.

The travelers had barely reached the river, whose clear gently flowing waters glowed dawn-red in the rays of the crimson sun, when they heard a commotion from the direction of the beehive houses. A flying swarm rose above the dwellings, and whirled in high excitement toward the retreating three. Soon they were swooping just above the explorers' heads, shrieking and shrilling until the eardrums of all three began to ache. The leader, perching for a moment on a tall rock above the river, with wings that slowly opened and closed like those of a butterfly just settling to rest, uttered a swift series of caws and cacklings, reminding the hearers of a parent scolding his unruly offspring. Several of his comrades meanwhile were dashing toward the earthlings, then dashing away again, as if warning them to retreat. The latter could see the dismay that convulsed the small milky-white faces.

"What do you think?" Dave barely managed to make himself heard above the uproar. "Are they objecting because we're going, or because we're going in just this direction?"

"Aw, who in thunder cares?" grunted Henessey. "We'd go plumb daft if we tried to figure out those blasted bird-things!"

"But there may be danger in this direction," suggested Eunice. "Maybe they're trying to tell us about it."

"Don't see why there should be more danger here than anywhere," growled Henessey. "One thing I can tell you, it'd be a harder pull if we turned uphill."

This argument proved decisive; although Dave, noting the agitation of the bird-people as they circled and screamed above, did have an impulse to turn back.

Not until nearly an hour had passed did the natives seem to weary of protesting and one by one, in a disconsolate drooping flight, go winging back toward the beehive houses. The last to leave was the leader, who swung round and round above the heads of the departing trio as if in farewell, his creased face looking sad and embittered in the unearthly light of the red sun, his flaming eyes brimful of reproach. Then, with a long-drawn wailing, more dismal than a lonely wolf-howl, he shot about and retreated almost with the speed of a jet plane. In a moment he was out of sight; but that dreary wailing seemed to remain, seemed to linger in the air like a forecast of disaster.

For a time they strode without a word along the riverbank, where plants like ruby-headed rushes stood up by the thousands, and swished with snaky writhings into the water at the strangers' approach. Now and then bubbles on the water's surface advertised the presence of aquatic creatures; and once a scarlet snout, three feet long and dominated at the tip by a glaring purple eye as large as a baseball, shot startlingly out of the water. High in the sky a fleet of lazy rose-hued clouds drifted, and between them and the observers a winged shape occasionally appeared. The foliage about them meanwhile was exceedingly varied: tall leafless trees, enmeshed in rope-like tendrils that mantled them with glossy manes, alternated with trees whose leaves of microscopic smallness, covered them with the softest, filmiest of curtains. Beneath the trees some of the bushes were like balls of pink down which later, when the blue sun had risen, turned to the color of forget-me-nots; others, with fronds first ruddy and then blue-green when all the suns were shining, swung their long twisted limbs above them like praying hands although there was no wind, still others, spiny and black, warned the adventurers away by the hissing and puffing of bladder-like globes, which spurted a blood-colored liquid that (as they later learned) would have been poisonous as snake venom had it penetrated their skins. Meanwhile small writhing, things with many legs, and with heads at each extremity, wriggled darkly beneath them; and inch-long buzzing creatures, so rapid that they made but a blur in the air, whizzed past their ears.

But at, first they scarcely noticed these sights, so absorbed were they in their own thoughts. As never before, each was feeling his aloneness, his isolation on this strange planet, his everlasting exile from mankind. Each was recalling his own small corner in a world that had ceased to be, each was remembering friends and kindred, the loved associations that would never return. Though he knew that it was useless to look back, Dave remembered the chums of his college days— remembered laughing-eyed Clem Buchanan, his one-time roommate: who most likely had been killed long since by the Cosmic Blight; and earnest Jim Hartley, with whom he had worked out his first plans for space-travel; and his own brother George, good old George who had worked in a bank and was always planning what he would do when he was old and could retire; and his sister Pam, dear Pam who had been so concerned about every cough and complaint of her brood of three, and foresaw careers as Presidents or at least as Secretaries of State for her two boys. Where were they all now? With a catch in his throat, Dave remembered how hard he had tried to get into touch with them during those turbulent last weeks—and how they had all vanished, beyond his reach, in the turmoil that swept the earth like a flood. Even if they had escaped to Mars—and the chance in each case was but one in many thousands—they were all dead now for years and years. There was not the remotest hope that any of them were alive, for those events on earth had all occurred a lifetime ago, maybe more than a lifetime.

His ruminations were interrupted by a low, thoughtful voice.

"I've been wondering, dear, about the bird-people. It's just like we've left the best friends we ever had. You know, not every traveler to a strange world could expect the sort of reception they gave us."

"I'll say not!" agreed Dave, as, glad of a warm human presence, he squeezed his wife's arm in an affectionate grip. "I guess they feel they've had a pretty scurvy deal from us."

Eunice gazed across the river, which was split by several islands whose massed trees shone like flamingo feathers in the light of the red sun.

"Well, dear, try to look at things through their eyes. First we came to them out of the sky. Nothing like it had ever been known before. Maybe they thought we were gods. Maybe they wanted to worship us. But then they noticed we didn't have exactly divine qualities. We had only two eyes. We hadn't any wings at all. We had a disgusting habit—oh, maybe a criminal habit, as they looked on it—of killing plants and animals and stuffing their remains inside us. Just the same, they tried to nurse and guide us, and do the best they could. After which, what did we do? Suddenly took our things and deserted them, without even a 'By your leave.' Then picked the very route they plainly warned us against. We must look like rather low, self-seeking, ungrateful vermin."

"Well, maybe," agreed Dave, with a sigh. "But I don't see just what we can do about it."

"Aw, shucks," grumbled Henessey, contemptuously. "Haven't you folks got anything better to do than worry about what a lot of crazy birds think about you?"

"Well it isn't only what they think," defended Eunice. "As I've said, maybe they wanted to warn us of some danger."

"When it comes to danger, I'd rather look out for myself," swore Henessey.

And just then they came across the footprints.

There were only a few of them, leading between two the same size as those they had noticed beside the lake, and had the same deep seven-toed or seven-clawed indentations.

Silently the three stared at these ominous markings. And then, with furtive glances into the brush, they started away.

"Better stick together as much as we can, folks," Henessey proposed. "And best keep to the open when we can, too. Didn't I tell you, I had my suspicions all along?"

Dave and Eunice nodded. Deep within them both, though neither would have admitted it, there was the old blind, primitive terror of the unknown.

For several hours they kept on near the riverbank, more warily than before. They crossed beaches covered with purplish sand, where crab-like creatures with eyes on foot-high stalks were waddling; they skirted the edges of yellow-ochre cliffs; entered meadows where fuchsia-red plants repelled them with uncannily aimed little stinging darts; and waded at the edges of swamps whose slime was composed of masses of minute worm-shaped creatures. But they saw not a sign of the makers of the tracks. The river meanwhile, joined by several small tributaries which the travelers had to ford, was constantly widening, until it moved with a steady current half a mile across.

It was during this long, hard trek that Dave began to feel an irritation at Henessey. It was all very foolish, he realized; but he did not like the self-conscious courtliness of the other man's manner toward Eunice, the bowing, nodding, too-attentive gallantry with which he deferred to her, the cloying sweetness of his voice and smile. They were now "Earle" and "Eunice" to one another—after all, it had been Dave's own suggestion that they drop formalities, which, under the circumstances, were absurd. But the use of their given names brought them unconsciously nearer to one another. Had Dave's wife forgotten her original dislike of Henessey? So Dave thought that time when Henessey grabbed her arm just as she was slipping down a steep slope. Her expression was one of childlike pleasure as she beamed up at him. "Oh, thank you, Earle, thank you so much!" But it seemed to Dave that Henessey held her arm unnecessarily long, and even—or did his imagination deceive him?—gave it a sort of squeeze.

Then, a little later, when they were resting in a tiny grotto beneath shadowing cliff walls, he chanced to catch the expression with which Henessey was staring at Eunice. There was wistfulness, there was sadness in those small gray-green eyes; but there was something more, there was suffering, and there was hunger. After all, Dave reflected, it was pretty tough on Henessey, leading a solitary existence, while the only other earthman on the planet was happily married—more than that, unavoidably waving his happiness right in Henessey's face. Dave supposed that he himself in such a case would become sullen and morose.

"You know, folks," Henessey ruminated, as if reading Dave's thoughts, "maybe I've been a prize fool—maybe I ought to've married long ago. But I never met the woman that I thought was worth half so much as my freedom—that is, not till near the end. Then I got just what I deserved, blind idiot that I was. When the tide turned against us, Imogene felt the same prejudice as everybody else against the Weapon Control Board. I got my ring back so fast you'd have thought I was a biting rattler. Maybe it's just as well, though, I can't imagine Imogene, with her ballroom ways, being very much for roughing it in these wilds."

"What was she like, Earle?" asked Eunice.

Henessey picked up a little transparent rose-tinted shell, and absently turned it over in his hands. A bleak reminiscent smile crossed his face; his long twisted nose seemed even longer and more twisted than usual.

"Well, she's been dead a long while now, I guess—why not let her rest in peace? But she wasn't at all like you, Eunice. She didn't have your verve—your spunk. She wasn't as pretty as you, either—didn't have those nice golden ringlets strung all over her face, and those blue eyes that make a man think of a field of flowers."

Eunice averted her glance, but could not quite conceal her flush of pleasure. And Dave, mumbling into his beard, hoped that the others did not observe his scowl.

But there were more immediate matters to hold his attention.

They were hardly on their way again when they noticed a change in the weather. A mist formed above the river and gradually developed into a fog, at first eerily red, and then after the white sun and the blue arose—an uncanny gray-blue, which deepened to blue-green and in places almost to indigo, making progress next to impossible. The wanderers managed to find refuge in a sort of half-cave, where a beetling ledge gave partial shelter. And barely in time! A wind had come up; and the fog, at its indigo deepest, gave place to such beating, lashing, pummeling rivers of rain as the observers had never seen on Earth. In nearly solid sheets, the deluge splashed down; while orange shafts of lightning stabbed the opacity, and the thunder boomed with a roar as of continuous artillery. Though they huddled together in the furthest recesses of their shelter, they were drenched long before the storm was over.

"I can't help wondering," Eunice burst out, during a pause in the commotion, "how those poor bird-people can live through all this."

"Oh, never worry about the bird-people," consoled Henessey. "While you and Dave were inside their house that first time, I amused myself by testing the material of the walls. It looked as soft as silk, didn't it? Well, it's really tougher than canvas. I know, because I tried to tear it and couldn't."

"Well, it stands to reason," Dave contributed, "that they must have gone through storms like this before."

A fresh rain-gust, followed by lightning and thunder put an end to the discussion.

Twenty minutes later, the storm ended as suddenly as it had begun. The clouds parted; the red, white and blue suns blazed above as if nothing had happened; and only the drenched and steaming ground, half covered with bogs and morasses and everywhere running with small streams and waterfalls, bore testimony to the deluge.

"Lord, I guess this solves the problem of a bath," said Henessey.

"Yes, but what about the problem of drying?" questioned Eunice, wryly.

"In this sun, nature will take care of that very soon," predicted Dave.

This proved, indeed, to be the case with all parts of their apparel except their boots, after they had removed as much as convention allowed and permitted it to dry in the sunlight. It was about two hours before, having refreshed themselves with the delicious brown berry of an ivy-like plant, they were once again upon their my.

"Well, we still haven't seen the makers of the tracks," remarked Dave.

"Wouldn't boast about that if I were you," counseled Henessey. "Before you get done, maybe you'll see heaps more of them than you want to."

Just then Eunice, who had preceded the others to the peak of a little rise, uttered a low excited cry.

The two men, rushing up to her, joined her in staring down into a hollow by the riverbank.

"What in tarnation is that?" demanded Henessey, who was the first to find words.

A thimble-shaped structure rose by the water's edge. It looked like a huge cocoon: about fifteen feet high and ten to twelve feet broad at the base, it was of a cobweb gray, and was constructed of some soft woolly substance, which trembled ever so slightly in the breeze.

For several minutes the adventurers stared at it in silence.

"It might be made by some large animal," suggested Dave; "Something like a giant silkworm."

"More likely a giant spider," muttered Henessey.

"In any case, I think I'll investigate," decided Dave, as, gripping his cane, he started down the slope.

"Please, dear, be careful!" pleaded Eunice, creeping after him.

But Henessey, perched atop the ridge, slowly and coolly drew out his pistol.

CHAPTER SEVEN

FOR SEVERAL MINUTES DAVE reconnoitered all about the cobweb-gray object, in the manner of an infantryman suspecting a minefield. He could see that it was supported on slender ribs, though he was not sure if they were of wood or metal. He noticed, also, that rope-like fastenings held it to stakes almost buried in the ground.

"Doesn't look like the work of an animal, after all," he whispered to Eunice, who kept close behind him. "Whoever made it, however, doesn't seem to be home now."

"For goodness sake, watch out!" Eunice warned, as Dave came close to the structure.

"Feels soft, like down," he reported. "But with a sort of tough stringiness behind it, and a little sticky too—clings to the touch. I'd call it almost clammy."

He lifted one hand to his face, which immediately was wrinkled with a wry expression.

"Whew!" he burst out. "It smells like a zoo!"

"Please, dear, don't be so careless!" Eunice insisted. "If there should be anything inside—"

"If there was anything inside, we'd have heard it by now. Suppose I take a look?"

Dave pressed an ear against the wall; waited; then pulled at the downy substance, which gave way with a faint complaining screech. But there was nothing inside.

Or, rather, there was an apparently waterproof floor, made of the same substance as the walls.

"Well, the one thing certain," he reflected, as his eyes searched, the interior, "is that some sort of intelligent creature made this. Who knows?—maybe even civilized man."

"Couldn't be very civilized, if this is the kind of house he builds," decided Eunice.

"Well, I wouldn't jump to conclusions. After all, if you came upon a camper's tent somewhere in the mountains it wouldn't be fair to judge our great cities by that, would it?"

"No, but is the owner only camping out?" Eunice argued, as she started slowly about the thimble-shaped structure. And then, with a gasp, she stopped short. "Look, Dave!"

With a leap, he was at her side.

She was pointing to a glittering object half buried in the mud.

"Holy Christopher!" he burst out; and reached for the article.

It was somewhat bigger than a man's palm, and clearly of artificial construction. The surface was of a glassy smoothness; the substance looked like metal, and seemed hard as metal, yet had the lightness of a plastic, and was actually a form of stone; the shape was that of the claw of a large animal, with attachments or fastenings of some brown material as elastic as rubber yet seemingly strong as iron. But the really striking feature was not evident until Dave had turned the object over.

On the undersurface, there were seven sharp indentations.

"Glorious saints! Just see that!" Dave almost shrieked, unable to keep back his excitement. And even Henessey, who had been parading above with his pistol, rushed down to see what the disturbance was all about.

Dave bent over and pressed the newfound object into the mud. Upon lifting it out, he pointed to the imprint—pointed in loud astonishment. "Just see that! Just see! Would you ever imagine?"

The imprint was identical with that of the mysterious creature whose tracks they had seen by the lake, and later by the river.

For several long laden seconds the three stared at one another in bewilderment.

"Well, folks, I—I'd say we'd better beat it out of here just as fast as our legs can make it!" sputtered Henessey.

Dave swept the landscape with a searching glance. "I—I don't see anything to be scared of."

"Come on, dear, let's go—please!" pleaded Eunice. Hesitantly he started after her, still carrying the seven-clawed object.

"Looks like some sort of shoe or sandal," he reasoned. "The wearer may have lost it without knowing it, or else didn't need it any longer. Those rubbery fastenings are rather clever. The seven indentations at the bottom, I guess, help the creature get a grip on rough or steep territory."

"Even so, why don't we see any of the tracks around here?" questioned Eunice, as she reached the top of the rise.

"You haven't forgotten the storm, have you? I'd say that was more than enough to wipe out the heaviest tracks. Most likely the animal left this temporary shelter—if it was a temporary shelter, as I imagine—just before the downpour began. May be a long distance off by now."

"The longer, the better!" mumbled Henessey.

"But how do you know it's dangerous? It may be well disposed, just like the bird-people. Certainly, it seems intelligent. It may even have human qualities."

"So have cannibals!" Henessey threw back, as he jogged on at a good pace. "What was it, let me ask you, that made the bird-people so scared of this brute?"

"We really don't know that was what they were scared of," contended Eunice. "And we don't know that the creature is a brute, either. We'll simply have to wait and find out."

"Me—I can stand a lot of waiting," Henessey muttered. "If we've got any brains in our heads, we'll be mighty careful of our steps from now on."

But all that day they saw no further sign of the strangers. They kept on for a few hours, then rested for an equal period, since, it was impossible to travel continuously during the twenty-six or twenty-seven hours of daylight. But they did not get much chance for sleep before the arrival of the brief night.

Then the best shelter they could find was in a little niche of the woods, where a plant with bluish leaves as large as house windows arched high above. Beneath them a bed of sweet-smelling spongy weeds offered a comfortable resting place; while openings in the foliage gave a view across a meadow carpeted with butterfly-shaped black-veined orange flowers.

"Should we make a fire to keep off the wild beasts?" asked Eunice.

"Not unless we're crazy!" countered Henessey. "It might keep the wild beasts off, all right, but it'd be the very thing to attract the wild men. About all we can do, as I see it, is take turns standing guard. I'm willing to handle the first watch."

The others nodded agreement; and Dave and Eunice were soon asleep, while Henessey kept solitary vigil with his pistol. His two assigned hours passed without incident, but Dave, who succeeded him, had from the first the uneasy sense of forces abroad in the darkness.

This feeling may have been due in part to the normal night sounds: a faint chirping and murmuring as of invisible insects, mingled with the occasional hoots, grunts and rustlings of creeping or flying small things. And in part Dave's apprehensions may have been stirred by the weird sky forma-tions, all the weirder as seen through the openings among the leaves: the pale bluish and faintly red clouds that moved raggedly, from east to west, at times wreathing bronze or ruddy mists about one of the moons, at times blazing out in sapphire fire, or a mingling of sapphire and ruby. After watching the cloud movements for an hour, Dave was hypnotized, awe-stricken, yet never without a lurking sense of danger.

Yet it was just when this sense was at low ebb that the apparitions streaked across his gaze. He knew, of course, that they were not really apparitions; knew them to be solid as himself. But they looked like specters, like things of fog and shadow; and their ghostly—yes, their grisly, other-worldly quality—was enhanced by their very silence as they drifted beneath the flowing colored clouds and the red-and-blue, banded moons. There were but four or five of them, and no more than a minute passed between the appearance of the first out of the borders of the woods and the vanishing of the last into those same concealing fastnesses. Yet in that brief time their aspect was stamped upon the watcher's mind with a vividness that a lifetime could not erase.

They were a little more than man-sized, and were dark of hue and squat and thick of form; and they stooped and shambled like apes. Their necks, which seemed normally of a gorilla shortness, appeared capable of indefinite extension; in at least two cases they shot out until almost of a giraffe's length, then instantly shot back again. Their legs were only two; but they had three pairs of arms, fastened to their shoulders and backs; and three pairs of tentacle-long hands waved incongruously in the air. Attached to their rear extremities, they carried wide brush-like appendages, whose purpose the observer could not imagine; and he had the impression that, like the bird-people, they had eyes both in the front and the back of their heads, which were human-sized but tapered to sharp, horny points.

For the rest of that night, Dave did not sleep. But as soon as the red sun had risen, he hastened across the meadow to the point at which the night-specters had passed. It was just as he had expected, though he let out a little dismayed gasp at the recognition. The soil of the meadows bore the new made imprint of seven-clawed feet.

CHAPTER EIGHT

DAVE WAITED UNTIL THEY had finished breakfast, which they made from the sweet gummy secretion on the stems of a wax-like plant. Then, without attempting to soften the dread reality, he told what he had seen.

Henessey began a low spontaneous whistling, but instantly checked himself.

"Lord, you can curse me for an idiot!" he muttered. "Hope that don't give us away."

"I don't suppose they're prowling around looking for us," Dave reassured him, shaking his shaggy head uneasily. "At least, they didn't seem to suspect our being here last night."

"Wind probably didn't blow them our scent. But how do you know some of them aren't snooping about now?" questioned Henessey, as he fingered his pistol and let his eyes range in all directions anxiously.

"Personally, I doubt it. From all I've seen, I'd say they're nocturnal in their habits. At least, we haven't run across any of them by day. When they visited the bird-people, remember, it was at night."

"Maybe they're what the bird-people were warning us against," contributed Eunice, pressing close to Dave. "Maybe they knew those awful beasts lived in this direction."

"Don't see what there was in it for the bird-people, to want to help us!" snorted Henessey.

"Don't see what there is in you to make you such a cynic, Earle. You don't leave room for such a thing as common good will. Why, I've heard that even birds in the forest sometimes try to warn other creatures, of other species, upon the approach of predators."

A thin skeptical smile crossed Henessey's narrow twisted face. "Tell it to the marines," his manner seemed to say.

"Oh, can't you men ever stop arguing?" Eunice protested, stamping one heel a little impatiently. "What we've got to decide is how to get away from those—those night-goblins."

"I didn't say they were goblins," objected Dave.

"Well, way I look at it is this," took up Henessey. "We don't know how many of those beasts are in the woods. Maybe they're everywhere, like mosquitoes. Maybe trying to get away from them is like trying to escape human beings if you're suddenly plopped down in the heart—well, of Ohio or Indiana. You'll find woods and fields, all right, where you won't see anyone, but if you keep going you're sure to run into people. I have a hunch that's how it is here. However, there is a long chance that if we change direction we can get away from those devils. So I'm all for the change."

"Which way do you think we should go?" asked Eunice.

"I don't think. Thinking wouldn't do any good, since we haven't any premises to work from."

He paused, and pointed vaguely westward, toward the saw-toothed mountains they had seen in the distance. "Why not have a try over that way?"

"I'll hate like anything to leave the river," meditated Dave. "On the other hand, there's sense in your suggestion. The river may attract those beasts. In fact, like some kinds of earth animals, they may never go far from the water. What do you think, Eunice?"

"I agree. But it just came to me, wouldn't it be wonderful if we could go back and live with the bird-people?"

"Yes, and starve to death!" growled Henessey.

Eunice sighed. "But we can't go on forever, just rambling around," she argued. "We'll have to find some settled place somewhere."

"Well, I'm willing, dearest," conceded Dave. "But where? I guess for the present it's the nomad's life for us."

"The hunted wild beast's life," amended Henessey. "Come on, let's get going!"

With a regretful last glance toward the river, they turned into a forest of spreading blue-gray trees. The space between the trees was wide enough to make progress seem easy; but their way led over terrain so boggy from the rain that they often waded ankle-deep in a glue-like mud. Then, before they had gone a mile, their difficulties began to multiply. Sometimes they were impeded by plants that they named the "porcupine bush"—which looked like nothing more than balls of bristling black spines, razor-edged and dagger-pointed, and with a habit of flying at anyone who ventured too near—as Henessey learned to his grief. Then there was a harmless-looking tree, about twelve feet tall, which had a way of letting down long looping tendrils, which wound with a constrictor's strength about the passer-by. Both Dave and Eunice in turn were caught by this monstrous plant; and it was fortunate that they had knives with which to cut themselves free.

As if all this were not sufficient, there were the plants that formed living nooses on the ground, ready to tighten over any unwary foot. Then there were the long garnet-red, splinter-like insects that, while apparently harmless, whizzed overhead continually in annoying swarms; there were the double-headed lizards with purple eyes and needle-toothed jaws, which hissed like snakes in the path; there was a crawling flat jelly-like mass, pale-blue and to be shunned like the plague, since every weed it touched instantly withered; there was the long-jawed thing with phosphorescent eyes, which came scuttling out of the hollow of a stump, and barked like a dog; and there was the fanged toad that hopped shoulder-high, and seemed to bode no good with his four great baleful eyes that constantly changed color from grass-green to carmine, from carmine to fiery orange, and from orange to blazing purple, steel-blue and sulphur-yellow.

"Whew!" complained Henessey, whose hands, once delicately manicured were calloused and blistered where they were not bleeding from thorns and scratched by nettles. "I wouldn't ask for many years more of this kind of travel."

"It seems like years already," sympathized Eunice.

"Don't know but that the river way would be the lesser of two evils—regardless of the night-monsters," conjectured Dave.

But after a few hours they came upon a trail of a sort. It was faint and narrow, and was obliterated in parts by weeds and fallen leaves. Had it been formed by man or beast? "It's the sort of path," Dave concluded, "that animals might have worn on the way to a waterhole. On the other hand, it might equally have been made by humans."

"Can't say which I want to meet least, the animals or the humans," contributed Henessey.

"Still, it's better than no trail at all," argued Dave. "At least, it may lead somewhere."

"Yes, but where?" demanded Henessey, pointedly.

Dave attempted no answer. He would not have admitted it, but he did have a foreboding as they set out along the vague, thin track. He had the feeling of one who trespasses on hostile territory; the feeling that unseen eyes were watching him, unseen ears listening to his every footfall. And this uncanny sensation was heightened by the eerie looks of the forest: the blue light and the white and red that, in broken beams, slanted down from the roof of dusky green and deep, almost inky blue; the blue shadows that haunted the depths of the groves and thickets; the rose-glow that sometimes hovered above, through which mysterious flying things would flash. Before they had gone half a mile, Dave wished that they had chosen some other course— almost any other course.

All three wanderers still found it hard to adjust themselves to the long day and brief night. It seemed that several days had passed when, after two or three hard treks interspersed with intervals of rest and sleep, they interpreted the deepening shadows to mean that the blue sun—the last to remain above the horizon—was setting in the east. This time, because of the overhanging foliage, the darkness was nearly that of a moonless night on earth. They managed to find shelter beneath a limestone cliff near a trickling stream, in a cave about fifteen feet deep, which contained desiccated bones of dinosaurian size. And there, after dining on a banana-shaped fruit with a walnut flavor, they were so tired that they gave little thought to the possible perils of the night.

"Just the same," proposed Henessey, suppressing a yawn, "we'd be blinking idiots if we didn't stand watch. "I'll take the first half of the night, Dave, and you can take the second.

"Indeed you'll not!" protested Eunice. "I'll do my full share!"

"I don't get the point of not taking what's given you," grumbled Henessey. "Anyway, let's not waste time arguing. And so after a brief discussion, it was arranged that he and Dave should take the earlier watches, while Eunice should have the period just before dawn.

Hours later when Eunice awoke with a start, glanced at her radio-dial wristwatch, and reminded Dave that it was time for him to be relieved, nothing but the usual forest noises had broken the peace of the night.

Eunice shuddered just a little as she took her post at the cave entrance, staring toward the boles of great trees and the tangled masses of verdure that were no more than the barest shadows against a shadowy background. Thankfully she would have felt the reassuring touch of Dave's hand on hers; he seemed withdrawn to an incalculable remoteness where he lay, ten feet distant, at Henessey's side on a bed of dry weeds, while the sound of the two men's regular respiration came to her through the darkness.

An hour, an hour and a half went by. Then suddenly the night silence was broken by a shriek—a woman's scream, abrupt, piercing, terrified, but almost instantly muffled.

With violently thumping hearts, the men leapt up. Dave, as he snatched at his knife, heard a hoarse growling, a sound as of scuffling. Yelling his defiance, he plunged forward. Just beyond the cave entrance, he could see two barely distinguishable shadows, huge and crouching, and with tentacle-like projections waving above. One of them was struggling with something smaller, and as vague as himself. Then—not a second later, it seemed—the roar of a pistol crashed in Dave's ears, and his eyes were blinded by the blaze of a shot.

At the same time, he could see the dusky shapes withdrawing—slouching rapidly away, as if frightened. With a bellow of rage, he started after the fugitives. But he was barely out of the cave when something invisible caught his foot and sent him sprawling forward—made the whole world erupt in an explosion of pain. A fraction of a second later, everything grew blurred, everything was blotted out…everything was quenched in silence and darkness.

CHAPTER NINE

EVEN BEFORE HE HAD reopened his eyes, he felt something cool swabbing his forehead. There was still a pain in his head, and a dazed feeling…he could not quite remember what had happened.

"Euny!" he murmured. "Euny...! Dear!" And he opened his aching eyes in the rosy dawn of the red sun, and stared up at a grim looking Henessey, who was bathing his brow with a dripping handkerchief.

"Take it easy, old boy. Quiet for a little while, and you'll be fit as a fiddle," he counseled, with more gentleness than Dave had thought him capable of.

"Euny...Euny...Where's Euny?" Dave kept repeating, still struggling with his recollections. He had had a frightful nightmare, that much he knew—but beyond that he could not remember.

"You sure gave yourself a whopper of a knockout when you tripped on that root," the other man went on, not answering his question. "The way you went down—*kerplunk!*—whanging your head against that tree trunk—believe me, it's a marvel the tree's still standing."

"But Euny...Euny...Where's Euny?" Dave reiterated, as terror began flooding over him.

"That swelling of yours is a beauty, too," persisted Henessey, dabbing his handkerchief in the little stream a yard away. "But don't you fear, we'll have her down in no time at all. You can congratulate yourself, old chap, your dome is solid ivory."

"Can't you tell me what's happened? My God, what's happened?" Dave rasped, as the mists began to clear from his mind. And then, all in one shattering burst, he remembered.

With a roar, he was on his feet. Horror such as he had never before known swept over him, chilled him, turned him into a frantic, crazed thing.

"Where's Euny? God in heaven, where is she?" he shouted. And he seized the other man by the shoulders, and shook him. But at the same time he looked into Henessey's eyes. And his grip relaxed. The bleakness in those eyes told him more than he wanted to know.

"I did everything possible, Dave," Henessey went on, with a hangdog look. "Believe me, I did. That shot I fired—I aimed it into the air, just to scare them—had to, because I couldn't tell where she was. Otherwise, I might have plugged her by mistake. Before I could put in any decent shot—you know how fiendishly dark everything was—those devils had gotten away."

"Gotten away? Gotten away?" Dave yelled, with the feeling of a man whose whole world is bursting about his ears. "Where did they get to? Lord above, where did they get to? Did they take her along?"

Henessey's head drooped.

"How could I stop them, there in the darkness? I hardly got more than a glimpse, when they'd slipped behind the tree trunks. What would have been the use of following? They'd only have gotten me too."

"Then we'll have to follow them now!" Dave raged, stamping about like a madman. "We'll have to! Right now! At once! Quick! Before they get too far!"

Even amid his distraction his eyes, searching the ground, made out the seven-clawed tracks.

"Here's where they went!" he clamored, pointing down the trail. "Come! Let's not waste any more time!"

Henessey fastened his knapsack about his shoulders, and made sure that his pistol was in place.

"Crazy fools we were to take that trail!" he muttered. "Guess it's a regular highway for those brutes, and that's how they found us out... Here, don't act like a lunatic. Take your knapsack!"

Automatically Dave strapped on the bag. His mind was still struggling with his misfortune, which he did not fully realize all at once. It was sometime before he had a coordinated idea of the basic facts. Those demons, those monsters—the same as he had seen the night before—had stolen up upon Eunice in the darkness, and seized her before she could do more than scream. They had muffled her cries, subdued her struggles, and carried her away—where? And for what purpose?

He could not imagine, he must not try to imagine. He needed all his energy, needed every atom of strength in order to rescue her. Surely, she was not beyond rescue; he had the desperate hope that the two-legged beasts were not carnivorous; for whatever reason they had seized her, they meant to spare her life. He believed this firmly, he had to believe it! True, when he had a vision of her writhing in the clutches of those six-armed furies— but for her sake, he must keep his mind from such thoughts.

"We've got to be as stealthy as cats, and wilier than wolves," he heard Henessey's whisper in his ear. "It won't help her any if those devils get a lick at us."

Dave nodded; and felt just a bit less gloomy as he set out along the trail, with Henessey close at his heels. His head still ached; everything still whirled; and that may have been why, as he staggered along, he seemed to hear her voice in his ears, seemed to hear her calling, "Dave! Dave! Come! Come quick!" And then, growing fainter, dimmer in the distance, Dave! Dave! Come…come, quick! If you love me, come…come quick!"

They had no trouble to follow the seven-clawed tracks that were clearly marked along their trail of yesterday, but after about a mile, the tracks abruptly branched to the right, where a thin second trail wound into the woods. It was at this point that Dave uttered a low cry, and snatched a tan-colored scrap from the ground.

"By God, Earle, look at this!"

Henessey joined in staring at a little torn, strip of khaki.

"From her shirt!" gasped Dave. I'll swear it! I'll swear it's from her shirt!"

"Well at least," Henessey reflected, "it shows she was still alive and kicking."

"Yes, and putting up a perfect devil of a scrap. Poor kid! She's got spunk! You can see for yourself, she was fighting like the deuce to get away."

"Either that, or she tore off that bit of cloth to show us which way she was being taken."

"That could be it, too. Come, let's get going!"

There was just a glimmer of hope in Dave's eyes as they followed the new trail, which was no harder than the old to trace, as it was everywhere marked by the freshly broken twigs and small branches of shrubs and trees.

"Can't make up my mind," Henessey pondered, as they pressed on regardless of thorns, burrs and spines, "whether all these twigs were broken in a struggle, or simply lopped off in passing by those brutes, who were too big for the trail. Or else, like small boys tearing things down—"

But he did not finish the sentence. Dave was not even listening; with an intense burning look in his eyes, and fingers that clenched and unclenched as if over some invisible adversary, he pushed steadily ahead, in the manner of one driven by some fury within.

Hours went by. The red glow of early morning had been lost in the white and blue of the second and third suns; but they still kept on their way, eluding the snares of clutching giant lianas and poppy-like large flowers that snapped at them with the clicking action of steel traps. Once or twice they paused to rest and refresh themselves with cool water from a stream. Yet they knew that, weighed down by their knapsacks and with the constant need to beware of snares, they were getting further and further behind the pursued.

"Holy Jerusalem!" Henessey at last had to vent his disgust. "It's like a snail chasing a racehorse!"

Dave glared. "What makes you think those beasts are racehorses? Guess we're snails all right, but by gum, a snail could catch up with a racehorse that lay down to sleep!"

"Well, I hope you're right, old pal. They can't lie down to sleep too soon for me, I'm beginning to get winded, you know. Back home I never went in for marathons."

As a matter of fact, he did look winded. His breath was coming by hard, fast jerks; his reddened face was streaming with perspiration; his footsteps dragged.

"We've got to keep fit," he went on, mopping his brow, "if we're to be any use to her when we do find her."

"Right you are!" agreed Dave, who was also panting and red. And automatically he fell into a slower pace.

But it was not five minutes before, preceding Henessey along the trail, he halted as if paralyzed. "What in God's name is that?"

Henessey sprang to his side at the crest of a small rise, beyond which the land dropped gently. In all directions the blue-green forest foliage reached about them, an almost unbroken sheet; but there was a meadow about a hundred yards wide on the ridge where they stood; and this, since it sloped downward, made it possible for them to see over the comparatively low trees ahead. And no wonder that Dave had called out and painted!

"I'll be jiggered!" was all that Henessey could say, as he too saw. "Better pinch me, old fellow! Guess I must be dreaming!"

Above the treetops and beyond them, something vast and cobweb-gray was projecting. It might have seemed a range of mountains, had it not been for its uniform dull color and regular outlines; in the center a tremendous projection, apparently rising hundreds of feet above the trees, came to an arrow headed point, over which long woolly tassels waved in the breeze. And on both sides of this summit, smaller summits towered—dozens of them, each with woolly tassels floating above, and each tapering to a slightly lower elevation than the one next to it, so that the whole was symmetrical as an architect's design.

The impression of some architectural intention, indeed, was inescapable, even though the lower portions of the edifices were hidden from view.

"Lord save me," Henessey muttered, "if it isn't a city!"

"Looks like it," Dave admitted. "But it can't be—can't be where those monsters live!"

"I'd say not," agreed Henessey. And then, pointing to the seven-clawed tracks, "Just the same, Dave, look where those footsteps seem to lead. However, maybe they turn off somewhere."

But they did not turn off; they led straight toward the mysterious structure. The travelers now moved more warily than ever, glancing suspiciously into every hollow and clump of bushes, lest it harbor invisible enemies. But they had not covered more than another half mile when a glare ahead indicated a new break in the woods.

They now crouched rather than walked, hoping thus to elude any reconnoiterers. Nevertheless, Dave could hardly put a rein on his eagerness. It was almost as if he knew that just ahead of him lay the clue he so fervently sought—the clue to Eunice's fate.

But when he did reach the opening, he crawled. Lying flat on the ground, in the manner of a spy or sniper, he looked out upon the most astonishing scene he had yet encountered on this planet of many surprises.

CHAPTER TEN

THE BOWL OF AN ENORMOUS valley lay beneath them, curved toward the bluish snows of far-distant sierras. But all the nearer landscape was covered with the cobweb-gray edifices. They were even larger than the observers had imagined; miles in extent, and taller than Manhattan's tallest skyscrapers. In addition to the dominating towers already noted, there were hundreds of smaller projections, all arranged symmetrically, and all connecting, with gracefully curved roofs between, so that nowhere in all the thousands of acres was there an uncovered square foot. Like a giant circus tent, the gray roof slanted almost to the ground around the structure's whole circumference; or, rather, it came to within about twelve feet of the ground before descending perpendicularly. And all over the roof and the twelve-foot wall, which formed the rim of a vast circle, thousands of flaps were visible, some only a few inches across, some a yard or more in diameter—designed as if to admit the air, though they could not have let in much light, as all were covered in such a way that, while the air could enter from beneath, the direct rays of the sun were excluded.

Minutes passed while the two men, still lying with chins pressed against the weeds, stared at this bewildering spectacle. "In Pete's name," Henessey finally spat out, "if that's a city, why don't we see some of the people?"

For reply, Dave nodded a puzzled head.

"I'll tell you why," his comrade rushed on. "It's just like you said—their habits are nocturnal. But Lord deliver me from such a city! You can argue it any way you want, but we guessed right about who lives there!"

He pointed toward the seven-clawed tracks, which led down across the bushy country, straight toward the gray walls.

They waited in impatience for another few minutes; but still there was no sign of life from the supposed city.

"Well, no use spending the rest of our lives here!" Dave exclaimed suddenly, as he leapt to his feet. "I'm going down!"

"Going down?" Henessey flashed back, unable to keep the consternation out of his voice. "Man! What are you talking about? Gone plumb daffy?"

"No, but I'll go daffy if I hang around here doing nothing, when every moment something is calling out to me, 'She needs you! Needs you! ' Heaven help me, if I've got any spunk, I won't let precious time slip by!"

"Having spunk isn't the same as being a babbling fool," argued Henessey. "You don't mean to say you're going to throw yourself right into the jaws of those ogres?"

"Not if I can help it. Didn't you just agree they're probably nocturnal in their ways? Even if they aren't, I've got to find— simply got to find out what they've done to her!"

"How do you know you can find out by risking your hide?"

"A man that wouldn't risk his hide hadn't better try space travel. But this dispute is getting us nowhere, Earle," Dave went on, plaintively, while his luminous big dark eyes caught the glare of the red sun in such a way as to send back a crimson flash of anguish. "I just have to go down and look around. Want to come along?"

"Not on your life!" refused Henessey. "One lunatic at a time is enough."

He still crouched low among the weeds, while fondly examining his pistol. He saw his comrade move warily down the slope; saw him reach the edge of the gray structure, and feel its substance appraisingly; saw him creep to one of the larger flaps, which he cautiously lifted. An interminable period went by. Surely, Henessey's watch lied; something in the planet's gravity or air-pressure had disturbed it; it was not true that Dave stared through the opening for only five minutes! No, the time was nearer a quarter of an hour, half an hour! But finally, when the watcher on the hill had begun to believe that something had gone wrong, Dave withdrew his head, and began excitedly motioning.

Even then, Henessey did not forget caution. He did not move precipitately; he gazed circumspectly, to all sides and behind him. As he approached the gray edifice, he noticed a vaguely unpleasant sour smell, a little like that of vinegar. And he observed the seven-clawed footprints that crisscrossed the ground.

"The fellow's plumb nuts!" he cursed beneath his breath, angry with Dave for having drawn him into such dangerous territory.

But the imbecile continued frantically to motion him forward.

"Just look at this! Just look!" Dave whispered, when Henessey was within touching distance of the wall. And he fingered the substance, which had the same soft woolly quality as the thimble-shaped house in the wilderness.

"Now take a squint inside!" Dave urged, still in a muffled voice.

Fighting down his repugnance, Henessey approached the flap which his partner held open. That same vinegar smell was in the air, though stronger than before, and mingled with a fetid odor that reminded him of a menagerie.

"Come on!" muttered Dave. "It won't bite you!"

Henessey plunged his head through the aperture, which was just large enough. And all at once he knew why Dave had stared so long.

It took him minutes to adapt himself to the main features— features so astounding, so bizarre, so horrible that they struck him as parts of some ghastly nightmare.

He was peering into an enclosure that hardly seemed an enclosure at all. Far above, at a height of thousands of feet, the gray cobweb ceiling curved like an actual sky. Though from without, it had looked opaque, from within he saw it to be translucent: the subdued and filtered radiance of the three suns penetrated it with a soft, even glow that appeared yellowish rather than red, white or blue, and that provided sufficient (though barely sufficient) illumination without glare. The walls were ribbed with thousands of strands of some fabric that looked like bamboo and crossed it irregularly, and yet somehow gave the symmetrical impression of a cobweb; and a continuous meshwork of branching supports, which likewise suggested a cobweb, curved and bent and twisted between the floor and the ceiling, with closely woven whorls and patterned spirals and platforms and slim long cables that swung faintly as if in an invisible current.

But strange as was this vast edifice and its furnishings, the inhabitants were stranger still. At the first glimpse, Henessey did not know if they were really alive, those monstrous, things that hung in giant webs stretched between the building's main supports. They were a bit larger than a man, and most of them clung to the web by means of three pairs of tentacle-like arms that reached above the shoulders, while a pair of legs dangled uselessly beneath. Their forms were squat, and almost rotund; wide brush-like appendages were attached to their rears; their mouths, like those of the bird-people, were toothless; and their heads, which terminated in horns, had not only two pairs of phosphorescent lidless greenish round eyes, but complete dust gray faces both in front and behind. In color, some were like granite; but others were coal-black, sandy-hued, cinnamon, bark-brown, cypress-green, or purple-blue; while a few had black and white zebra stripes, or black leopard spots against a yellowish brown background, or curved lines and crescents like no beast the observer had ever seen before. But each, sprawled sideways in his own tangle of the web, and moving his eight monster limbs but slightly if at all, looked like nothing so much as a giant relative of a certain well-known flycatcher.

"God preserve us," mumbled Henessey, as he jerked his head out of the opening, "it's enough to turn your stomach."

"But didn't you see?" demanded Dave. "Mean to say you didn't see? You didn't see about *her?*"

"See—about her?" threw back Henessey, bewildered.

With the expression of one who resigns himself to a second dose of asome disgusting medicine, Henessey thrust his head back through the opening.

This time he did see something moving along the floor, among the patches of green things that miraculously throve in this odd environment. But here surely was nothing connected with Eunice. It was a child-sized drab creature, ash-gray and with four lusterless eyes; its translucent soft yellow hair had been shorn off; and its shoulders were disfigured by the stumps of two pairs of wings. It moved slowly, bowed under some shapeless dark burden, a little like an aged wood carrier beneath a too-heavy pile of faggots. As it drew near, Henessey saw welts and gashes over its body. It drooped so disconsolately, it uttered such groans, its whole appearance was so lackluster, it was so unlike the multi-colored, flying, singing creatures of the woods, that Henessey did not at first recognize it as one of the bird-people.

But even he, though he cared little for the bird-folk, felt a twinge of pity as he reported what he had seen.

"Reminds me of an old beaten nag. A regular slave-laborer, if you ask me."

At any other time, Dave would have been interested.

"Glory, you'd make a swell detective!" he burst out. "Looks like you're still stone-blind! Here! I'll show you!"

He placed his head beside Henessey's at the opening, and pointed to something small and subtle on the floor. At first Henessey didn't see what he meant. Then, as the fruit of Dave's excited insistency, all that he made out was a faint shining at the edge of a patch of green growing things. After several seconds he identified the object: the golden disk of a woman's wristwatch.

CHAPTER ELEVEN

"LOOKS TO ME, DAVE, LIKE she lost it in a struggle."

"But where's there any sign of a struggle? It may have simply become unfastened while she was being carried."

"At any rate, we know she's somewhere in those labyrinths."

"Yes, we could bet our last penny on that."

The two men had withdrawn to the shelter of a clump of cane-like shrubs, and stood talking in whispers, while casting furtive glances all about them.

"Well, there's only one thing to do!" Dave decided, with a sharp up thrust of his bearded jaw.

Henessey said nothing.

"If we don't go and take her out," Dave rushed on, "she won't have a caught sparrow's chance. Are you with me, Earle?"

Henessey turned halfway about, and spat on the gray-blue weeds. He was staring as if in urgent entreaty toward the red sun, which had sunk halfway toward the eastern horizon.

"You know I'm with you—that is, unless you're going to poke your head into the fire like a raving fool. I've got to be frank, though: if you've got the brains of a four-year-old, you won't jump right into the enemy's lair. Wouldn't it be wiser just to browse around for a time, and sort of get the lay of the land?"

"Got the lay of the land already!" Dave snapped. "Every minute we wait, she's in there, in terrible need—maybe terrible suffering. That's why I'm going in after her, I still hope to heaven you'll come too."

"Don't see what she'd gain if you and I got caught by those spidery demons. Why, man, if they once came after you with their six octopus arms, there wouldn't even be mincemeat left."

"Oh, good riddance to you then!" Dave vented his disgust. "If that's your state of mind, you'd be a liability, not an asset. But maybe you'll be a good sport and lend me your automatic?"

Henessey took out his weapon, fingered it fondly, started to pass it to his companion, then abruptly slipped it back into its holster.

"Nothing doing!" he decided. "A nice fix I'd be in if you didn't bring it back. A gun wouldn't help much anyway against a gang of those fiends."

"Well then, keep your precious pistol!" Dave angrily acceded. "All I ask is for you to wait here for me. If I don't come back in twenty-four—no, thirty-two hours—you can give me up for lost. I know well enough I'm taking my life into my hands, and you may think I'm crazier than a howling Piute; but she's worth it, you can take my word she is."

"Lord, just see what comes of being in love!" Henessey derided. "They do say it's like a poison in the system—turns a fellow plumb batty... But watch your step, man! Believe me, I want you to save her, but I want you to come out whole yourself. If you don't—" He tried to speak lightly, but could not quite keep a plaintive note out of his voice. "If you don't, try to picture what a swell time I'll have, the only human being left in a topsy-turvy world."

Dave grunted; then made sure that his knapsack was properly fastened. "May need some of these things," he muttered. He snatched out his clasp-knife, in readiness for instant use; took his steel cane in one hand; and started down the slope toward the gray edifice.

"So long, old fellow!" he waved farewell. "See you soon—I hope!"

"For God's sake, keep both eyes open—and leave a path clear behind you!" Henessey threw out his last warning.

But Dave, not seeming to hear, strode on at a steady gait.

Henessey watched him fumble about the wall, and, after a moment, draw open a large flap a foot or two above ground level. His head and most of his body disappeared; with a swift sliding motion, the lower portion of his legs passed through; the flap fluttered for a few seconds, and became still—and

Henessey, for the first time in his life, knew the meaning of lone-liness.

An incalculably long period went by. The red sun sank low, and vanished in a crimson flare; the white sun declined and set, and then the blue; but Dave did not return. The watcher, lying well concealed in the bushes of the hill, seldom took his eyes off the mountainous edifice; seldom ceased scanning the long rows of flaps, from one of which he hoped to see a familiar form emerging. But as the hours crawled past, his twisted face became more bleak and drawn; his little gray-green eyes stared out like those of a Crusoe searching the sea for the sail that never appeared. Long before his wait was over—indeed, just when the blue sun was sinking—his impatience bade him mutter half aloud, "Crazy fool! Crazy fool! Couldn't he see he was throwing his life away?"

He shifted position slightly; absently munched a biscuit from his knapsack, and moistened his lips from the water bag; but did not leave his post. Where, in fact, was there to go? The night, when at last it settled down, was unusually dark, for a veil of cloud had blotted out the stars and moons. And yet Henessey was not without light. For as the illumination of the outer world diminished, a pale radiance became visible within the gray edifice. A greenish yellow glow, sepulchral in its phosphorescence, spread inside and transfused the walls, not as if from a central fire, but as if from some source distributed evenly throughout the entire structure. Even at its brightest, it did not approach brilliance; rather, it had a sort of glowworm quality.

Now, from inside the city—or the hive, as Henessey preferred to think of it—a stirring of life became manifest: The sound of a great murmuring arose, as if thousands of sleepers had awakened all at once; buzzing, humming, whirring, grating, whizzing, and screeching noises began to mingle; and the din, though never for two instants the same, did not for a moment cease. Now and then something like a shout or yell lifted itself above the general commotion; and once the night was stabbed by a fierce, heartbreaking scream.

"Beastly place," Henessey mumbled to himself. "Beastly place!" Almost instinctively he began to creep away. But he checked himself when he remembered that his only chance—his one slight chance of ever again having a human companion—was to remain where he was.

Even as he settled back to wait, several of the nearer flaps were raised; and half a dozen squat, slouching creatures, each with six arms waving above it, came slowly trooping out. The watcher crept deeper into the bushes as he saw how one of them, in the manner that Dave had already reported, shot out its neck until it seemed of ostrich length, then shot it back again to a gorilla shortness. "Heaven save me now!" he thought, fighting with the impulse to flee.

Fortunately the beasts, seeming not to suspect his presence, turned in another direction.

But still Dave did not return. What in the name of all the saints had happened to the fellow?

Henessey wondered whether it would be safe to venture a little closer, so as to look through one of the flaps into the lighted interior; but, of course, he knew that he would never do anything so foolhardy. Then all at once, as when a theatre curtain is lifted, invisible hands pulled at invisible strings, and a section of the wall several hundred feet square was folded out of sight. And Henessey gasped, and stared with popping eyes into the unexpectedly exposed hive.

All the observable parts of the interior—the walls, the floor, the high curved ceiling, the meshwork of webs and cables were glowing with an internal light, a cold yellow-green in-candescence, which did not differ in intensity in any two regions. By contrast with this radiance—though it was much fainter than that of the average electrically lighted room, and was nearer in degree to sparse candlelight—the inhabitants appeared dark, sinister and grotesque.

All the eight-limbed creatures, who previously had sprawled as if asleep in their webs, had awakened to crawling and monstrous life. They were like giant crabs as they crept and sidled along the luminous network, some ascending or descending in a perpendicular line, some moving upside down horizontally. With their six long tentacle-like hands, each of them clung to the web, over which they moved with assurance and evident security; and every now and then one of them would show a spurt of speed, as of a spider that attacks a fly. But only a few were to be seen on the floor; and many had climbed to towering heights. About one quarter of them were undersized (the young of the tribe, Henessey thought); but otherwise there appeared to be little difference among them except in the colors and markings of their ungainly bodies.

Henessey, as he watched in shuddering fascination observed two of the creatures that had just descended to the floor. With surprising agility for animals of so heavy a build, they circled one another in the crouching manner natural to their kind. As they drew near each other, their heads would shoot out, lengthening several feet on their expandable necks before snapping back into place; and the pointed tips, which looked sharp and hard as dagger points, were evidently aimed like deadly weapons, which they did their best to dodge. Henessey couldn't decide at first whether or not this was a mere sporting affair; but after a time, with a terrific head thrust, one of the adversaries impaled its rival in the breast. Because of the other noises of the hive, Henessey could not hear the cry of the struck beast; but he did see the foot-long gash; he did see how the creature reeled and fell, covered with a flowing yellow liquid; while its opponent, with its head popping rapidly back and forth in triumph, shambled vaingloriously away.

The watcher's eyes had hardly left this spectacle when he noticed a commotion just inside the nearer wall. Through the open section, two of the beasts had entered, one of them struggling with something much smaller than himself. Henessey caught a glimpse of a milky white convulsed face, and four trailing dragonfly wings as the captive ineffectively threshed, squirmed and fluttered in its jailor's six arms.

"Lord save me, it's time to get out of here!" Henessey thought; and he could hardly control the chattering of his teeth. True, he was seemingly well enough hidden; but when he pictured himself in the place of that unhappy bird-creature—

His motions were catlike; like a cat, he kept to the ground. Where should he go? He only knew that he must put as great a distance as possible between himself and that ungodly hive. Dave and Eunice? Both of them, if they ever got out of that verminous lair—which was unlikely—would have to take care of themselves. No one could expect him to stay until those spider claws tightened about his neck.

He did not know how long it took him to crawl fifty yards, a hundred yards up the hill. With the fury of an abysmal terror gripping him, it was all he could do to keep inching forward rather than yield to the primitive urge to dash frantically away.

He had covered a considerable distance, keeping always to the screening brush. And then, by the pale yellow-green light radiated from the open hive, he found himself at the borders of an open patch. He was about to dive back into shelter when several dark bushes to his left flashed into action. He had barely time to make out the squat crouching forms, barely time to send a shot flaming through the night, when the attackers closed upon him.

CHAPTER TWELVE

SOMEWHAT TO HIS SURPRISE, Dave attracted no attention as he slipped into the hive. With unblinking and doubtless unseeing phosphorescent open eyes, the web-creatures swung in their meshes, all of them seemingly asleep; the menagerie smells, mixed with the sour odor as of vinegar, caused the invader to wrinkle his nose in disgust.

Once inside, he paused; snapped open his clasp-knife; threw circumspect glances to his right and left; then started off along a floor of some spongy dough-soft material. His first action was to rescue Eunice's wristwatch; he could not hold back a sigh as he clutched it to his breast and the memory of its owner rushed back over him. Apparently it was just as he had suspected: it had worked itself loose as she writhed in her captors' arms; there was no other reminder of her anywhere, though his eyes explored the vicinity exhaustively.

But there were tracks on the floor, which took impressions in the manner of slightly moist clay. He could make out the marks of two of the seven-clawed creatures—most likely, Eunice's jailors.

Scarcely reckoning the possible price, he pursued the tracks. They wound in and about as if their makers hardly knew the way; followed the curve of the wall; twisted under low-hanging meshes; looped across wide, mostly open spaces; then kept briefly to the great rows of gray roof-supporting pillars, which, as thick at the base as cathedral columns, seemed made of some form of stone or cement. Yet clearly, despite all his meanderings, Dave was taking the right path. For after he had gone a good distance, his gaze was attracted to a little yellow object on the floor. As he snatched it up, his heart did a wilder dance than if he had unearthed a gold mine. It was a carton of matches!

"Sure enough," he reasoned, as he stood fondly turning his find over and over in his hands, "either it fell out of her knapsack, or she dropped it on purpose, to show me the way if I ever got this far."

But what if the track led on endlessly? He could see no sign of its destination; and here and there, where it was crisscrossed by other newly made tracks, it was a bit hard to follow. Besides, would he not get so deep inside the hive that he would be unable to make his way out?

Overhead the translucent ceiling curved enormously, with intricate meshed supports and innumerable great dangling webs; hundreds, maybe thousands of sleeping natives hung at various heights. But the wall, hidden by the gray of the webs, was already so well concealed that the intruder could only guess its direction.

"Henessey's right," he reflected. "I'm an infernal fool to've come in. Heaven knows how I'll get out again." But when he remembered Eunice's peril, he knew that he would rather be a risk-taking fool than remain safe like Henessey.

Just as this thought flashed over him, he heard a gabbling, cackling noise; and wheeled about to face half a dozen creatures. They were not hostile, that he knew instantly; but they were curious, and surprised, and just a little afraid; and they huddled together in a group, like girls giggling before some unpleasant but not too dangerous beast in a zoo. They were all just like the miserable slave-creature Henessey had seen; they were each from three to four feet tall, and stood on ostrich-slim legs; and their scaled bodies were not gaudy and iridescent like the bird-people Dave had known, but were buff or ashen; and the stumps of their four shorn-off wings stood out on their shoulders; and their two pairs of eyes were almost lusterless. But a faint glitter, of interest or amusement, did light the gaze of one or two.

Wondering if they could not be friends, Dave motioned to them. But one of them, misconstruing his gesture, squawked in fear; at which they all whirled about and went scurrying away like panicky barnyard fowls.

Although none of the web-monsters had seemed to notice, Dave felt more uneasy than ever. Might those flighty bird-things not betray him? But no, there was nothing malicious about them. However, what of that striped black-and-gray creature that swung on a net twenty feet above? Surely the big wide-open eyes, cold and inhuman as a cuttlefish's, were scrutinizing him!

Instantly Dave started away. But even as he withdrew, the monster's head shot out, seeming to cover half the distance between them. The phosphorescent eyes, in the dust-gray face, glowed frigidly, with alertness and malignity. For the barest fraction of a second, Dave saw the creased features indented with lines of astonishment, fear, hatred, and malevolence. And then an amazing thing happened. With a spring-like snapping motion, the creature swung its head about, so as to show its other face, complete with eyes, flat one-nostrilled nose, minute mouth, and long, scaly, horned head. But this face had a wholly different expression. It was smiling amiably, almost benignantly!

"My God!" Dave reflected. "This beats old Roman Janus!"

But which face was the true one, and which the false?

However, Dave did not wait to find out. Half expecting to hear the shrilling of an alarm, he dashed away, still following the tracks of Eunice's captors—after all, he was so deep in the hive that he might as well take this direction as any.

But no alarm shattered the silence: most of the web-creatures continued to sleep and swing as calmly as if no being from another planet had invaded their community.

Nevertheless, Dave's nerves did feel a mounting tension. Angrily he told himself that he was being frightened by shadows. And yet it was as if an impalpable menace were growing all about him, as if something vague and sinister were pursuing him, dodging his every footstep, tracking him like a leopard. He found himself glancing behind, warily, doubtfully, though nothing was there except the same undisturbed tangles of webs. "What's getting into you, you old rummy!" he mentally rebuked himself. "Getting so interested in your own precious skin that you're forgetting about Eunice?"

For several minutes, he refused to glance behind. But that same tormenting feeling was with him—the sense of something intangible, something terrible creeping up from the rear. Everywhere the great webs, with their prodigious whorls and geometrically spaced loops and long connecting cables, stretched about him just as when he had entered. Everywhere the denizens of the webs lay seemingly asleep. Then why did a rising, unreasoning terror command him to flee?

Why should they have carried Eunice all this distance? Would he ever find her? Was his search not a little like the mythical quest of Orpheus for Eurydice in the Underworld? How, even if he did find her, would he charm the natives into letting her leave?

This thought had barely crossed his mind when he felt something gripping at one foot. He looked down, and removed a strand of some soft gray sticky substance that had begun to curl about his left calf. He whipped out his knife; but had hardly detached the strand when a second caught at his right calf. This too he easily threw off, when something clutched at one arm.

As he tore at the newest obstruction, he gazed up in apprehension—and his fears were confirmed. Three monsters were dangling just above, each gripping the web with three pairs of long, seven-fingered hands. One of them was a doubly large beast, horrible in its scaly coat of glistening blue-black. Another was banded snake-like in black and tan. The third was of a dirty-looking mottled reddish brown. But all were moving energetically; and all let down dangling gray streamers from the brush-like appendages at their rears—streamers that seemed to unwind in the manner of cables being released from a coil.

Impulsively Dave started off. But at the same time a gray strand caught him about the waist like a lasso. To throw it off was a matter of several seconds, for it clung to his hands and clothes. And before he had removed it, another had joined it; and ropes of the same substance had wound themselves about his arms. Not if he had had three times his natural energy could he have competed with that gray, soft, adhesive material. Though he slashed vigorously with his knife, loop after loop entangled him; within a minute, both his legs had been lashed together, both his arms were as if strapped to his sides, his neck had been enclosed so that he could barely breathe; and, kicking and squirming like an overturned beetle, he toppled to the floor...

Then, from just above, he heard a clicking, clucking sound, and a whirring as of gigantic insects. And while he still threshed futilely, he saw the three monsters descending from the web; saw them standing over him with evil phosphorescent green eyes.

CHAPTER THIRTEEN

FOR A WHILE THE BEASTS paraded all about him, inspecting him from every side. One of them plucked at his clothes with long gray fingers—five jointed fingers that were extraordinarily supple; another tore a strip off his sleeve and passed it to his comrades, each of whom examined it with a pained expression on one face, although the other face was blank and inexpressive. The third creature meanwhile, with a disgusted grimace on his rear face, pointed to Dave's hair; pulled it as if to discover whether it would come out; and then, with a roar of mirth, passed one probing hand over the shaggy back of the victim's head.

Their swift nimble fingers, cold to the touch as steel, now began to feel all over the man's face, arms, and neck; while one of the creatures pried his mouth open, and shrieked in astonishment to observe the teeth. A second went so far as to jerk at his tongue; but he snapped his jaws together in time to bite the intruding fingers savagely; at which the creature shrieked, and, nursing the bruised members, withdrew to a distance. But Dave's mouth burnt with a taste as bitter and unpleasant as iodine.

The two remaining monsters, who had howled in amusement at their comrade's injury and seemed not at all disturbed by his suffering, now apparently held a conference, at least, they stood face to face, crouching in their usual attitude, while each in turn uttered a painfully harsh combination of grating, grunting, and chirring noises, at times like the sounds of insects, at times like wild beasts in a wood. This went on for a long while, varied by intervals of, silence; and all the time the captive, squirming and gasping in his meshes, remained unnoted on the floor.

Then all at once one of the creatures uttered a long drawn hoot, reminding Dave of a locomotive whistle. And as if forgetting all about the captive, he and his companions started away.

It may have been ten minutes later when half a dozen of the bird-people arrived. They were drab and bedraggled wingless specimens. With a dull, disheartened appearance; and they seemed to act automatically as they fastened long sticky gray ropes to Dave's, helpless form, and then, working together machine-like while uttering occasional gurglings and cluckings, began slowly to drag him away.

They may not have gone far, but it seemed miles as they bumped him along the floor, while he struggled to save his head from a fatal blow. At last they pulled him through a curved, irregular doorway into a web-shaped circular compartment, of about the size of a large room on earth. He noticed the faintly self-luminous hammock-like meshes that dangled from the ceiling twelve feet above; and the equally self-luminous webbed curtains that fluttered at one side. He also observed the queer creatures that squirmed and scuttled about: blue-red things with three-forked tails, running over the walls and ceiling; purple moth-like things that whizzed through the air, or stood on the floor, whirling about so swiftly as to be almost invisible; and little eight-limbed beasts that looked like small replicas of the web-creatures, except that they had each only one well-defined face and no horns. Seeing how some of his attendants fondled and caressed these little monsters, Dave knew them to be household pets.

As the bird-people untied him, Dave wondered whether he too was not now regarded as a domestic animal. Perhaps the web-beasts had contemptuously turned him over to their slaves or servants to amuse their spare hours. Might that not be why his captors hung over him as they did, chirping and cooing and pecking? After his cramped arms and legs had been unbound and he had stretched them gratefully, the bird-things fluttered about him a little like small boys about their first puppy. Every gesture, every motion of his fingers or twisting of his lips, was the theme of murmurous comment. Then suddenly two pairs of the creatures, as if realizing that they had forgotten something, rushed away and in a minute returned, each pair weighed down with a large clay jar containing several gallons of clear water. They motioned him to drink; and being thirsty, he complied, bending down and lapping up the liquid dog-fashion; while some of the attendants daintily sipped from the other vessel.

But there was no sign of food. Like all the bird-people, they evidently thought that a jar of water was a banquet.

However, Dave was too excited to eat, even if food had been brought to him. He glanced anxiously toward the doorway, which had been partially covered with waving strands of the sticky gray material; but whenever he started toward it, one or two attendants interposed themselves, with warning caws and squawks.

"Good heavens!" he thought. "Am I going to be locked in this cobwebbed den? Then how'm I going to help Eunice?" What if she too were imprisoned in a hole like this?

But before he had had much time for thought his attention was diverted. His captors' minds, evidently, were like those of children; like children, two of them began fumbling in his knapsack, curiously inspecting every object. Heedless of his protests, they were dragging out the contents: the packages of food, which they examined in an amused, bewildered way; the flashlight, which they turned over and over, and tried to look through, as if it were a telescope; the medicines; the water bag; and, finally, the matches, a carton of which one of them seized as a special prize.

"Hey, there!" Dave yelled, foreseeing danger. And with a dexterous movement, he wrested the carton from its possessor.

"Might as well show 'em what it's for," he reflected. "Then they'll be less likely to get into trouble."

Instantly he struck one of the matches.

Shrieks, screams and screeches, mingled with cacklings of glee, broke out as the little flame leapt up—brighter if somewhat briefer than a match-spurt on earth, because of the higher oxygen content of the atmosphere.

One or two had begun timidly to withdraw; the others, like small boys intrigued by a sleight-of-hand performance crowded closer, with babblings that plainly said, "Do it again! Again!"

Although he disliked wasting another of the precious matches, he repeated the performance, to the clamorous amusement of his audience. Was it possible that they had never seen fire before?

While he was asking himself this question, two of the bird-people slipped away...to return after several minutes along with a pair of their masters: a black-and-gray speckled brute with one half-closed front eye; and a coal-black monster at least a foot larger than the average.

Both these creatures, after squeezing their way into the room, stood glaring at Dave with phosphorescent greenish eyes. What had he done that these fearsome beasts should be summoned?

But he was reassured when the bird-creatures began pointing to the matches with squeaks and squeals whose meaning was unmistakable. Light another! Light another!"

Evidently there was no help for it—he must squander another of these irreplaceable treasures.

The effect of the new match-flare was strange and unexpected. The web-monsters both uttered yells of pain and threw two hands in front of their forward eyes, to shield them from the light. Clearly, they were unadapted even to the moderate brilliance of a match-flare! Could that be why they lived in faintly illuminated enclosures, and seemingly never ventured abroad except by night?

As this idea came to Dave, it occurred to him to try a fuller test. He snatched at the flashlight, which one of his attendants had dropped just in front of him; and sent its rays sparkling toward the eight-limbed beasts.

As before, they yelled; threw up two hands to protect their eyes; and at the same time shrank back to the further wall. Then, with heavy rumbling shouts, the black monster began pointing to the flashlight, plainly ordering Dave to put it down. And Dave hesitated a second or two, then reluctantly complied; after which, shading their front eyes with their hands, the creatures again drew near. But only for a second. Both of them simultaneously let out a deafening howl; while shrieks of agony burst forth from behind. And Dave, wheeling about, realized what had happened.

One of the hammock-like meshes was afire. Highly inflammable, it burnt with a vivid orange blaze, as if gasoline had been poured upon it. At the same time, two of the bird-things were hopping about as if mad, with fires licking at their wing-stumps. While Dave's back was turned, the idiotic creatures had been playing with the matches!

It was frighteningly clear that none of the bystanders knew what fire was. Instead of quenching the flames, they swept about the room in a shrilling pandemonium, fanning the conflagration into greater activity. Already the air was acrid with smoke; in a moment, the whole place would be ablaze. Dave had a vision of the entire hive burning—and horror seized him when he remembered who else was held prisoner in its obscure recesses.

Automatically, even as this thought stabbed his mind, he did the obvious. He lifted one of the earthen jars; and splashed gallons of water over the flaming meshes. And as the fires sizzled and went out, he turned to the two shrieking, burning bird-creatures, and poured the contents of the other water jug over their backs and shoulders. And finally he tore down a smoldering portion of the web, and extinguished the last spark underfoot.

Pausing for breath, he was aware of the effect he had created. Now that the commotion had subsided into a faint babbling and murmuring, all six bird-people were staring at him with eyes no longer dull, but glowing with wonder, awe and admiration. Even the phosphorescent greenish orbs of the two web-animals, as they slowly returned after scurrying into the distance, seemed to shine in a less cold, unfriendly way. But what Dave chiefly noticed were the two burned creatures. Still moaning and sobbing a little from their wounds, they approached him. One, he observed, was a slightly undersized thing that limped a bit, and was covered with yellowish brown scales. And the other was full-sized, and had steel-gray scales, and a large crescent star on its milky brow and left cheek. Both, as if by one will, approached their rescuer; dipped their hands low before them; then rested their chins on the floor, in a position of abasement in which they remained for several minutes.

A grunt from the coal-black web-creature distracted Dave's attention. He was reeling like a man who has been bludgeoned on the head. Then, in a swift sibilant voice, extremely unpleasant to Dave's ears, he began addressing two of the bird-people. And at this they set up a great gabbling and cackling, and turned toward Dave with suddenly kindled eyes. It was evident that an important decision had been reached.

*   *   *

An interval of comparative calm followed. Because of the awe he had evoked by putting out the fire, Dave was treated as something better than one of the lower animals. He was permitted freedom, though of a limited nature; and he was allowed to regain the articles in his knapsack. True, he had to pass most of his time in the webbed room with the domestic pets; but he could now and then go out for short distances into the hive, though always surrounded by the bird-people who crowded about him in numbers precluding escape.

The next important episode was the arrival of Go-glabbo. This, he learned, was the name of the large wrinkled old bird-creature who first visited him an hour or two after the fire. Like all his fellow captives, he had only the clipped-off stumps of wings; but his greater size and majestic sorrowful presence indicated a personage. Apparently he was older than the others; apparently, also, he had not their simple, childlike mind; his face, gray-brown rather than milky white, showed deep ruts and furrows, and his sunken eyes had a profound, otherworldly glow.

He immediately made his purpose plain. He began stalking about the room, and let out various clear sounds in a bell-like tinkling voice that reminded Dave of the free bird-people. "Kal-len! Kal-len!" he said, meaningfully indicating one of the webs. And Dave knew at once that Go-glabbo was trying to tell him the native term for this object. "Kal-len! Kal-len!" the pupil repeated, in a way to bring a ripple of laughter from most of the onlookers, though the tutor nodded approvingly. Then Go-glabbo pointed to the floor. "Yolup! Yo-lup!" he exclaimed. And Dave repeated these syllables, and did his best to remember the word for floor.

It was slow work, of course, and slower still when Go-glabbo began to link verbs to the nouns so as to form short sentences. He would, for example, make a spurt across the room, then point to himself, and utter repeatedly, "Blun-zu! Blun-zu!" And thus Dave got the idea that this meant, "I run! I run!" Having a good retentive memory, he was able to fix the phrase in his mind; and though he confused it at times with expressions such as "Mur sdar" ("You drink!"), and "Kun gton" ("He sleeps"), his tutor smiled continual encouragement.

A long period went by...many of the thirty-two-hour days...enough to make several weeks, though Dave lost all exact count of time. And meanwhile he spent most of his waking hours learning and practicing the native tongue. Meanwhile also his contacts were almost entirely with the bird-people; the web-creatures, he observed, still remained for the most part somnolent during the long spells of daylight, but Were roused to immediate activity whenever the third sun set.

Dave's training had barely begun when he learned that the web-monsters and the bird-people spoke the same language (because the masters had absorbed the language of their slaves). At the same time, he discovered that the art of writing was well developed. The writing substance was a tissue-thin clay or stone composite with a corrugated surface; marks drawn on the ridges had a different meaning from those made in the depressions. The writing instrument was a long flinty stick, which left a luminous mark, so that all writing could be read as easily in the dark as by daylight. Thick volumes of the corrugated tissue had been compiled, ordinarily cut into sheets about two feet square; Go-glabbo proudly displayed some of them, turning the pages with reverence; for just as his people had created the language, so they had written the books and devised the very system of writing.

Rapidly as he was learning, it seemed to Dave that he did not progress nearly fast enough; he could hardly restrain his, impatience to speak the language. It was not only that there were a thousand matters on which to satisfy his curiosity. The chief, the overwhelming motive was that he must be able to converse before he could hope for news of Eunice, the thought of whom was like a burning goad in his mind. He would see her in his dreams; she would call out to him constantly, "Dave! Dave! Come help me! Come! Come—come soon!" He knew that she could not be far away; he felt sure that she was in need of him—yet she might have been back on earth, for all he could do for her now.

True, Henessey (so Dave supposed) was still free. But no hope lay in that direction. How, by the way, was Henessey managing to exist, all alone in a venomous world?

Dave himself meanwhile was finding it hard enough to live. While the bird-people still brought him water—sufficient water for drinking and bathing—in the beginning not a scrap of food was on the bill of fare. For a day or two Dave kept himself alive from the reserves in his knapsack; then, fearing to exhaust these supplies, he began to forage about for other means of subsistence. But at first he could find nothing. Then, when he could see the shadow of famine just ahead, he turned to some of the green things (or, rather, the blue-green things) which he had seen growing here and there on the floor of the hive.

These, he learned, were carefully cultivated, and were watered regularly by the bird-people; they had been intended, as he suspected, not for beauty, but for utility. Their stems exuded a sticky sweetish juice which was the best preservative for the webs; without repeated coats of this substance, a web would decay and split apart, resulting in dangerous and possibly fatal accidents. (Three of the web-creatures, according to Go-glabbo, had plunged to their doom some time ago because the preservative or Yxion had not been applied to some of the upper meshes. And six of the bird-people had been punished with death for this mishap).

Dave found that the secretions of the plants, which gathered in dime-sized gummy globules along the hirsute stems and under the long sword-edged leaves, were fairly palatable and quite nutritious. Having sampled some of these, Dave wondered if the whole plant might not be edible; and, accordingly, he uprooted one, although not without lacerating his hands on the sharp leaves. The root, he discovered, was bulbous and about as large as a good-sized turnip; and its deep purple flesh, when he slashed it with his knife, was of a rewarding sweetness—even more nourishing, he thought, than the gummy secretion.

But he had hardly bitten into the pulp when a ferocious growl caused the booty to drop from his hands. One of the web-creatures, dangling ten feet above, had suddenly awakened; and looked down with a menacing glare. With the hoots and snarls of this beast still in his ears, Dave started off at full speed, while the bird-people cackled and fluttered in wild excitement at his side. To poach upon the Yxion preserves was evidently a serious offense.

Nevertheless, when he awoke next morning in his circular prison-chamber, several Yxion plants—roots and all—were lying at his side. And while he wondered who had brought them he saw two pairs of faintly glittering eyes peering from the doorway—the eyes of Tintle and Glarr, the bird-people he had saved from the fire. And then all at once he understood. They had observed that he wished the Yxion plant; and though the need for eating was something beyond their comprehension, they had obtained the treasure out of gratitude, and at heaven only knew what risk!

Thenceforth, two or three times a day, Dave found at least one Yxion plant near the wall where he slept. A ring of the bird-folk would look on with luminous knowing eyes; and when he had eaten, the remains would be furtively cleared away. All seemed to share the knowledge of danger and the zest of doing the forbidden, though probably none but Dave realized that they had saved his life.

And now that the food problem had been settled, he could concentrate the better on the local language.

CHAPTER FOURTEEN

AS DAVE BEGAN TO LEARN the language, he had daily talks with Go-glabbo—talks that shed strange and often startling light concerning the Lil-bro, or bird-people; and their masters, the web-creatures, or Ugwugs.

But on the all-important question he gained no light. "Is there anyone else of my race in the hive?" he asked. "Have the Ugwugs not captured some other member of my species?"

"I know of no other member of your species," answered Go-glabbo, with a displeased squawk. "We Lil-bro are not taken into the confidence of our masters. If they have captured any other such as you, it has not been their pleasure to tell us."

Whenever Dave returned to the question, he received the same answer. Nor could he wrench any better response from any of the bird-people. In growing dejection, he realized that he would have no news until he could find some way of looking for himself.

Meanwhile, in his daily sessions with Go-glabbo, it was the latter who most often sought information.

"Who are you? Tell me of your people," Dave asked one day, as he sat in his usual fashion opposite his tutor on the cobweb-gray floor, supporting his back against some hammock-like meshes.

"But who are you? Tell me of your people!" Go-glabbo countered, his minute mouth opening in curiosity and wonder. "By my four eyes! It is not for your own sake that the Ugwugs are educating you! It is so that they may learn who you are, where you come from, and whether you fulfill an ancient prophecy."

"What ancient prophecy?"

"That a traveler from an undiscovered land would enter their city, and do strange and miraculous things, and after a while leave in a great puff of light. Since you have already done strange things, and made a great brightness that wounded two of our people, the High Webbed One thought you might be the traveler the soothsayers foretold long ago."

"Who is the High Webbed One?"

Go-glabbo, ignoring the question, blinked oddly, and turned his head so as to reveal the two scintillating rear eyes.

"What is your name? Where do you come from?"

"My name is Dave Harrowell. I come from a world in far-off space."

Go-glabbo clucked softly to himself, so softly that at first Dave hardly realized he was laughing.

"That cannot be, Dave Harrowell." He pronounced the words so that they sounded like "Glabe Glarrowell— No living thing has ever come out of space. You have risen from the depths of Sar, our own planet. That is so clear that a half-grown Ugwug would know it."

"What makes you think that?" Dave asked, not quite certain if Go-glabbo were serious.

"I am not alone in thinking it. All the Ugwugs think it. You look in some ways like us Lil-bro, but you have no wings, nor even wing-stumps: and no arms for climbing like the Ugwugs. Therefore you are built to live in some place where you neither climb nor fly. Again, you have but two eyes and those of rudimentary power, proving that you are made for life in a dim, underground region. Your legs are strong, as befits one who has to roam much in caves below. Your skin is soft showing it has not felt the light of day; and is so sensitive that you have to cover it with patches of some ugly foreign material, we know not what. Again; being unable to use the sunlight like the higher forms of life to make your food within your own bodies, you have fallen to the level of the most rudimentary animals; you are a parasite, who absorb the food produced in the bodies of other organisms. All this makes a chain of clear scientific proof, showing that you come from the depths of this planet. There is nowhere else you could have come from."

"And how do you suppose I came up out of the depths?" demanded Dave, who hardly knew whether to be irritated or amused.

"That is not important. Since you are here, obviously you had a way to come up. However, we know that there are caverns, reaching down further than any of us have ever gone; also, the craters of dead volcanoes, which send their tunnels down for great distances."

Dave had not been able to follow all Go-glabbo's words; but he did catch their general drift.

Now suddenly a shocking realization burst over him; he had no way to prove that he was not from this planet, Sar! He had no way to paint a picture of the earth; to demonstrate that the earth existed, or had ever existed. When he admitted that he could not say how far away his native world was, and could not identify its parent sun nor even be sure of its direction he did not wonder that Go-glabbo's large round eyes twinkled incredulously.

"Dave Harrowell," the latter chided, "you would do well to heed an ancient saying of our people, 'He who cannot honor the truth should bind his lips together.'"

Thenceforth Dave knew better than to discuss his place of origin.

"I see that your mind is almost empty, Dave Harrowell," the tutor said a few days later, as he sat scratching absently at his gray scales with a curved little claw-like hand. "You know less than a fledgling. Then let me tell you about my people. There was a time when we, the Lil-bro, possessed the whole planet of Sar. Our colonies were everywhere, with their shimmering, fluttering hives. Our people, lifted on their four gorgeous wings, spent most of their time singing and dancing and whirling in the air, in the joy and pride of existence. Since we had not your brute need of filling our bodies with the substance of other creatures, but found all our nutriment in the water we drank and the air we breathed and the rays of the three suns that showered down upon us, there was no cause for us to quarrel over the means of subsistence. We led a happy life and a carefree one, and thanked the bright Spirit of the Light that we were alive. Thus we had been for countless cycles, and expected to be for countless cycles more. Each of us lived his allotted seven cycles, and then quietly, without pain or regret, went down to his rest—"

"How long is a cycle?" Dave interrupted.

"The time required by our planet Sar to make one complete revolution about the center of gravity of the three suns, it is a very long time, thirty-seven thousand, three hundred and eleven of our days."

Dave did a rapid mental calculation. Figuring one of the local days as thirty-two hours, a cycle was equal to a bit more than a hundred and thirty-five earth-years. If the bird-people lived seven times that long, they would approach the good old age of a thousand!

Could it be that their plant-like metabolism, which enabled them to produce their food without intake of poison from alien bodies, was what made this longevity possible?

"Our life was so easy, so gay and merry," Go-glabbo went on, his gray-brown face furrowed with a profound sadness, "that we fell into a false feeling of security. Doubtless, also, we lost track of the realities in our search of pleasure, and became too soft. At all events, in the course of hundreds of cycles, one of the lower animals gradually spread across all the continents."

He paused; glanced about him to make sure that there was no eavesdropper; then solemnly went on.

"This was the web-creature, the Ugwug, which for ages built only low hives in the deserts and waste places, and harmed no one. It was too mean and lowly for us to notice, since it had not even wings; and what was more, it could not endure the daylight, the splendid bright daylight in which we gloried; and went abroad only at the time of darkness, when we slept. We scarcely thought it worth a glance, even when its hives kept growing, until they reached the size of hills and mountains. And then one day sad news came to our people. In a night raid, the Ugwugs had entered one of our colonies, and had captured some of our brothers in great nets and carried them off. This was but the first of many raids, which became more and more common, until we could not roost at night except with a great terror upon us, and with guards posted about our hives that we might flee on the enemy's approach. Even so, the Ugwugs stole up so often that our people became fewer throughout the world, and their hives not nearly so many as of old."

"What did the Ugwugs want with your people?"

Almost instantly, however, Dave regretted the question.

Reproachfully Go-glabbo glared at him out of big hurt eyes. He did a turn or two about the room on his ostrich-like legs; took up one of the small blue-red domestic animals by its three-branched tail as it streaked across the floor; examined it absently; and replied in a pained voice.

"Do you look at me and have to ask? Do you not see my comrades with their wing-stumps? They, like me, could once fly with glimmering scales on rainbowed wings in the glory of the sunlight. But having been caught, we must serve the Ugwugs, who are enemies of the light. What else can we do? They have cut off our wings. Without wings we could not reach the island of Laro, which is the only inhabitable place in the world where there are no Ugwugs, and is located as far to the sunrise as a Lil-bro could fly between the rising of the red Sun and the setting of the blue. But as it is now, even if we could escape, they would pursue us with a cruel vengeance. No! we must all be slaves till our seventh cycle ends. Even I—I who was revered as one of the Knowing Ones of my tribe—must be a slave till my seventh cycle ends. Thanks to the Lord of The Three Suns, that will not be long now!"

Go-glabbo's head sagged; all the light had left his four eyes.

But in a moment he had revived, and a little wearily answered Dave's further questions.

"When your seventh cycle ends, will your children have to serve the Ugwugs?"

"My children?" Go-glabbo threw back in a rasping voice. "Do you think any of us captives are so wicked as to have children? If by any chance an egg were laid, we would destroy it instantly. No! far better that our race should die out in the first generation of enslavement."

"But if you do not reproduce, will the Ugwugs not raid other communities for slaves?"

Go-glabbo uttered a low hiss; stepped to the door to make sure that no spy was about; then went on, sadly.

"The Ugwugs will raid other communities, no matter what we do. They are a greedy race, whose desires know no boundary. Their whole life-system rests upon greed."

"But how so?" asked Dave.

Go-glabbo placed himself on the floor, in the position of a roosting bird, with his legs tucked under him.

"I may do them wrong," he went on solemnly, "for we Lil-bro are of such different minds from them that they are harder to understand than the insects of the fields. We believe that life should be a free and joyous thing. We believe that the great Lord of the Three Suns has given us wings, and that we were meant to fly. We believe that he has given us gay hearts,. and that we were meant to be gay. We believe that he has brightened the world with rich tints and colors, gorgeous scents, musical winds and streams, and radiant landscapes, and that we were meant to love and enjoy those colors, scents, winds, streams and landscapes. We believe that we have been granted all that we need, and more than we need and were meant to live together harmoniously. This is not my philosophy only, Dave Harrowell. This is the philosophy of all free colonies of Lil-bro. And that, until the Ugwugs came, was the religion by which we lived."

"And the Ugwugs believe differently?"

"Differently?" Go-glabbo shifted his legs uneasily, lifted his wing-stumps as if obeying some ancient impulse, then settled down with an unhappy grunt. "Do you have to do more than open your two eyes to know that the Ugwugs believe differently?"

"But their bodies are not as yours," Dave suggested. "They have no wings. Maybe they cannot thrive on air and water, but have to take food into their bodies, even as I—"

"No, no," Go-glabbo interrupted, sharply. "They are not under that bestial necessity. They need not struggle in order to live. Nevertheless, they allow themselves neither joy nor peace. In the battle for what they do not need, they have enslaved not only us but themselves. Indeed, they threw an even viler bondage about themselves; they have put fetters about our bodies, but have tied cords around their own minds and spirits. Thus they have destroyed love and even good will along With freedom and happiness, and have let selfish competition, envy, hatred and every other evil take their place."

Go-glabbo waddled toward the door, and looked up into the vast spaces wherein hundreds of the webbed creatures hung motionless on their nets.

"For saying this," he resumed, as he re-seated himself, "I might be condemned to strangle on one of the webs. But that disturbs me not. I have often prayed to end my seventh cycle."

"But if the Ugwugs have no need of food," Dave argued, "what have they to compete about?"

Go-glabbo sighed. "That is what we Lil-bro have long been asking. Again I may do them an injustice, for the channels of their minds are blind spaces to our eyes. But there, as We Can see them, are the facts. Their lives are built about their webs. These are made from secretions of their own bodies, which unwind through those wide organs you may have noticed in their rears."

"I did notice," said Dave, remembering the brush-like appendages. "You know," he added, hastily, "in my native land we have a small eight-legged animal with similar habits."

"As you have learned," Go-glabbo hurried on, "the webs can be preserved by means of the Yxion plant. Thus they can be kept for many cycles. Hence an Ugwug may not only have the web which he himself wove, but those that his father and his father's father wove before him. More than that, he may have as much of any neighbor's web as he can seize. You have seen two Ugwugs fighting?"

"That I have!" acknowledged Dave, as he recalled the two monsters battling by means of their horns.

"Quarrels among these beasts are very common, and are often fatal. In that case, the winner takes over the web of his foe. Thus one Ugwug may win a great spread of web. The more web he takes, the higher in the hive he may sit."

"But what is the use of all this web?"

Go-glabbo uttered a puzzled squawk. "I have passed whole cycles, my friend, trying to answer that question. All that we know is that the webs originally were places of rest, sleep and shelter. Of old the Ugwugs would build low huts or nests of the same substance to protect themselves from the elements; they still do this when caught out of doors in a storm or in the light of day. They also—"

"Ah, that explains the small hive-shaped gray houses we saw in the woods!" interrupted Dave.

"They also," Go-glabbo continued, ignoring this remark, "used them and still do use them as swinging sleep nets or berths. But after all, there is only a small amount that any one Ugwug could use. That is why I say they are a greedy race, whose desires know no limits. For every Ugwug's aim is to get as much web as he can."

"And what when he gets a lot of web?"

"As I have said, the more he owns the higher in the hive he may sit. The higher in the hive he may sit, the more he is honored and respected. And the more he is honored and respected, the more he is courted and flattered, the more his neighbors crouch and fawn before him, the more he is envied and hated, the more he has to fight to protect his webs, the more in danger he is of being thrown down by treachery or force, and the less his peace and joy of life. But all Ugwugs strive to rise in the hive."

"And is there no gain from all this?"

Go-glabbo paused, while scratching with the fingers of one talon-like hand at the gray substance of the floor.

"There is much gain, in Ugwug eyes. If they climb high enough, they can order their people around, since all will rush to do the bidding of a Webnate, as they call one with much web. Also, every Ugwug hopes that he may climb to become the High Webbed One—the one who perches at the topmost pinnacle of the hive, and so has the greatest distance to fall. The High Webbed One, as befits the most hated, slandered, abused, envied, praised and admired of all the Ugwugs, passes most of his time trying to capture the webs of subjects who are trying to capture his webs from him. Since he has so much web already, he usually finds it easy to get still more. And in recognition of this merit, the Ugwugs let him make their laws. But at the same time they do their best to throw him down. The life of a High Webbed One is usually not long, but while it lasts it is very full."

Dave felt a chill traveling down his spine.

"Is the High Webbed One," he asked, "just like a common Ugwug in most ways?"

"Yes, in most ways. But usually he has an especially good double face."

"Just what do you mean by that?"

"Well, you've noticed, of course, that every Ugwug has two faces. They think this necessary—to use one of their silly phrases—if they are to get ahead in life. One of the faces, usually the rear one, expresses just what they are thinking and feeling, and so they try their best to keep this out of sight. But the other face expresses what they want you to think they are feeling and thinking. By putting this face forward, they make great progress in taking their neighbors' webs; the most successful Ugwugs are very skillful at using their false faces. And that is why, as I have said, the High Webbed One usually has an especially good double face. He has to, if he wants to rise."

"Well, after all…" Dave started to reply…when all at once he sprang to his feet, and stood listening as if electrified. From somewhere in the far recesses of the hive, a penetrating sound had shrilled.

It was such a sound as he had often heard on some traffic-crowded street on earth. He was ready to shout in amazement as he recognized the blast of a police whistle.

CHAPTER FIFTEEN

"HOLY MOSES!" HE CRIED, so excited that he did not notice that he was mixing an English expletive with the local speech. "Hear that?"

"Hear what?" gasped Go-glabbo.

The sound was repeated—a long, shrill outburst, seemingly coming from a considerable distance.

"God preserve us!" Dave almost screamed. "It's one of them!"

"What do you mean by them?" asked Go-glabbo, his eyes faintly troubled, as if he feared for his pupil's sanity.

The police whistle shrilled once more.

"But heavens above, don't you hear it?"

"I only note the savage noise that comes from your lips. What you hear, my friend, is in your own mind only—"

"Like fun it's in my own mind!" raged Dave, in English. Then, as the blast came again, in three short rapid notes, he raved on, still in English, "Euny! By glory, that's Euny, sure as I'm alive! That's just how she'd blow!"

Go-glabbo was beginning to look more concerned at the barbarian's jubilant, wildly excited expression.

Dave meanwhile was acting more and more weirdly. Obeying a sudden idea, he dived into his knapsack, and brought forth a little piece of shining metal, which he placed to his lips, sucking at it in a peculiar way.

"Sorry to blow that right in your ears," he apologized, after a long, powerful blast.

"Blow what?" demanded Go-glabbo, the creases of bewilderment deepening on his ancient gray-brown face.

Even as he spoke, a responsive whistling came from outside.

Then another idea flashed over Dave. He blew three short blasts. After four or five seconds, three short blasts came from without. Then he blew three long blasts, and was answered by three longs; then a long and a short, and was greeted by a long and a short, followed by four shorts in swift succession.

"By the Lord!" he cried, once more in English, as he mopped an invisible perspiration from his brow. "It's Euny, all right! I'd recognize her style in a thousand! She's trying to tell me she's all right!"

But instantly another thought, far less consoling, burst over him. Could she be in peril, and signaling for help? Besides, if she was able to call him now, why had she never done so before? He remembered how, before their present misfortunes, he had suggested to her and Henessey that they use the police whistles to locate one another if they were ever separated.

"Will you tell me, Dave Harrowell, why you are chewing at that strange instrument?" asked Go-glabbo, pointing in scowling displeasure at the whistle.

"If you haven't heard it, old fellow, you're deafer than a board!" snorted Dave.

"On the contrary," denied Go-glabbo, drawing himself erect in injured dignity, "I have always been commended on my exceptional hearing." And then, calling to his kinsmen Tintle and Glarr, who were on guard duty just outside. "Listen, my people! Do either of you hear anything?"

Once more Dave whistled his loudest. And from far away, after several seconds, a clear shrill blast replied.

"Well, don't you hear?" he demanded.

The two guards looked puzzled.

"Hear what?" questioned Tintle.

"There are only the usual hive sounds," said Glarr, breaking into a low rippling laughter.

"You see!" concluded Go-glabbo, with a triumphant nod toward Dave. "Didn't I tell you?"

They were all so transparently honest that Dave could no longer doubt. The truth was that they did not hear! Their ears were not adapted to the same wavelengths as his. Just as on earth a dog-whistle would be heard and obeyed by canines while man heard nothing at all, so a police whistle was too high-pitched for the ears of the bird-people who detected not the faintest sound.

But what of the Ugwugs? Not pausing to consider the risk he was taking, Dave rushed to the door. The web-creatures were sprawled above by the hundreds, asleep on their intricate nets. But not one of them stirred when he blew the whistle.

"By thunder," he thought, "if they could hear that sound, the whole community would be astir." As far as the whistle was concerned, they were all stone-deaf!

Before he had had time to consider all that this discovery implied, Go-glabbo plucked at his arm and drew him back into the circular prison chamber.

"I realize, my friend," he stated, his face wrinkled anxiously, that you have had great troubles. These have unhinged your mind. With rest and self-control I doubt not that you will recover."

Across from Dave, Tintle and Glarr were tittering.

But at the same time he heard the whistle once more from outside, two shorts and two longs; and answered it in the same manner.

"I've got to get out!" he shouted. "Got to get out—out there—and find her—find her, where she's whistling—find out why—"

"Now, now, now, soothed Go-glabbo, again taking one of Dave's arms. "Sit right down on the floor, and rest your limbs. This fit will pass in time."

"It's no fit!" Dave stormed. "I tell you, she—Euny—is out there, waiting. I've got to get to her!"

"Just control yourself," urged Go-glabbo, making long hypnotic passes with his hands: "Many of us, when overly excited, suffer from these fantasies. We think we see things, creatures in the air. This Euny or Euncy of yours will pass, like other vapors of the mind—"

"But can't you understand, it's not an hallucination, it's real!" Dave pleaded; and then broke short, seeing Go-glabbo nod as if to reply, "Yes, that's what they all say." The grim simple fact was that there was no way to convince him. In Go-glabbo's eyes, and all the bird-people's, it would seem self-evident that this stranger from a far land had a diseased mind, which made him think that he heard things where there was nothing to be heard, and saw things where there was nothing to be seen. Even Eunice would appear but a ghost created by his imagination!

Yet all the while the realization burnt deep into him that she was somewhere out there in the hive, calling to him, perhaps desperately needing him.

Urged by his raging emotions, he started again toward the door. But Go-glabbo placed himself in the way, while Tintle and Glarr stood beyond, gently deterring him.

"I must go into the hive!" he insisted.

"If you go into the hive at a time that the Ugwugs do not permit," Go-glabbo pointed out, in sad reproval, "you must pass our guards. That would not be easy, but if you do pass and are caught, who will the blame fall upon? Who but us Lil-bro, into whose charge you were given? The Ugwugs look down upon us enough even now, deeming us a base inferior race with no rights except to serve and be beaten. But if we give them an excuse, such as letting their prisoner escape, they may break out into a rantangle."

"What's a rantangle?" asked Dave, though his mind was upon the mysterious whistling, which had now ceased.

Go-glabbo sighed. "It is a form of madness that darkens the minds of the Ugwugs now and then. A great crowd of them gather, with growls, howls and hoots; and blaming us Lil-bro for all their troubles, they seize all whom they can catch, and tie us by the neck to the webs, so that we may die miserably, while all the Ugwugs dance and grunt with pleasure."

"Why should they want to kill you, if they need you to do their work?"

"The Ugwugs, alas! are not logical animals. They say the lives of creatures so inferior as us do not count. They say they must chastise us to keep us in our places. But the real reason is that they are secretly afraid of us—and secretly jealous, for in their hearts they know that we have minds and abilities that they cannot equal. That is why their feelings explode now and then in these murderous rantangles, which keep them from feeling inferior. And that is why I beg you, Dave Harrowell, not to try to escape, so that they may have no new excuse to rise against our people."

"I—I do not wish to bring any rantangle down upon you," said Dave.

He had hardly spoken when he raised the whistle to his lips, and waited—waited in vain—for an answering blast. Why had the other whistler all at once become silent?

After Go-glabbo had gathered together his writing materials and gone shuffling off for the day, Dave turned to the two guards.

"Be good people, and let me out," he begged. "Till the end of my last cycle, I will be grateful!"

The guards stared back at him with large round troubled eyes. Tintle arched up his back, and ruffled his yellowish brown scales; Glarr turned at an oblique angle that seemed to make the crescent scar on his milky brow and left cheek glow with an inner radiance.

"You know our devotion, O Light-Maker," the latter said. "You know that we would gladly pass our whole lives serving you. Ever since you slew the demon that lived in the great brightness, and saved us from ending our cycles before our time, we have known you as one of the shining creatures from the skies. So we have felt love and gratitude, and have longed to do your bidding. But we cannot let you go, O Light-Maker. If we did, the Ugwugs would punish not only us but all our people."

"Their punishment," added Tintle, "is worse than the storm that breaks with a great noise over the hilltops."

Dave, peering out of the doorway, let his glance travel stealthily to all sides, to make sure that they were not overheard. But the web-creatures swung drowsily in their meshes far above, well beyond eavesdropping distance.

"I do not wish to see you or your people punished," Dave pleaded. But the Ugwugs would not see me if I went out now, when the suns are still in the sky. Before the suns have gone down to their sleep, I will be back. I promise you, Tintle and Glarr, I promise to be back. Think! are you more eager to help me or the Ugwugs?"

"We are more eager to help you. The Ugwugs—may their cycles end soon! hissed Glarr, his eyes taking on a sudden brilliance at his own blasphemy.

"We would not care if you left," acknowledged Tintle. "If you were not seen, and came back before all the suns were out of the sky. Still, there is always danger that some Ugwug will be about even by day."

"I will elude them all, be sure of that! None will see me!" Dave swore. "As I love my life, I take my oath to be back!" Following some further pleas and promises, the guards conferred among themselves. And finally Tintle, limping slightly, crept stealthily up to Dave.

"Go!" he whispered. "There is an old law among the Lil-bro that we must deny nothing to him who has saved our last cycles. But by my lost wings! you must crouch down, and move softly. Be back before the third sun has gone to sleep lest the Ugwugs smite like a fury from the sky!"

CHAPTER SIXTEEN

ARMED ONLY WITH HIS clasp-knife, Dave felt like an aviator who has crash-landed in a jungle. All about him the webs stretched in loops and ladders, hammocks and spider-like concentric circles; one direction looked as unpromising as any other. Which way should he go? The whistling had seemed to come vaguely from his right; and so he started to the right, while staring apprehensively at the striped and spotted, the snake-banded, the reddish brown and the blue-black occupants of the webs, who swung and shifted and stirred in their sleep but showed no sign of recognition in their wide-open and (he hoped) unseeing greenish eyes.

"God help me, but I'm a reckless crazy fool," he thought, as he remembered how he had been captured before in the slimy coils. "If they catch me again, how'm I going to keep my promise to the bird-people? But they just won't catch me!" he swore, to reassure himself, when he remembered that not only the Lil-bro's fate and his own was at stake but Eunice's safety and maybe her very life.

Anxiously he blew the whistle—without response. With savage eagerness, his eyes searched the gray tangles of the webs. But there was no sign of Eunice. There was no sign even of any place where she could have hidden.

Then suddenly the gray substance of the floor gave way beneath him, and a circular trapdoor sprang open, revealing a long corridor. This gallery was round as the bore of a pipe, and not more than seven or eight feet across; and it glowed with the faint inner radiance of all the hive material. It stretched in a straight line as far as Dave could see; and was filled with bird-people, hundreds of them, stood with drooping necks and lusterless eyes, one pounding at something with his small hands, another polishing a glistening object, a third scraping at some tiny article with a continuous rasping, and still another pecking away industriously at the floor or digging at a spot on the wall. Spaced at regular intervals, Ugwug guards crouched among the workers; and a huge crimson-and-black beast, posted as gateman, turned upon the intruder a pair of baleful phosphorescent eyes that shot almost into his face upon the long distendable neck.

With a low cry, Dave retreated. The trapdoor snapped back into place, and one more peril had been averted—so he hoped. But in his flurried haste, he had stepped into a tangle of low-hanging webs, which began to tighten their nooses about his legs. As he was pulled to the floor, the thought of Eunice flashed across his mind—Eunice, whom he now could not help; and the bird-people, who would be betrayed by his absence, and subjected to God only knew what punishments.

Even as these thoughts swept over him, his clasp-knife was busy. Automatically, with the fury of a strength that he hardly knew he possessed, he was slashing at the meshes. They were thick and strong; but to cut them was only a little more difficult than to free his hands from the slimy, sticky cords. Only after minutes that seemed hours long did he manage to struggle free.

"Just my rotten luck!" he swore softly to himself, as he noticed how large a piece of the web he had hacked to bits. "I didn't mean to leave my signature."

There being nothing else to do, however, he retreated rapidly, whistling as he went—partly to keep up his courage, but chiefly in the hope that Eunice would respond.

He did not know just when it was that he began to have the sense of being observed. It was just as when he had first explored the hive—he seemed to be alone, and yet felt, or rather knew, that he was not alone. Some subtle sense, such as may warn a cat of a dog's proximity, cautioned. him to be upon his guard. The webs seemed just as before, swinging faintly in the pale light filtering down from the high ribbed ceiling; the web-creatures hung sleeping and unperceiving as ever. Or so Dave thought, while he continued to whistle and to strain his eyes in the hunt for Eunice And then he made an observation which, slight in itself, almost froze his blood.

His gaze had been attracted to one coal-black monster which, because of its unusual size, seemed somehow more sinister than most. But the beast's front eyes, of a sickly green, appeared as empty and unseeing as any; his face registered the blankness of sleep. However, the creature stirred slightly and shifted its head; and Dave, after walking a slight distance, caught a glimpse of the animal's other face, which it revealed in a careless instant. And Dave gasped, and went white. The features were convulsed with malevolence; the fiery emerald eyes were contracted in a look of cunning and malignity that belied utterly the bland harmlessness of the forward face.

It was then that Dave took to his heels. In his terror he scarcely knew where he ran. Several times he tripped and fell; more than once he narrowly escaped entanglement in the looping webs. Did the monsters, above notice this panicky thing that raced in and about, winding among the dangling screens and curtains? When at last he paused for breath, a greater alarm clutched him; the meshes on all sides looked precisely like the meshes everywhere. He had lost his way! He might wander aimlessly for hours…might wander until nightfall and the awakening of the hive had signaled his doom!

But, like many primitive men and most wild creatures, he had a sense of direction that was surer than his conscious mind. This, which had once saved him in a forest at night, came to his rescue now. He closed his eyes; swung himself about at random; and then, as some subconscious prompter took command, started forth with absolute assurance. And, not five minutes later, he saw the welcome faces of Glarr and Tintle beaming at his prison door.

Still, his mood was far from a triumphant one. His trip abroad had failed in its one purpose. He was no nearer than ever to contact with Eunice.

He had barely seated himself on the prison floor, in his usual cross-legged position, when Tintle and Glarr burst in with bobbing excited heads and shining eyes.

"O Light-Maker," they shrilled, in one voice, "there is someone to see you!"

"To see—me?" gasped Dave, as he rose unsteadily.

"To see you. One of the Ugwugs, O Light-Maker!"

Across Dave's mind there shot the terrorizing thought that he had been followed. His prowlings about the hive, possibly him breaking of one of the webs, had been reported to some higher authority, and retribution was at hand! Things must indeed be serious if one of the web-creatures, who did not ordinarily travel by day, had come for him now!

"A few Ugwugs are ordered to do duty when it is light," said Tintle, as if reading Dave's thoughts. "Especially the young, who are not hurt so badly by the glare. Come! the visitor waits outside!"

"Tell him—tell him I'm not here!" gasped Dave. "But he says, O Light-Maker, he saw you enter."

Then truly Dave knew that all was lost. Despairingly he glanced about the small circular room, wishing for some way of egress through the walls.

"Very well. Very well, I'll come," he heard himself saying, in a faint, unnatural voice.

Just outside the door, an undersized Ugwug was waiting. His body, with black stripes on a background of buff, was much slimmer than the majority, proving him to be a mere youth; his head was marked by a peculiar star-shaped purple scar on the left, of, the horn, which was not yet fully grown. He edged to within a foot of Dave, and the greenish front eyes examined him questioningly.

"Ah," he said, in a throaty voice, "you're the one I've been sent to see!"

Dave said nothing, waiting to hear his sentence. But he fingered his knife, resolved to sell his life dearly.

The Ugwug glanced at a small sheet of corrugated writing-tissue in one of his fore-hands.

"Yes, you're the one!" he affirmed. "I was told to seek an animal with only two hands, two eyes, and one face, and no horn on its head, and wearing a strange unnatural substance above its body."

One of the beast's hands fumbled appraisingly at Dave's shirt. His nose wrinkled in disgust. "Yes, you're the one. When I saw you going through this door, I knew it must be."

"What in the name of the three suns do you want with me?" demanded Dave.

"I? It is not I that want you. I have orders from above."

Dave groaned, and peered appraisingly down the aisle, wondering if there was not just the barest possibility of flight.

"I was told to get you," the Ugwug went on. "One of your own kind sent me for you."

"What's that?" cried Dave, stunned and incredulous. "What's that? One of my own kind?"

"One of your own kind. One with a sickly pale skin like yours, a small body, and only two hands, and nothing but a thin stringy substance on the back of his head where his rear face should be."

"Thank God!" Dave exulted; and reeled, and almost broke down beneath the frenzy of his joy. "It's Eunice!"

His informant, he knew, had had to use the masculine gender, since, in the language of Sar, there was no feminine.

"Thank God! Thank God!" he repeated, unable to keep his joy silent. "So all this time, when I was looking for her, she was sending out for me!"

Evidently it had not been possible for her to come herself. But that did not matter! Soon, very soon, they would be together again!

"Where is she? Where is she?" he shouted (literally, of course, "Where is he? Where is he?")

The emissary had turned to Tintle and Glarr and displayed a little stone strip marked with quaint characters. "This proves my position," he said, "and my right to ask for the prisoner."

Tintle and Glarr dropped to the floor in fluttering abasement.

"Oh, treat him well!" begged the one.

"See that no harm comes to him!" pleaded the other.

But the messenger, as if to show his contempt, butted each of the pair in turn with his half-developed horn.

"Come!" he commanded Dave. "I was told to lose no time!"

All a-tremble, Dave wasted not a second. He was surprised, however, when his guide started to climb. With a spider's agility, he scaled a long ladder of cobweb-gray, ran out across a rope-balcony that swung frighteningly beneath his weight, mounted hand over hand up a trellis as long as a city block, and sprinted across a two-foot-wide railless bridge above a hundred-yard abyss. With his three pairs of arms that enabled him to clutch at the strands above, and his feet that clung to the sticky substance below without being retarded, he was as well adapted to his medium as a fly to ceiling-walking.

But Dave, though he had scaled Andean cliffs and Alpine glaciers, made a very poor second. Terrified by the sagging of the web beneath him, he crawled along cautiously, making sure of every foothold, while his head swam when he stared into the immensities beneath…looked down hundreds of feet at meshes where eight-limbed creatures somnolently swung. Meanwhile his breath was coming faster and harder, for he was weighed down by his knapsack and provisions (which, as a precaution, he had thought it best not to leave behind). And his guide, now and then running back impatiently, would urge him on, "Faster! Faster!"

"Lord save me, how did Eunice ever climb so far?" he kept wondering. He knew, of course, that she was slim, spry and agile; and remembered how like a mountain goat she had seemed when they had picnicked together among the canyons of the San Gabriel range. However, this web was a different matter entirely—how nimble and brave she must have been! Her elevation would account, of course, for his not having seen any sign of her in the hive; it hadn't occurred to him to look above. She would have known, too, that it would be hard for him to follow. But doubtless she hadn't any choice; doubtless everything would be explained when he saw her.

The climb seemed never-ending. They clung to swaying cables over half-mile gulfs; crawled through funnels like the ventilators of a steamer; circled around nets patterned like acre— large cobwebs; scaled the precipitous slopes of the branching ceiling supports; and elbowed their way past sleeping monsters whose phosphorescent green lidless eyes seemed somehow malevolently aware. "Will we never reach the end?" Dave kept asking. And his guide would reply, laconically, "Further. A little further."

And now a dreadful suspicion shot across Dave's mind. What if all this were only a ruse? What if Eunice had not sent for him at all? What if she were merely being used as a pretext to entice him to his doom?

None the less, he kept plugging and panting on his way. Though his hands felt like bags of glue from contact with the sticky web-substance; though more than once he slipped and almost went plunging into unknown depths; though his arms seemed nearly wrenched from their sockets by the effort of clinging to the overhead cables, and though he ached in his chest and in every limb, still all the torments of the horrible climb were as nothing beside the chance to see Eunice again, to hear her voice, glimpse the sparkle in her clear blue eyes, and know that she was safe and well.

As he made his way skyward, he would not have suspected that gravity on this planet was less than on earth. He could not calculate the distance he had traveled; surely, he was a thousand yards, perhaps twelve hundred, perhaps nearly a mile above floor level when one of the peaks of the irregularly ribbed roof loomed just above, penetrated by the subdued radiance of the three suns in a soft, even glow that appeared oddly yellowish or yellow green rather than red white or blue.

"Thank the Lord, we can't go much further now!" he reflected, as for the fiftieth time he paused to regain his breath. But where, where could Eunice be?

Then he noticed, not far beneath the ceiling, a thickly woven horizontal web. It was elliptical in shape, perhaps a hundred feet long and half as much across; and its meshes were so close together that it was quite opaque. Toward this the guide mounted; then stood on the swaying hammock like platform, which was held to the roof by stout cables and began motioning to Dave as, with a fresh spurt of energy, the latter hurried toward him up a long rope ladder.

"This way! This way!" he called. "Here is one of your kind!"

Dave's head reeled; he almost lost his grip on the cords. He could see the elliptical web above bending as beneath the rapid motions of some two-footed creature. Eunice, Eunice was hastening to the edge to greet him! In a moment, he would see the flash of her big blue eyes!

A minute later, as he puffed his way almost up to the webbed platform, he did see two eyes staring down at him. They were wide with surprise, but were small and grayish-green.

CHAPTER SEVENTEEN

FOR A LONG STARTLED moment the two men stared at one another.

"By God!" cried Henessey, as, lying almost flat, he leaned out over the edge of the web-platform. "So it's you!"

"Euny? Where—where's Euny? Isn't Euny here?" Dave was barely able to stutter.

"Come on up off that ladder, old fellow, and we'll talk about it," urged Henessey, nervously. "It gives me the jitters to see you dangling there like a tightrope walker."

Somehow Dave managed to scramble on to the platform, which rocked threateningly. He saw at once that it was nothing but a bare gray surface, featured only by a half-empty knapsack, and by some cables stretched low above it near the middle. At this sight, everything went blank before him-there was no sign of Eunice!

"Come on over here, old chap, away from the edge. Hold on to those cables if you feel wobbly," Henessey was instructing. "Holy mackerel! I didn't know it was going to be you. I thought-I thought Eunice—"

"Then you know-you mean, you know where she is?" demanded Dave, as, still dazed, he began slowly to recover his senses.

Henessey shrugged. "No, old sport, wish I did know. When I heard that whistling, I thought it was her. Sounded somehow like a woman. So I sent for her, to get her out of those pesky Ugwugs' clutches. Not that I wouldn't have been just as glad to send for you, seeing that I couldn't go down myself."

Now for the first time Dave really saw Henessey. He noticed that the man was thin—many pounds thinner than of old, even though he had always been lean. His cheek bones, above the hollow cheeks, stood out prominently. His high, narrow brow seemed higher and narrower than ever, his long twisted nose longer and more twisted. His eyes had an harassed, a hunted look.

"Lord help us, Dave," he said, as he gripped the other man's hand and crept with him to the center of the sagging swaying platform, "you look like you've been through a clothes wringer! Lost weight, too, haven't you? Well, guess we've both got a pretty good idea now of Dante's Inferno."

"But Euny—Euny," Dave kept repeating, unable to forget the one obsessing idea. "Sure you don't know anything about her?"

"Only about the whistling," stated Henessey, as he pushed Dave to a seat, with his back supported against some taut cables.

"But that was her whistling. Part of it, anyway," Dave insisted. "That is," he added, swiftly, as a horrible suspicion smote him, "if it wasn't you!"

"Me?" flung back Henessey. "Do you think I'm fool enough to call attention to myself by whistling?"

He tapped meaningfully at the holster of his pistol, as if to indicate his one reliance.

"But you wouldn't be heard!" denied Dave, who was slowly regaining his breath. "Haven't you found out? Those brutes wouldn't hear a thing!"

"No?" Henessey asked, in a manner that seemed to say, "Tell it to Sweeney!"

For answer Dave snatched the whistle from his knapsack, and while Henessey strove to deter him, blew a long blast.

The Ugwug guide, who stood motionless at the edge of the web, gave not a sign. Through a peephole in the platform, the two men looked down at scores of web-creatures. But all remained sleepily dangling on their nets.

"In Pete's name! Who'd have thought it!" was all that Henessey could say.

"I was in touch with her by whistle, Dave reiterated. "I thought she was the one who summoned me up here. I swear to you Earle it was a fiendish climb."

"Don't I know it?" muttered Henessey. "It took me much longer, but I thought I'd never make it. A hundred times I expected to end like a rocket."

He turned toward the buff-and-black striped guide. "Hey, Xangrl, come here!" he yelled, using the local tongue so crudely that Dave, for all his own imperfections, wanted to laugh...

Xangrl obediently came crouching forward. To Dave s surprise, he put his head against the webbed floor in token of subservience.

"What orders did I give you?" demanded Henessey.

"Why, Master," he said, in tones a little like those of a pupil before a glowering pedagogue, "you told me to find one of your kind and bring him here. You said I would recognize him easily, and so I did when I saw him crawling about the hive bottom. Have I not done as you asked?

"There is another of my kind somewhere in the hive," Henessey went on, slowly, while making the most ludicrous errors in grammar and pronunciation. Have you seen nothing of her?"

A smile of amusement illuminated the web-creature's gray rear face. But the front face remained blandly respectful.

"If I saw another of your kind, O Master, could I forget it?"

"But there is one such, and you must find her. No! wait a bit!" he deterred, as Xangrl started off over the edge of the platform, "I have some things to say first to my friend."

Then reassuringly, to Dave, "We'll do our best to locate her, old fellow. I've just now gotten to my present position, otherwise I'd have hunted for you both sooner.

Over Dave's mind the suspicion flashed that Henessey was slightly touched in the head. On the other hand, there was no question about Xangrl's deferential attitude. And how, in any case, did Henessey happen to be perched on this high web, not far from the ceiling? All at once, in a stunned way, Dave remembered Go-glabbo's statement that the Ugwugs were honored according to their height on the web—that they schemed and battled all their lives for a high position.

"Congratulate me, old man!" Henessey went on, with just the trace of a sardonic smile. "I'm a Webnate now. Yes, Sir, I own a mighty rich stretch of web, and there isn't anybody above me except the High Webbed One himself, I in a self-made man—a power in the land. And I owe it all to my trusty little gun."

He tapped significantly at his pistol; made a wry face; thrust himself close to Dave in a confidential manner, and muttered, "Heck! I feel like someone's run over me with a threshing-machine. It's a great life, however if you can stand it."

"What in fury has happened?"

"Come, better turn to a pleasant subject, old fellow. Let's hear of your own sweet adventures."

"They've been about as sweet as a term in Sing Sing. I've been a prisoner all this time, and that's really all I have to report. But you, Earle—I can see you have a story to tell."

"You bet I have! Henessey admitted, grimly. "The kind it's a blazing lot more fun to hear about than live through."

Apprehensively he glanced toward the edge of the web.

"I'm always having nightmares of falling off. When I take a nap, I lash myself to one of the cables, just so I won't roll overboard when the bunk sways."

"If that's the way you feel, why in the name of common sense did you come up here?"

"Couldn't help myself. That's the solemn truth, Dave. Want me to tell you about it?"

"Naturally."

Henessey settled himself as comfortably as he could on the platform, which jerked and swayed every time he moved.

"Well," he began, slowly, "let's go back to the day when we parted. You know how scared I was for you—just felt it in my bones that if you went into this devilish hive things would go wrong. When you didn't come back, it wasn't any satisfaction at all to know I'd been right. I waited till night, when I was attacked by a gang of those web demons. I fired a shot, but it went wild. They caught me in their villainous ropes, and had me all strung up like a goat ready for the sacrifice. I sure thought I was a goner. But after a while, when they had me inside the hive, they untied my arms, thinking, I suppose, that my legs being still bound, I was as helpless as a steer in the slaughterhouse. Believe me, that's where they made their fatal mistake."

"Fatal?"

"Take my word, it was fatal—for some of them. My hands being loose, I worked them around to my pistol, which must have looked like a harmless little stick—they evidently didn't know what made the flash when I was captured, and after what I've learned about the whistling, I doubt if they even heard the report. But I was raving mad. I tell you, I saw red after the way they'd pushed me around and manhandled me and half suffocated me with those ropes. So, without thinking, I snapped out my automatic. The shot caught a big blue-black beast right between the front eyes. He let out an awful howl and keeled over, bleeding a sort of sticky yellow blood. While this was happening, another of those beasts made a grab for me with all six arms at once, and I let him have it, too. Got him through the breast. He roared like a lion, but listed over, and was dead in less than a minute."

"Lord help us, that's what I call asking for trouble!" commented Dave. "What under the sun could you do if the whole gang fell upon you?"

Henessey mopped his brow; his little eyes squinted fearfully, as if he were re-living his peril.

"Well, I've always tried to lead a cautious life, Dave," he declared, solemnly. "It's been my motto that a reckless man is likely to leave a young widow. But this time—and you'd better kick me for it—my excitement did get the better of me. When I came to consider what might have happened if that whole beastly army had set upon me— However, they didn't. No, thank God, instead of exterminating me then and there, those brutes formed themselves in a wide ring around me, putting their heads low to the floor, in a way to make me think of subjects worshipping a sultan."

"Mean to say they didn't resent your killing two of their friends?"

"Well, as I found out later, it was my good luck that the ones I shot were of the lowest caste—the webless ones, who lived at the pit bottom and weren't held to be of much value. Nobody called it murder to kill such common trash. It was something like swatting a fly. Just the same, they were awed at what I'd done—I tell you, they thought I was a god, or maybe they thought my pistol was a god. Nothing like it had ever been seen before on this whole blamed planet."

"But all that still doesn't explain how you got up here."

"No, by jiminy, it doesn't. Take my word for it, I've been competing with the monkeys for high-climbing honors, and no monkey ever went through half what I did. The start came right after that first little shooting contest. Some of those six-armed devils began climbing rope ladders, motioning me to follow. I was wary, of course, but the whole gang kept on in such a way that I finally got it into my head their intentions weren't unfriendly. About twenty feet above the Boor there was a sort of swinging platform, a little like this one, though much smaller. I thought I could make that easy enough, and I did, with one hand on the pistol, just in case they started any funny business. There wasn't a thing on the platform, and I was glad to rest there a bit, while those crazy beasts balanced themselves on the ropes and ladders all around me, and bowed their heads low, as if to say I was the great Lord Jehovah. It was lucky, though, I kept my weather eye peeled for trouble."

"They didn't try to throw you off, did they?"

Henessey shifted position uneasily, and stared through one of the peepholes into the intricacy of nets that reached below him for thousands of feet.

"Well, as a matter of fact, that's just what they did try. Rather, one of them tried it—a large, heavy-set beast, with a skin the color of dry grass, sprawled over with some sickly-looking dark-red sausage-shaped markings. He came at me with a growl like an angry dog—I'd been poaching on his preserves, as I afterwards learned—and he was going to deal with me in short order. Well, as he rushed forward, with his head popping in and out all his long elastic neck and his horn aimed for business, there was only one thing I could do. As bad luck would have it, a bit of the web deflected the first shot, and it didn't do any more than chip his horn. At this he yelled like a Piute, and believe me I didn't waste any time about finishing him off with the next bullet. As he crashed to the floor, the others let out a tremendous shout, and then everybody bowed lower than ever."

"And so you stayed on that platform?"

"Yes, for quite a time. They sent some of the bird-people up to teach me the language—not that I was much of a pupil and anyway it's the rummiest language you ever heard. It must have been weeks before I could talk in any sort of a way, and then I could never open my mouth without making those crazy birds laugh. Just the same I did learn some things. I found that the way to get on in this idiotic world was to rise in the webs. So I got on, all right—me and my little pistol."

Henessey paused; gave his thin face a crafty twist; thoughtfully stroked his long, ragged beard; and continued.

"I'll let you into a secret, Dave. See this pistol. Well, she's as worthless as a broomstick. Fact is I fired my last shell in killing that third monster. I thought I had another clip of ammunition somewhere, but it must have dropped out. So I said to myself, 'Earle W. Henessey, now's the time to show guts. If those beasts know you're powerless, they'll make an end of you quicker'n you'd step on a worm. Only thing you can do is put a bold front on, and go right up. How can they know the pistol won't work?'"

"Mean to say you bluffed them into your high position?"

"Well, not all at once. Maybe fifty feet above, there was another platform, and I climbed up into it one night when the owner was away. He was a fiendish-looking black monster, and when he came back I trembled so you'd have thought I had palsy; you can just bet I was ready to scramble down the ladder at his first move. But all I had to do was lift the pistol. He yelled, and ran, looking funny as the deuce with all six arms waving in the air above him; and never came back for his property. A day or two later I went higher still; and I've been rising until just today I took this platform and became a Webnate. No way of going any further now unless I challenge the High Webbed One himself."

"And no one ever challenged you?"

"Well, usually it was enough just to lift the pistol. However, I did have quite a fright once, when a purple-spotted demon started toward me from below. I couldn't see him very clearly, so turned my flashlight upon him. Then the rays hit him in the eyes, he screamed like he was being murdered and fell off the web. So I took the hint, and used the flashlight whenever these furies became pestiferous. It never failed, either. Only things that did fail," finished Henessey, with a sigh, "were the batteries. Just today I found they were burnt out."

"I can lend you mine," volunteered Dave. "But you still haven't told me all. How the heck did you get enough to eat?"

Henessey twisted his lips wryly. "Well, that's a good question. Here you see me one of the moguls of the hive, up here in an honored position that most of these half-witted Ugwugs fight and scheme to reach, without much chance of ever succeeding. But Lord! wouldn't I trade my high post for a good juicy steak! Yes, sir, or a dish of good old-fashioned pork-and-beans, or ham and eggs, or even corn beef hash—I tell you, I never go to sleep without dreaming of them!"

"But surely, you've gotten something to eat!"

"Well, in a way—but what a way! First, of course, I finished the provisions in my knapsack—they seemed to vanish by magic. Before they were quite gone, I noticed a sweetish-smelling paste the bird-people spread over the webs—to preserve them, they said."

"From the Yxion plant," stated Dave.

"Yxion? I could never get that name straight. Anyhow, it was edible. After it's been on the web a while, some chemical change sets in, and makes the sour odor you notice all through the hive. But when it's fresh it's about as nutritious, I guess, as beets or carrots. God! am I sick of the stuff! But I've been getting the bird-people to bring it to me regularly, and that explains why—skin and bones as I am—I'm still able to hold on to life. Feeling famished the way I do, I tell you, Dave, the costs of fame come high!"

"Well, I wouldn't mind joining you in a fillet mignon or two," laughed Dave. "Way I feel now, I could eat a whole cow."

"Question is, how're we going to get out of this infernal mess?" questioned Henessey, as he stared mournfully at the ribbed, translucent ceiling.

"Well, old fellow, I'd suggest you get down, off your high horse, and come with me to hunt for Eunice."

Several large Ugwugs had appeared at the edge of the web, and after bowing low, slowly retreated."

"Can't come," refused Henessey, glumly. Don't you see how they're prowling around? If I left, one, of those beasts would instantly take the web, and when I tried to get back they might discover my bluff. But that's not the worst. It's an unwritten law in the hive that any Webnate who comes down loses caste. Once he's up, up he stays. It's considered beneath him to mingle with the common herd; that is, if he doesn't want to become a mertum—a plebeian a target for everybody's scorn—and everybody's horn. So you see, I can't take the risk. I'm simply stuck here."

"But my God. didn't you realize that before climbing so high?"

"No, I didn't," Henessey admitted, with a low moan. "Guess I'm a doggone Jackass all right, but I didn't have the ghostliest idea of this rule till Xangrl told me about it just this morning."

"Who the deuce is Xangrl anyhow?"

"My servant, of course. He's attached to this part of the web, no matter who the master is. Only Webnates have personal servants—and I wasn't a Webnate till today. That's why, as I've explained, I couldn't send any sooner for you and Eunice."

The mention of Eunice seemed to touch off some secret spring in Dave's mind.

"Well, Earle, guess I'll have to be going," he burst out, suddenly starting up. I'll never find Eunice up here. It's been great chatting with you. If you can help now in locating her—"

"Hang around just a bit, old man. It won't do you any good to rush away. I'd better send Xangrl first to make some inquiries."

"Hey, Xangrl!" he called. And then, in words that again brought a smile to the Ugwug's rear face. "Go to the High Webbed One! At once! Ask him where the third creature of my kind is to be found. He will know, since he has all information. Now hurry!"

"I will hurry, O Master," acceded Xangrl, bowing submissively. And clinging with his six arms to a parallel pair of long, tight-drawn cables, but with no foot support whatever, he started across a deep abyss, and, at the speed of a trotting horse, retreated into a maze of webs and was soon lost in the gray distance.

CHAPTER EIGHTEEN

YOU HAVEN'T ANY IDEA, old man, what it's like to see a real human being once more," Henessey ruminated, as he lay flat on his back, looking at the spidery ribs of the faintly glowing ceiling. "Actually, it was like being sentenced for life to solitary confinement. Then, when I thought of the earth, and all my old pals, heaven knows how many trillions of miles away, and dead whole generations ago—"

"I know just what you went through," Dave sympathized. "As for me, I try not to think of the earth—it makes the little shivers run all the way down my spine. However, I wouldn't say we're exactly alone here, considering the bird-people—"

"Well, they're not so bad as those vile Ugwugs," Henessey conceded, begrudgingly. "But somehow I can't get chummy with a lot of gawky birds. I'm going to be lonelier'n the Sahara after you've left, Dave—something like a lost orphan child, and that's no exaggeration."

Dave was silent for a moment, while the web swung gently beneath him.

"You know," he proposed, "there's no reason we can't keep in touch even after I've gone. How about the whistles?"

"Well, what about them?"

"You still have yours, haven't you?"

"Sure, here she is!" reported Henessey, as he felt about in his knapsack, which lay on the platform at his side.

"When Euny and I were whistling back and forth," Dave went on, "I wished like the devil we'd had some sort of code. It wouldn't be hard, you know. Suppose we cook up something of the sort while we're waiting for this Xangrl of yours to return?"

"All right. How would you proceed?"

Dave drew out his whistle, and blew three short blasts. "We can let that be S. O. S."

Henessey replied with three equally short swift answering blasts. "O. K. S. O. S. I'll remember."

"One short and one long," suggested Dave, after making the indicated sounds, "can be, 'Hurry! Straight ahead!'"

"And one short and two longs," added Henessey, "can be, 'Hurry! Go back!'"

"And two longs and a short, can be, 'To the right!' Two shorts and a long, can be, 'To the left!'"

"Good enough!" agreed Henessey. "Now suppose we go over all those and fix them in our minds."

During the next hour, they made and memorized about fifteen signals, including, "All's well," "Come," "Stay away," "Watch out," etc. And having completed this task, they settled down again to the wait for Xangrl—a wait that seemed protracted needlessly, inexplicably.

"Wonder if that slowpoke has gotten lost?" Henessey growled. I'll sure give him a piece of my mind!"

"Maybe he's plumb forgotten," surmised Dave.

"Or else the High Webbed One wasn't in a good mood. They say he can be darned nasty on an off day. As I understand it, he's suffering from, the disease they call the grums, which is a contagious irritation that particularly affects holders of high office. I can understand that, all right—I'm sort of beginning to feel the symptoms myself."

By this time a gradual dimming in the ceiling-light showed that the red sun had left the sky and the white had followed.

"If Xangrl doesn't come back soon," predicted Dave, nervously, "I'll be marooned up here all night."

"Marooned is the word," agreed Henessey. "Sorry I can't offer you hotel accommodations, old chap. A mat to sleep on, and a dose of this—what do you call it, this Yxion plant?—for dinner tonight and breakfast in the morning. That's the best I can do. But believe me, you're welcome. Besides, the night here is mercifully short."

"I know. That's one thing that's always puzzled me, too. Not, of course, the shortness of the night, but that the Ugwugs crowd all their activities into those five or six hours, then sleep away the other twenty-six or twenty-seven."

"Does seem peculiar, doesn't it? The way it's been explained to me, Dave, is something like this. In the old times the Ugwugs used to stay awake much longer; even now, you know, they're well able to go about in the hive by day, though they couldn't stand the sunlight outside. But not having to work for their bread, they were bored to death; and didn't know anything to do with their spare time except spend it fighting. The result was the most fiendish turmoil, until some clever religious leader said he'd had a message straight from the gods; it was wicked to stay awake at day (though exceptions were made for necessary workers, including the bird-people). This fitted in with the natural inclinations of the Ugwugs, who are indolent beasts; and the rule, according to all I can make out, has now been in effect for thousands of years. It's praised as a social measure, because it makes life so much more peaceful; as a health measure, because the average life span has tripled since the amount of fighting has been reduced; and as a humanitarian measure—though of course they don't use this term—because the most merciful as well as the most useful way for the Ugwugs to pass their leisure is in sleep, which avoids the problem of how to kill time. Besides, they've found that five or six hours a day of struggling for their places on the webs is about all that the hardiest constitution can stand."

"Well, thank God, I wasn't born an Ugwug!" rejoiced Dave. And just then his eyes, staring out into the gray tangles of webs, detected a black-striped buff figure rapidly approaching. "Look! Isn't that Xangrl?"

"Yes, by gum! High time, too, that rascal got here!"

"Hope to heaven he's brought word of Eunice!" Dave fervently prayed.

Xangrl, stepping on to the web platform bowed low to his chief. His forward face expressed frankness and pleasure; his rear face, of which Dave caught just a glimpse, had the screwed-up cunning look of one who knows more than her cares to reveal.

"O Master! O great Webnate!" he began, in a voice that seemed composed of silk and oil. "I have done your bidding! I have been even to the august doorway of the Lord of All, the High Webbed One himself."

"Good!" snapped Henessey. "Did you get any news?"

"Did you—did you find out about the other person of our kind?" Dave demanded, unable to hold back his impatience.

The smirk on Xangrl's rear face did not at all accord with the ingratiating smile on his forward countenance.

"I have done all that you asked, O Master! But the High Webbed One is not easy to see. What is more, the grums caused him much pain. There were three healers in attendance; but after he took the advice of them all the disease became three times as severe."

"But did you talk to him? Did you learn any facts?" shouted Henessey.

"Yes, O Master, I talked to him. This was not permitted, however, until I had shown the writing tablet proving I was sent by a Webnate. Otherwise, as you know, they would have thrown me off the web."

"Yes, yes, yes," insisted Henessey, nervously. "But what did you learn?"

"I learned that the High Webbed One, O Master, is fierce and hard. His eyes are greener than any other eyes. The fingers of his six hands are longer. His horn is bigger and sharper. His head can stretch out further on his neck. And his body is all red and black, and magnificent to see."

"In the name of all things holy," burst out Dave, mixing English with the native speech, as he usually did when excited, "what did he tell you? Where—where's the other person of our kind?"

"I asked him that. But one can do no more than put questions to the High Webbed One. It was long before he answered. At first he said he was not interested in the lower animals. But I told him he did not understand. This did not concern the lower animals; it had to do with the kindred of a Webnate. At this he wrinkled up his front face, and said he had some recollection that a queer beast was caught some time ago by a scouting party in the woods. It had only two arms and one face, and they thought it to be a degenerate relation of the Lilbro, though it possessed not even wings."

"That's Eunice! That's Eunice, all right!" cried Dave, shaking so violently that Henessey feared he would slip off the web.

"For a time," went on Xangrl, "the High Webbed One did not remember what had happened to this creature. After all, he is a busy Ugwug, and has many important matters on his mind. But soon everything came back to him. The prisoner being useless for ordinary purposes, he had sent it to Sub-Web Z."

"Sub-web what?" Dave almost shrieked. "Where's that?"

"He did not know if the prisoner was still there," Xangrl continued, not seeming to hear Dave's question. "By my horn! much could have happened in all this time, and the turnover in Sub-Web Z is very fast."

"Know where Sub-Web Z is?" Dave demanded, turning to Henessey with a long, drawn face of distress.

"Haven't the dimmest idea," Henessey confessed. And then to Xangrl, with a roar of command, "Take my friend down to Sub-Web Z! At once!"

"I can take him there," said Xangrl. "But I cannot promise what he will find."

He paused, and pointed to the ceiling, whose internal greenish yellow light was becoming more and more evident. "The time of wakefulness comes. Soon my people will be crawling all over the webs. Soon I must take my rest. I cannot go to Sub-Web Z till the time of sleep comes back."

So speaking, he seized some overhead cables with his six long twining hands; and being comfortably settled in a dangling sidewise position, began to swing with the motion of the web, and was soon giving forth the low, regular murmurs of peaceful slumber.

CHAPTER NINETEEN

ONCE MORE THE HIVE was crawling with activity. Huge wall-flaps had been drawn back like curtains, admitting the air and revealing unfamiliar constellations to the watching men. A confusion of noises—buzzings, hummings, whirrings, gratings, screeches, mingled with occasional shouts and screams—indicated the renewed life of the populace, who scuttled or sidled back and forth crabwise, ascending or descending, each with six long waving tentacle-like hands; while a few of those near the top showed brilliant flashes of color from the tips of their horny heads. And the light, which pervaded everything with a cold yellow-green incandescence, gave the whole spectacle a nightmare weirdness.

To the two men on the high swinging platform, it did indeed seem a nightmare. Sometimes taking turns in napping, but more often lying awake and chatting, they waited for the night-hours to pass. More than once Henessey shot up alertly when some six-armed monster, the point of its horn flaming a brilliant scarlet, emerald or purple, climbed to the edge of the platform and looked across with burning greenish eyes, Dave smiled to see how, on every such occasion, Henessey reached for his pistol, which he would hardly have time to point before the intruder, with astonishing agility, had flashed from sight.

"It's a good trick so long as it works," muttered Henessey. "But I'd feel a darned sight safer with a few solid shells in that gun."

"What do you do most nights?" asked Dave. "If I was you, I'd be afraid to go to sleep."

"If I went to sleep, I'd probably wake up doing a dive like a shooting star. No, at night I'm mighty particular about being on guard. Time enough to sleep by day, when the coast is clear."

For a moment the two men stared in silence at the sepulchrally glowing web. From far below, the bellowings of two beasts in mortal combat came discordantly to their ears.

"I've been wondering about that light here," said Dave. "It comes from the whole web, yet there doesn't seem to be any heat. I can't quite figure out the source."

"Well, what about glowworms, or fireflies, or the lamps of deep-sea fishes?"

"It may be something like that, but I've another idea. Sort of seems to me to have the looks of radioactivity. There may be much more radioactive material on this planet, you know, than on earth—"

"In that case, wouldn't it be about time for your death-warrant?"

"Not necessarily, any more than from the radio-dial of your watch, or your dentist's X-ray machine. It may be in a very diluted form. Besides, the natives may have a much greater tolerance than we for the radiations. That's just what has me worried—*If.*"

"You mean—"

"I mean we can undoubtedly absorb a certain amount of the radiation. But the effect's cumulative. If we pass the limits of toleration—and without Geiger counters we can't even estimate when that may be—then the end may be slow, but it'll be as certain as tomorrow's sunlight. That's one reason I'm anxious to get us, all of us, out of this infernal place just as soon as we can."

Henessey's face, beneath the unnatural illumination, looked a sort of sickly green.

"Oh, I wouldn't worry too much about it," Dave went on. "My diagnosis may be all askew. But it's just as well to keep these possibilities in mind when we plan our next step."

"Curse it all, I never asked to come to this filthy hive in the first place!" swore Henessey.

To Dave, as time wore wearily past, it seemed impossible that the night could be but five or six hours long. He was impatient, frantically impatient, to be up and looking for Eunice. During his few brief snatches of sleep, he had dreams of Sub-Web Z, which appeared as a cavern where creatures like cavemen were hanging upside down on dark curtains; and then, awakening, he asked himself over and over whether he would actually find her, whether he would really lead her back to safety.

At the first red glow in the west, the hive-flaps rustled to a close the inhabitants all scrambled back to their places on the web, the hubbub of movement and contention ceased, and relative quiet returned, while the green-yellow light gradually gave place to the filtered yellow of day. Then, after what seemed a long time, Xangrl opened his eyes, yawned, and crept down to the platform with the remark that the night always went too fast.

"Ready to leave?" demanded Dave.

"If my master wishes."

"Your master does wish!" ordered Henessey.

There was a dimness in his eyes as he held Dave's hand in a long clasp.

"Well, old fellow, good luck! May you find Eunice—and mighty soon, too! Give her my regards. When the two of you are free together down below, remember me stuck up on this web all by myself."

"Oh don't you worry!" promised Dave. "We'll find some way of getting you down!"

"Hope to God you do! groaned Henessey, looking anything but optimistic. And then, tapping meaningfully at his whistle. "Don't forget, we've got to keep in touch.

With the speed of one who thinks nothing of a thousand-foot drop, Xangrl started down the web. But Dave, whose head swam at sight of the monstrous abyss, found the descent even harder than the ascent. "Should have gone to sea in an old-time sailing vessel, and practiced dashing over the rigging in a storm," he reflected, as he let himself down the ladder at a fifty-degree angle, clung to cables, wove his way around an intricate meshed lattice-work, swung himself in air upon swaying ropes from balcony to balcony, and set his feet upon slanting webbed floors that quivered and rocked, while all the time Xangrl preceded him, urging him on and jeering, "Quelp! Quelp! Quelp!"—a gibe roughly translatable as "Snail! Snail! Snail!"

But finally, reeling as if on a gale-battered deck, he found himself on the floor, with the vast web-tangles stretching mile-high above. He saw Xangrl motioning him to the right, and suspected that the ordeal was not yet over. A minute later, in fact, he knew that it was not over, for his guide threw open a trapdoor in the floor, and dived into apparent vacancy. From somewhere in the darkness below, he could be heard calling, "This way! This way!" But Dave stood hesitating at the rim of what seemed a bottomless pit.

"I can't follow!" he yelled down.

"Crutl! Grimax! Grusson!" came back Xangrl's disgusted tones. And Dave knew just enough of the local slang to interpret these words as, "Weakling! Fool! Idiot!"

There followed something that sounded like profanity, though Dave was not sure just what insults were hurled at him.

Then, still in a contemptuous voice, the guide called back directions which, after they had been repeated several times, Dave was able to translate: "Imbecile! Dolt! Go to the left. Take the babes' and invalids' entrance!"

Another trapdoor burst open, revealing a narrow sloping tunnel that glowed with yellow-green phosphorescence. Down this Dave descended, and, after several twists and turns, found himself beside the irritated Xangrl, who had swung himself down by the shortcut of a fifty-foot rope. The scorn on the young Ugwug s rear face, which he made no effort to conceal, clearly showed his opinion of Dave.

"This way!" he snapped. "Sub-Web Z!" And he threw open a small round door, and plunged out of sight.

Dave, as he followed with a furiously palpitating heart, found himself in a huge octagonal chamber pervaded with a weak greenish-yellow glow. The ceiling, about thirty feet above, seemed woven of one intricate many-stranded giant cobweb. Each of the eight walls likewise looked like an enormous cobweb; the floor—or as much of it as was visible—also appeared to be a colossal cobweb: and cobwebs of various sizes hung here and there at various angles In the vaguely lighted spaces above.

But what held the visitor's attention were the creatures sprawled on the floor. Most of them were bird-people— scrawny, disconsolate-looking bird-people, who sat, with fireless eyes and drooping necks, while they held bits of web which they listlessly repaired by means of long needles. Here and there among them, swaggering back and forth, were several Ugwugs who lashed the workers now and then with their whir-like tentacled hands, or lacerated them with the tips of their horns. But the victims never answered except with low groans, and, with downcast eyes, continued drearily plodding away.

"Eunice! Where's Eunice? Can she be here?" Dave wondered, muttering to himself in his anxiety. And then suddenly he saw.

Seated on the floor among the drooping bird-people at the farthest end of the room, a golden-haired being was languidly polishing a bit of stone with a small black brush.

"Euny! Euny!" he shouted.

He thought that one had risen from among the dead as she sprang to her feet, cried out hysterically, and, with outflung arms, staggered toward him.

CHAPTER TWENTY

EVEN IN THAT EAGER FIRST half second, he noticed how pale she was, how haggard and thin, with a haunted light in her burning blue eyes.

"Dave!" she shrieked, as she rushed to throw herself into his arms. "Dave! Thank God!"

His answering cry was interrupted by a six-armed thing that propelled itself between them like a war tank. His arms, just as they opened to enclose her, were blocked by the chill metallic scales. His fervent exclamation, "Euny! At last! At last—" was cut short by a savage rumbling, "Back! Back! By my tail! Back!"

He stood facing her across a three-foot gulf, which was filled by the unyielding bulk of an Ugwug.

"It is forbidden!" snorted the guardian, a particularly large, vicious-looking beast, whose hide was all a gray and black checkerboard design. "It is forbidden to touch the prisoner!"

"Forbidden!" roared a second jailor. "It is forbidden! She is under sentence of seclusion, as a punishment for trying to escape!"

"But I have word from the High Webbed One!" protested Dave. "Here, Xangrl, show them!"

Xangrl displayed a little slip of writing stone.

"We have read that already!" snarled the checkerboard monster. "It gives permission for you to see the prisoner, it says nothing about touching her."

"It says you may see her for a short time!" growled the second jailor, who was distinguished by worm-shaped orange markings on a background of purple-blue. "It is for us to say how long. You may remain for just one jupthrum."

Dave groaned, knowing that a "jupthrum" was less than twenty-five minutes.

"Oh, my darling," he heard Eunice's voice wailing in his ears, "I've been waiting for you so long, so long! Oh, but it's blessed to see you!"

"It's heaven, seeing you!" he flung back; and his hands unconsciously reached for hers across the Ugwug barrier. But a pair of powerful tentacle-like fingers seized him, and hurled him back amid a low threatening grumbling.

"Better not try that, dearest," she warned, though she lifted her arms, panting with eagerness to clasp him. "Let's make the best of our short time. Tell me about yourself. Where have you been?"

"And you? What about you, Euny?" he demanded, glancing with a disgusted grimace about the great cobwebbed room. "Been here all this time?"

"Yes, all this time—with one brief exception. After catching me in the woods, they carried me right here. They seemed to think I was a sort of wingless bird-woman. They made me go to work. I have had many jobs, all dull as ashes, like weaving together broken webs, and—"she pointed to the bit of stone she had been polishing with a black brush—"working at those awful things, which the web-creatures wear when they're away from the hive."

One glance at the object showed Dave its similarity to the seven-clawed sandal they had found in the woods.

"It's been, oh, more boresome than I can ever tell you," Eunice went on, while he noticed how her eyes were reddened about the lids; while the lovely cheeks showed trenches of suffering that made them all the more lovely in his sight. "If it hadn't been for the hope of escape, I don't know how I could have kept up. But the chance didn't come for a long while, until one day they were bringing down some of those poor bird-people, whom they'd just captured and Were putting to work, after snipping off their wings. There was, oh, a terrible amount of shrieking and confusion, and I saw that the door was open, and the passage outside unguarded, so I just walked out. I actually got to the floor of the hive without being noticed, and then of course the thing I wanted most in all the world was to find you, dearest. I was simply panicky, but I thought of the police whistle, which was in the knapsack I always carried on my back—if I blew it, there was just a chance you might hear me!"

"You bet I did hear you!"

"Oh, so it was you! Thank heaven for that! I couldn't tell, of course, maybe it was Earle—but anyway, you don't know how glad I was that someone did hear, and answer. I thought at first I was taking dreadful chances, but pretty soon I noticed that none of the web-creatures heard. So I kept on whistling, and answering your whistling, hoping maybe I'd find where you were. You can imagine, however what happened next."

"You were recaptured?"

"Yes, as soon as they noticed I was gone, they set out after me, and I didn't have the ghost of a chance. Anyway, I was more hopeful from that time on, thinking you might be somewhere near, looking for me. But ever since that day I've been watched more carefully; those terrible animals have been even crueler than before. Just look!"

She unbared one arm, displaying a series of blue welts.

"Oh, you poor child!" he sympathized. And on a wave of pity for her and rage against her oppressors, he again forgot himself and tried to press across the blank wall of the checkerboard monster.

A growl stopped him short. The head of the orange-marked jailor shot out until the razor-edged horn was within inches of Dave's face.

"Keep back! Please! Don't take any chances, dear!" Eunice begged, as she hastily wiped a tear from one eye.

"Listen, Euny!" he went on, hastily. "I don't know how much time we have left, so before I go I want to tell you about the code Henessey and I have made—"

"Oh! So he's all right?"

"Well, in a way, poor fellow! He's stuck about a mile up on the web—has one of the highest places in the land, and is thoroughly miserable about it. But let me get on. We've arranged a whistling code. Three shorts are S. O. S."

And he went on to ten of the key signals, which Eunice, who had a naturally retentive mind, was able to memorize after one or two repetitions.

"Now tell me, Euny," he asked, as soon as she had the better part of the code in mind, "how in perdition have you managed to live? I notice you're a bit thin—and no wonder! What have you had to eat?"

"Well, not too much," she admitted; and now it seemed to him that she had the pinched expression of a poverty stricken waif. "But you don't look as if you've been exactly feasting on caviar and roast chicken yourself, dearest. Maybe I've done better than you. First, of course, I cleaned out the knapsack. Then for a day I starved, before I noticed a little bluish white mushroom growing all along the webbed galleries just outside, where they let me go now and then for a few hours' sleep. I was so famished I had to sample it. I knew I was taking chances, it might be as poisonous as arsenic. But it tasted good, and didn't leave any after-effects; so ever since then I've been gathering all the mushrooms I could find. See! there's one over there."

Dave glanced at what looked like a commonplace toadstool. "But could you get enough of that?" he asked.

"I don't suppose I could have—without help. But when the bird-people and the web-creatures saw me eating, they were all so amused they crowded around to watch, none of them having ever seen anyone eat before. At first their laughter annoyed me; but I forgave them when they began gathering mushrooms and bringing them to me, just for the fun of seeing me eat. I guess it's about the way small boys feel to see monkeys gobbling peanuts at a circus. Anyhow, they've never tired of the sport, which is why I haven't died of hunger. But mercy, when I get out of here, dearest, I never want to see another mushroom in all my life!"

And then, turning to Dave solicitously, she burst out, "Goodness gracious, here I've been raving on all about myself. Now tell me about yourself, darling. What's been happening to you? I'm ever so anxious to hear."

"Well, tell the truth, Euny," Dave began—when a stertorous voice jarred upon his ears.

"Jupthrum's up!"

"What's that?"

"Jupthrum's up!" repeated the checkerboard beast, with a snarl. "By my six arms! you have interrupted work in this sub-web too long already! If you had not had a message from the High Webbed One, we would not have permitted this nonsense. Now, praised be to all Webnates! the jupthrum's up. There's the way out!"

"Just one minute longer!" pleaded Eunice, as she threw out her arms, straining toward Dave.

"Just one minute!" he appealed.

Two horned heads shot out from two monstrous bodies, one just grazing Dave's face, the other thrust almost into contact with Eunice's bosom.

"One jupthrum was too long! You did nothing but jabber in some coarse-sounding foreign language. Perhaps there was no meaning in what you said. But what if you were saying something seditious?"

"What if they were conspiring against the High Webbed One?" shrilled the second guard. "As surely as I fear the light of the three suns, if they stay one wink of the eye longer, they will know the feel of a horn through their flesh!"

Not liking the malevolent look in the creature's two greenish forward eyes, Dave drew back a step.

"Never mind, dearest," he called, as his persecutor prodded him toward the door, "keep up your courage. We'll come for you, we'll get you out of here—I swear to God we will!"

"You—you—take good care of yourself, dear!" Eunice bade farewell, in a choked voice.

As Dave made good his retreat, with Xangrl at his side and two horns pressed against his rear, he had barely time to throw Eunice a kiss. Even before he had passed through the round doorway into the dim outer corridor, a woman's muffled sobbing followed him from the yellow-green gloom behind.

CHAPTER TWENTY-ONE

SURELY, THERE WAS SOME way to make good his promise, some way to wrench Eunice free! So Dave reflected as he trudged dismally back to the main hive, while Xangrl jeered him on. Yes, of course there was a way! and one that gave immediate hope! He would make the long, hard climb up the web, and see Henessey once more; and Henessey would send Xangrl to the High Webbed One with a request for the girl's immediate release. As a Webnate, Henessey certainly could obtain so small a favor. Thus, before the last of the three suns went down tonight, Eunice's prison door would swing open!

So Dave planned; and the scheme at first seemed flawless. But he had barely reached the hive-floor when he received the first of several shocks.

"Take me up to your master!" he ordered Xangrl. "I have a message for him!"

Xangrl turned toward Dave with a calm, almost deferential look on his front face, but his rear lips were wrinkled in an angry curl; his rear eyes shot out little daggers of green light.

"I cannot take you to my master," he objected. "By my horn! he did not command it. But I have made other promises. When I saw your Lil-bro guards at your prison door, I promised to bring you back to them."

"I will come later," stipulated Dave. "First I must see your master."

"I cannot take you to my master," argued Xangrl. "I will bring you back to your prison."

Indignation blazed over Dave. But at the same time fear shot through him, though he could not see the hostile look in his guide's, rear face.

"What if I refuse to come with you?" he challenged.

Xangrl spat out something halfway between a snort and a laugh.

"Refuse? Unless I am weaker than a Lil-bro's sheared-off wing, you cannot refuse! Where would you go? What would you do if I called to one of my people to send you into a sub-web?"

He pointed vaguely above, where some striped, spotted and pitch-black monsters dangled at various angles.

"It would not be long," Xangrl went on, with a contempt that he made no effort to conceal, "before you were tied in every limb more tightly than a captured Lil-bro."

Dave remembered the constricting webs that had once entangled him, the helplessness, the feeling of near-strangulation; and decided upon a change of tactics.

"Very well, I'll go with you," he conceded, knowing that it would be easier to escape from his prison guards than from the enmeshing webs. His problem, to be sure, had been complicated; he would have to plan craftily, and would have the devil's own time to make his way mile-high into the hive and find Henessey without a guide. Still, he did at least have a chance—more of a chance, anyhow, than if he were caught in new webs and sent, like Eunice, to some underground cell.

He did not, however, foresee the next stumbling block.

Passing through a long webbed corridor, they came within sight of his former prison. Tintle and Glarr, with drooping heads, were standing near the door; and they showed no joy at Dave's return, but slowly and mournfully slouched forward to meet him.

"O Light-Maker," said Tintle, "we have waited for you long."

"We have waited long," confirmed Glarr. "But we were not the only ones. You are wanted, O Light-Maker."

"Wanted?" echoed Dave, catching the ominous note in that word; and he glanced about him hastily, wondering which way to flee. But Xangrl blocked the path in one direction, and a curtain-like web walled off two thirds of the remaining space. And even in that dread half-second while he stood hesitating, two monsters started down the nets just overhead.

Both were evil-looking creatures, of exactly the same gray as the webs, which may have been why Dave had not noticed them sooner; and both glared malevolently out of their rear eyes, though their front faces showed a smiling affability.

"You are wanted!" said the larger beast, as Dave retreated before the horned head.

"You are wanted! Wanted!" repeated the other Ugwug.

"What for?" Dave was barely able to demand, when the first brute seized him in six powerful arms.

While he was ineffectively struggling, the second monster answered, in mechanical tones, "We Guardians of the Hive never ask why a culprit is wanted. It is merely our place to take the criminal in charge when our masters command."

"O Light-Maker! O Light-Maker! What is to happen to you now?" Dave heard Tintle wailing.

"All day they have been waiting for you," mourned Glarr. "By my lost wings! we had no way to warn you!"

"Silence, you clod of a Lil-bro!" commanded the smaller Ugwug. And he shot his homed head at Glarr, who screamed and fled, side by side with Tintle.

"The lower classes are getting out of hand," the Ugwug remarked, grimly. "What is needed, Oesle, is a good rantangle to shock them into obedience."

"As I love my web, Kpelke," agreed the other, "I have often thought a nice big rantangle would give them respect for their superiors. Would you believe it, my neck has been getting sore from hitting them, and my horn has several dents at the tip, and still they are more disobedient than ever!"

"It wasn't like this in the old days," mourned Kpelke. "Our fathers were worthy of the name of Ugwug, unlike us degenerate modems. Whenever one of those insolent Lil-bro showed any will of his own, they used to massacre a few hundred in a good old-fashioned rantangle—the kind we haven't seen of late, so much the worse for us! Well, let's be going! We've got to dispose of this miscreant, and after that there's still a whole long list."

"Yes, the task of a Guardian of the Hive is a hard one," lamented Oesle, as he started slowly away. "We have to work at all hours, even by day, when decent citizens should be respectably asleep. And what thanks do we get? They blame us whenever one of the inferior races shows an unlawful glint in its eyes."

"Ah, well," took up Kpelke, sadly, "there's nothing much we can do about it. The lot of the people's true defenders always was hard. Who but us, I ask you, can clear the hive of vermin? Yet we can't even strike for a higher place on the web without being called—"

Dave never did learn what his oppressors might be called. He was still struggling in the six iron arms; and just now a vicious twist at his throat made him gasp for breath, and, for one horrible moment, feel that he was being suffocated.

When he began to recover, he was already on his way into the web. Oesle, carrying him in his six arms as easily as a man carries a small dog, was starting up at a forty-five degree angle. Held on the monster's back in such a way that he faced toward the ceiling, Dave had ceased to struggle; if by any unlikely chance, he could fight his way free, he would fall to fatal depths.

Around and around they went, and up and up, spiraling and twisting and weaving along the intricate gray webbed tangles. Once he caught a glimpse of Xangrl, who was self-invited to accompany them, and whose rear face beamed with mischievous glee, like that of a small boy who follows a police patrol. And most of the time he heard his captors chatting as nonchalantly as poundmen who have made the routine capture of a stray dog. He felt indeed, a little like a dog seized by unknown captors for unknown purposes.

He could not even estimate how long they were on their way. All that he did know was that they went far and high; he was able to twist his neck just sufficiently to catch glimpses of bottomless abysses. Why had he been seized? He scarcely dared ask himself this question; one thought, so insistent as to dominate all others, kept recurring in his mind, "Now I can't help Euny! Now I can't get her out! What will happen to her now? O God, what will happen to Euny?"

But finally the ordeal—or, rather, its first phase—was ending. "By my four eyes, here we are at last!" he heard Oesle mumbling. And he was carried through a funnel-like entrance into a high closed conical structure, which, built out of the web material, was held in place by long diverging cables that reached about it, above it, and below it in all directions, mooring it so that it looked a little like a house fastened in the air.

The edifice wavered slightly, but only slightly beneath the tread of the Ugwugs as Dave was carried into a large oblong faintly glowing yellow-green chamber. Kpelke instantly retreated; but Oesle, having dropped the captive to the floor, remained to block the entrance. And Dave, as he squirmed and writhed, flexing and unflexing his cramped muscles, only gradually took in the nature of the place.

At the room's far end, on web platforms swinging a few feet above the floor, three particularly obnoxious-looking Ugwugs were perched. One of them was all a smudged gray-black, as if he had been through a fire; the second had ash-tinted scales that seemed to have been splashed with ink; and the third, the largest of the trio and the central figure, was colored like a great frog, with a dark-green body crossed by stripes of still darker green.

On the floor beneath these monsters, a number of abject creatures were crouching. Most of them were Lil-bro, but one or two droop-necked Ugwugs were among them, their front eyes registering respectful attention, their rear eyes shifty and furtive. They were kept in place by several Ugwug guards, who now and then would discipline them with a horn-thrust.

Just as Dave arrived, one of these creatures was being goaded forward until he stood beneath the three swinging web-monsters. As the beast bent low, his six arms trembling, his legs shaking, and, his dust-gray face even grayer than normal, it was evident that he was begging for mercy.

There was a peculiar unpleasant rasping in the voice of the frog-colored monster when, after glancing at a stone strip handed him by the guard, he turned toward the suppliant.

"Do you confess to the crime?" he demanded, in a bored and routine manner.

"Yes, O Wise One."

"Do you repent?"

"I repent, O Great One, I was wrong. Ten thousand times over I was wrong."

"Are you willing to suffer the penalty?"

"I am willing, O Glorious One. It is but my just desserts."

Being in a position to see both faces of the criminal, Dave noticed that the forward one had a look of pious humility and resigned repentance. But the rear face was convulsed with terror, rage and vindictiveness.

"Your meekness does you credit," commended the judge. And after a mumbled consultation with his colleagues he decided. "Since you have confessed, we will be merciful." And then, to one of the guards, "Judl, take this evildoer in hand, and see that he ends humanely by the seven coils of strangulation."

The condemned beast groaned, his rear eyes flashed with malevolence. But he made no resistance as the Guard butted him out of the room.

The frog-colored brute now turned to the next in line, one of the bird-people. This time his tones were a bit more severe, but he asked exactly the same questions as before and was answered in exactly the same words, although the defendant was so weak that he more than once toppled to the floor, and had to be supported by a guard. He too, as the reward of his confession, was treated with civilized leniency, and was sentenced to die by being hurled "over the brink of the black pit."

After several more prisoners had confessed in precisely the same manner and had been rewarded with various merciful punishments, varying from laceration by sharp knives to asphyxiation by poison fumes, Dave began to shift nervously from foot to foot and to clench and unclench his fingers, while wondering what he had done to bring him before the court. He noticed that no specific charge was ever mentioned, but that none of the defendants escaped the sentence of "Guilty!" If he too was declared guilty— But that could not be. What, indeed, was he guilty of? And besides, he must, he must get free in order to rescue Eunice!

CHAPTER TWENTY-TWO

AFTER A WAIT THAT seemed hours long, Dave felt Oesle's powerful arms shoving him forward to a position just beneath the judges.

The first thing that he noticed about them was an evil odor— and did, it come from the webs in which they hung? In any case, it was unpleasantly suggestive of decay. The bodies of all three, bloated and over-sized even for Ugwugs, seemed alarmingly like those of overgrown spiders.

The central judge thoughtfully examined the slip of stone passed him by Oesle. He frowned, and displayed it to each of his colleagues in turn; and they also frowned.

"What do you think, Nunkez?" he asked the gray-black magistrate.

"For my part, O Yurduz," grumbled Nunkez, "I have never believed in treating foreigners like rational beings."

"I too, O Yurduz," growled the ink-splashed one, "see no point in being sentimental. Nevertheless, even the lowly and ignorant should have the benefit of equal treatment under the law."

"A wise saying, O Whackthu. A wise saying," commended Yurduz. "I will take your advice, and judge this wrongdoer by the regular procedure.

Turning to Dave with balefully glaring greenish eyes he threw out the usual question, "Do you confess to the crime?"

"What crime?" asked Dave.

A murmur of surprise and consternation ran through the Courtroom.

"Grudl!" he snapped (this being an untranslatable term of rebuke, implying "Fool!" "Wretch!" and "Rascal!" all in one). "You are not here to question the court! I give you one more chance. Do you confess to the crime?

"If I knew what crime you meant—"

"If you knew?" howled the judge, shooting, his head several feet out of his body, with the horn projecting directly toward the accused. "Great Webnates! who does know if not you? If you committed the crime, how can you help knowing?"

"These foreigners have no Idea of logic, remarked Whackthu.

"They lack common sense," agreed Nunkez.

"For the last time, I ask you," roared Yurduz, "did you commit the crime?"

"No!" denied Dave, resoundingly. "I committed no crime!"

For a long dreadful minute, an unnatural-seeming silence filled the court. Several Lil-bro, who had been herded in while awaiting sentence, forgot their own terror in staring at Dave in wide-eyed astonishment.

"By my six arms! This is most irregular!" trumpeted Yurduz, when, after a moment, he had regained his equanimity. "It is customary for defendants to plead guilty; in fact, it is expected. This hastens court procedure, and enables us to execute justice more efficiently."

"Also," added Nunkez, his rear eyes twinkling maliciously, though his forward ones were bland and, friendly, "only the prisoner who confesses can expect merciful treatment."

"Nevertheless," Whackthu pointed out, with a snarl, "there is a law for cases in which the prisoner is uncooperative. Not, however, that any in recent cycles have been so imprudent."

"As I value my green scales, I am well acquainted with that law," returned Yurduz, "even though it is now so nearly obsolete that there is talk of abolishing it. It is provided that the defendant, at his own risk, may choose not to confess. Personally, I regard all this as a tiresome waste of the court's good time. But by my horn! the law is the law, and may never be openly disobeyed."

"A noble sentiment, Yurduz! It does you credit!" approved Whackthu.

"Well, in the name of the High Webbed One, since we must have evidence, let's have it and get it over with!" decided Yurduz. "If there were no evidence, clearly, it would be much simpler to condemn the prisoner. But then, of course, if it were simple it wouldn't be legal."

Bowing so low that his chin almost scraped the floor, Oesle had crept forward.

"O Wise Ones! O Great Ones! O Glorious Ones!" he exclaimed, when he was practically beneath the three judges. "Here is the evidence!"

"Let's have it! Quick!" grumbled Yurduz. "By the Holy Web! this court is already working overtime, far into the day hours, when good citizens should be asleep—and all because we have so many people to condemn!"

"You will have one more now, O Magnificent Ones!" proceeded Oesle, casting Dave a malign flash of his rear eyes. "Agents of the Official Inspection Service have been following him, as is their duty with all citizens, and have found that he has been chummy with the Lil-bro servants. This, as you know, is against the law. It provokes thoughts in the lower orders. It fills their heads with foolish hopes. It makes them imagine they have rights. Worst of all, it encourages them to contaminate the air we breathe by intruding on the preserves of us Ugwugs."

"A vile crime, if true!" muttered Yurduz.

"Nor is that all!" rumbled Oesle, warming to his theme. "The scoundrel has not been content with one crime. As you know, there are various tangles of Sacred Webs throughout the hive. They are gloriously old and dusty, and, naturally, like all relics, have no practical use; but for that reason we hold them all the more in the most worshipful esteem. One of the dearest and dustiest of all these Sacred Webs is in the Lower Districts, near the entrance of Sub-Gallery GY."

"By my: tail! I remember!" confirmed Yurduz. "I have often paused there in wonder and meditation. But what has that to do with the offender?"

"Everything, O Wise One. Not long ago he trespassed upon those holy preserves, with the plain intention of defiling them. Worse than that! having been caught in the loops placed there to trap violators, he sacrilegiously cut his way out, breaking some of the web-strands that are more than a hundred cycles old!"

"Monstrous!" growled Nunkez.

"Devilish!" squeaked Whackthu.

"Abominable!" charged Yurduz. "But by the light of my four eyes! how do you know it was this particular fiend?"

"We know, O Great One! because they were hacked with a barbarous tool such as no Ugwug ever used. We know because some of our people, awakened by the noise this ruffian made In escaping, watched him from above and reported to us Guardians of the Web. We know because we have traced him to the cell where he lives. We were not surprised to find him but an ignorant foreigner."

"Is this true, you low one-faced miscreant?" Yurduz demanded, turning angrily to the prisoner.

Dave knew too well that it was true. He remembered how, only yesterday, when he had left Tintle and Glarr to search for Eunice, he had been entangled in a portion of the web near the trapdoor, and had hacked himself free with his knife. Even at the time, he had been afraid that this would lead to trouble; but he had forgotten the danger amid the subsequent more startling events.

"Is this true, you vile scoundrel, you four-limbed freak, you worse than Lil-bro?" Yurduz shouted.

"Even if it is true, there were reasons beyond my control."

"Beyond his control?" shrieked Yurduz. "Great Webnates! Listen to that! This monstrosity, this two-handed absurdity, who cannot, even speak without an outlandish accent, pretends he is not responsible for his own misdeeds! As surely as I have forty-two fingers on my six good hands, he will not deceive us with any such foolish plea! He has now, by his own, confession, been proved doubly guilty. The crime of being intimate with the Lil-bro was bad enough. The outrage of cutting the Sacred Webs was even worse. Hence he deserves death twice—death in two horrible forms."

"Scales of my arm!" Nunkez reflected, with a sigh. "I fear we face a limitation in the law. No matter how many times a criminal deserves death, we are able to inflict the sentence but once."

"I have often thought of that," admitted Yurduz, mournfully. "No, not even the High Webbed One, may his cycles be many! can do anything about it. However, we might sentence the rogue to two forms of death: if the first is not effective, we can try the second. Suppose we begin by tying him to the web and having him gored by the horns of ten of our mightiest citizens?"

"And after that," suggested Nunkez, "just to make sure, we can take him up to the peak of the web and drop him off."

"I suspect," decided Yurduz, his greenish front eyes smoldering with unholy relish, "that between them, these two sentences will serve the purpose. They will be a lesson to law-breakers."

Oesle had already stepped toward Dave with six tentacle-like arms extended.

The intended victim, shrinking back, knew that if he did not save, himself immediately he would be lost beyond hope. His mind was working clearly, though in desperation. Even as he felt Oesle's fingers closing about him, he shouted his appeal.

"Hold there, one minute! Or you will bring great trouble on your own heads! I am a Webnate's friend!"

A wave of derisive laughter rippled through the room.

"You? A Webnate's friend?" jeered Yurduz, shaken by such mirth that his web swung as if in a gale. "What would a Webnate want with an insect as his friend?"

"The three suns preserve us! What sort of a Webnate?" roared Yurduz.

"One very much like me," swore Dave. "Really, my brother—a creature of my own kind—"

Oesle, with a wrench at the prisoner's neck, choked off these words. "Come, you ragged beast!" he snapped, and tugged at Dave's beard, just for the sport of it.

"Hold! Hold!" ordered Whackthu, giving his ink-splashed body a delighted twist, while his rear eyes glittered with the glee of one who anticipates a good time. "By my six arms! this sounds inviting. Here I have been bored night after night and day after day by cases that were duller than a cast-out web. And now for a change something amusing comes up. Unless my neck be as stiff as a Lil-bro's, I want to hear this out! Let this beast tell us about his Webnate friend!"

"This court is already half a cycle behind on its schedule," grumbled Yurduz. And then, with a growl, to Dave, "Go on, let's hear about the Webnate. But be quick! If we find you are only wasting the court's time, by my scales! we will condemn you to death in a third terrible way!"

Released from Oesle's hold, Dave began to tell about Henessey—only to be met by incredulous laughter. Apparently Henessey's rise was too recent to be generally known; and, besides, the fact that a foreigner had become a Webnate might have been kept secret lest it lower the other Webnates' prestige.

"There never was a Webnate such as you described!" decided Yurduz. "There never could be!"

As Oesle's grasping arms once more reached out, Dave thought of Xangrl. It seemed but a straw to clutch at—yet if he had not known the Webnate, how would he be able to tell about his servant? And so Dave described Xangrl. in detail: his under-developed, youthful frame, his buff body with the black stripes, the peculiar star-shaped purple scar on the left of his horn.

"We waste the court's time!" fumed Yurduz, his surprised rear eyes showing him to be more impressed than he would admit. "But we will prove he is wrong." And he reached deep into the web, and pulled out a two-foot-square book, containing the latest list of Webnates and their servants.

As the judge clattered the pages, Dave drew hope from the thought that Xangrl, being attached to the web, would be listed even if the information pre-dated Henessey's rise.

"Ah, in the High Webbed One's name, here it is!" Yurduz burst out, while his two fellow judges projected their distendable necks so as to peer over his shoulders.

His rear face registered disappointment, although his front one was expressionless as he reported, "Xangrl... A servant of Web E 11... By the High One! It is true! He has a purple star-shaped marking."

"That does not prove the prisoner to be the Webnate's friend!" snorted Nunkez, as his smudgy body settled heavily back on his own side of the web.

"It proves nothing!" agreed Whackthu. "Nevertheless, it does bring up some important issues, on which we should consult."

Immediately the three judges withdrew to the depths of the web, where they were barely visible to Dave as they conferred in whispers.

"It is no slight matter," remarked Whackthu, when they were out of the general hearing, "to execute the friend of a Webnate. I have not forgotten what happened to our poor old colleague Blucktho. Was it last cycle or cycle before last?"

"Cycle before last," stated Nunkez. "It was a sad affair. He was a wonderful web-spinner, too, just at the beginning of a promising career."

"That's proof enough that we have to watch the way we weave," acknowledged Yurduz. "It's a long, hard drop to the bottom of the hive."

"My motto," took up Whackthu, "is better free a thousand criminals than anger one Webnate."

"Sound practical advice! Commended Yurduz. "But it doesn't tell us what to do with this prisoner. The troublesome brute! I'd like to wring his neck! After all, have we not convicted him legally? That being the case, what can we do but execute him?"

"He has been proved to be a law-breaker in two ways," pointed out Nunkez. "That, as I love the hive! leaves us no choice. The only legal way is to execute him."

"Poor Blucktho followed the legal way, too," sighed Whackthu.

Yurduz pondered. His rear eyes were grave with perplexity.

"I am not a credulous Ugwug," he finally reported. "I do not for a moment believe this two-armed beast ever so much as saw a Webnate. Just the same, if we made a mistake, it would be our own scales that had to pay. I am a family creature, with six young Ugwugs in the web. So I must consider the future."

"Just so," coincided Nunkez. "Having recently taken a new mate—in the respectable legal style, of course—after throwing the last one out of the web—"

But Whackthu, whose rear eyes showed the dull green of boredom, broke in impatiently.

"Listen, friends! As you know, it is lawful, and therefore ethical, to do anything we want so long as we can find a ruling to justify our choice. Just the other day, ongoing over some forgotten ancient books—they were a few hundred cycles old, as I remember—I found just the thing to apply to our case. Shall I not send for it?"

The others nodded; and Whackthu motioned to a Lil-bro servant, and mumbled some instructions. Meanwhile Yurduz, on a sudden impulse, summoned another Lil-bro, and likewise muttered some secret orders.

Fifteen minutes later, three bent and aged Lil-bro staggered into the web, puffing beneath the weight of a thick tome, about four feet by four. This they deferentially placed before the judges, then hastily withdrew.

The three officials all stretched then necks to examine the contents, while Whackthu hurriedly turned the pages. Several anxious minutes passed.

"Ah, as I honor the name of Webnate, here it is!" he finally reported, in a subdued voice. "It is the case of an Ugwug named Vilchum-thum, who was a prodigy at crime. He broke more webs than he had fingers, slew more Ugwugs than there were cycles in the lives of his nine children, and stole more of his neighbors' property than mathematicians could compute. That, of course, was in the simple old days, when stealing for the sake of web-position was not yet considered respectable. For anyone of his crimes he could have been sentenced to be hurled to his death from the top web. But that, in the opinion of the seven judges, was just the trouble. Let me read their decision."

Dave, standing impatiently below the web, saw Whackthu pause, and heard him clear his throat, with a noise as of a reluctant car motor just warming into action. But he could not catch the judge's words.

"Decision of the Seven Web Sages in the case of Vilchum-thum. 'Whereas we find that the accused deserved death for each of his numerous crimes, we submit that it would be unthinkable to punish him for anyone of them and so leave the others unpunished. Such a miscarriage of justice would only encourage criminals in future to break the law as often as possible, knowing they would suffer no more for a hundred outrages than for one. Since, however, it is impossible to punish the culprit with death for any particular crime without leaving most of his crimes unpunished, obviously we cannot hold him for anyone of them. But if we refuse to hold him for anyone, we cannot discriminate and hold him for any other. Consequently, we must take the broad view, and not hold him at all. Case dismissed! '"

The three judges were silent for a moment.

"An admirable piece of logic!" commended Yurduz, as he pored over the book.

"I fear that we have no such astute legal minds nowadays," Nunkez lamented. "Oh, by the way what happened to this Vilchum-thum?"

"He lived to commit many more crimes," stated Whackthu, and became a Webnate. He died cycles later blessed by wealth and honors, after laying the cornerstone of one of our foremost families."

"Altogether an estimable character!" remarked Yurduz. "But what I am trying to decide is just how this case applies to our own problem. Of course, it does supply precedent for releasing an offender who has offended more than once. Nevertheless, I am against being technical if we can avoid it."

"In other words," suggested. Nunkez, "you agree with me in wanting to execute the prisoner unless he is under a Webnate's protection?"

"Sacred scales, I want to execute him soon!" snorted Yurduz, with a fierce flash of his shrewd rear eyes.

"Ah, who comes here?" demanded Whackthu.

Attended by two Lil-bro, an undergrown Ugwug had entered. His body was buff-colored, with black stripes; there was a star-shaped purple mark to the left of his horn.

"By my tail! that looks like him!" muttered Yurduz. And then, to his colleagues, "I thought it best to send for him and learn the truth at first hand."

The young Ugwug came forward without enthusiasm. His head drooped; his whole form trembled. Though his front eyes showed respectful attention, his rear ones were almost popping out of his head with fear.

"What's your name?" demanded Yurduz, as soon as the newcomer stood beneath his web.

"Xangrl, what, O Wise One have I done—"

"Speak when you're spoken to!" snarled Yurduz. "My horn! If you have done anything, you will hear of it! We called you here to ask some questions. As surely as this is a High Web Court, you must answer honestly, or you will repent in the Steaming Caverns!"

Dave noticed how Xangrl's rear eyes still flashed distress signals of terror.

"Put your horn to the floor, and swear, in the name of the High Webbed One, that you will let yourself be slain by the light of the three suns if even one syllable you say be not true!"

Xangrl put his horn down, and hastily mumbled something that nobody could make out.

"Now for the first question!" Yurduz bellowed, in a bullying manner. "Answer in one word! Are you a Webnate's servant?"

"Yes, O Great One!"

"Just as I thought!" boomed the judge. "Now for the next and last question! Think long before you reply. This too may be answered in one word. Is your master, the Webnate, built to resemble the prisoner?"

Xangrl's dust-gray face was discolored to the hue of putty. His voice was barely audible.

"Yes, O Supreme One."

There was no expression on Yurduz's front face. But his rear one, which had shone with an expectant glitter, suddenly froze.

"That is all, you base commoner!" he snapped at Xangrl. And the latter, almost tripping over a fringe of the web as he backed out, was gone in a second.

Again the judges withdrew to the depths of their webs, and once more conferred in whispers.

"By the shadows of the black pit!" cursed Yurduz. "I fear that, after all, we must respect the precedent of Vilchum-thum."

"It is fortunate that we found legal grounds of action," reflected Nunkez.

"I would be a poor judge if I could not find legal grounds for anything!" mumbled Yurduz. "But glorious webs! I still do not like to let the prisoner go."

"It would be gratifying," meditated Nunkez, with a thoughtful twist of his smudgy body, "if we could find some way to punish him without offending his protector."

"By the seven fingers of my front right hand! an idea comes to me!" exclaimed Whackthu. "Why not make him a smardl?"

"A smardl? You are a genius, Whackthu!" applauded Yurduz, his front eyes beaming with pleasure, though his rear ones showed a jealous flash. "Yes, we will make him a smardl. We will use him to decoy the Lil-bro."

"Only a few sleeps ago," recalled Whackthu, "we were mentioning how hard it is nowadays to get decoys to catch the Lil-bro. We cannot use other Lil-bro, since the low beasts would be unfaithful to us. We cannot use Ugwugs, as the Lil-bro have grown so monstrously suspicious they fly off at the first sight of one of our people. Yet we need more Lil-bro than ever to do our work—and the old ones die off while the ungrateful young will not breed."

"It comes to me," deliberated Nunkez, "that the prisoner will be a perfect decoy, since, as we have seen, he is friendly with the Lil-bro. They will never suspect him."

"If we use him," Yurduz remarked, with a low chuckle, "not even a Webnate can object, for it will be but a loyal web service.

Nevertheless, he will be doomed. Nothing is more certain than that the Lil-bro will slay him when they learn he has betrayed their kind."

"On the other hand," pointed out Nunkez, "he will be honored with a hero's last rites."

Yurduz meanwhile was motioning to Dave. His front face beamed with friendliness. Only his colleagues saw the screwed-up, wily expression of his rear countenance.

"My friend," he reported, smiling like a father, "my associates and I are merciful. Since you are a foreigner, and have had no chance to learn our laws, we have decided to overlook your crimes—on one condition."

"What condition?" demanded Dave, who sensed the hypocrisy behind the mealy-sounding words.

"That you act as a smardl. We will have you taken to the nearest hives of the free Lil-bro. You will mingle with them. You will pretend to be their friend. The Lil-bro are childishly simple, and will believe you. Then one night we will make a raid. You will lull the Lil-bro's suspicions, if indeed they have suspicions. You will lead them near the borders of the woods where our hunters will be hiding. Then we will spring out, and seize all of them we can lay hold of with our nets. You will be honored if we capture many."

Dave muttered an oath in English.

"What's that?" he demanded, his face going pale. "You—you want me to be a traitor?—pretend friendship for the Lil-bro, and then, like a miserable spy—"

"Now, now, now, my friend," soothed Yurduz, "you rush to conclusions. As I honor my web, this is not treachery that we ask—it is a noble deed, for the good of all the hive. After all, it is the end that counts; it is a first principle of politics, known to all half-grown Ugwugs, that it matters not how filthy the methods so long as the end be pure. In fact, there are no such things as filthy methods when the end is pure enough."

"Besides," Whackthu clinched the argument, "who are we asking you to betray? Only the Lil-bro! And were the lower forms of life not put into the world to serve the higher?"

"Moreover," reasoned Nunkez, "you will do them a service to capture them. Here in the hive they will be secure, with regular work for the rest of their cycles, instead of flying about foolishly and wasting their time in the open air and sunlight."

"That is to say," sneered Dave, "I will be blessing them by betraying them?"

"Come, come! My scales! we waste time arguing!" decided Yurduz, the friendly light in his first eyes changing to a glare of menace. "The prisoner must make his choice—at once! Either we sentence him to die, or he acts as a smardl!"

In Dave's mind, the situation was luminously clear. If he refused to serve as a decoy, his chances would be small But if he pretended compliance, he might find some way of betraying the would-be betrayers. He would be playing a desperate game; but he would leave no stone unturned.

"Let it be as you say, O Wise One," he heard himself assenting. "I will be a smardl."

CHAPTER TWENTY-THREE

HENESSEY, AS HE HALF SAT and half lay on the web-platform peering down through a peephole at the endless tangles of meshes, could not be sure quite how long it was since he had seen Dave. The accursed thirty-two-hour days had confused him; but as nearly as he could figure it, the time was somewhere around two weeks, though it seemed much longer. What had been happening to Dave and Eunice all this while? He felt certain, he sensed that something grim had been going on. And yet he had no facts at all. He laughed a little ironically when he remembered that he, a Webnate, was supposed to be second in power only to the High Webbed One himself, yet could not obtain the simplest information. That might be because of the law, made long ago by the so-called Wise Ones: "All truth must be licensed by the Public Inspector. If it is not licensed and properly stamped, it is not truth." But more largely the fault was with Xangrl.

Henessey, glancing at the web where Xangrl lay swinging in quiet sleep, remembered bitterly his efforts to drag Some facts out of that worthless servant of his. The first time had been when the latter had returned after taking Dave to Eunice. "Well, did he get to see her?" Henessey had asked. But Xangrl had coughed out a monosyllabic reply. "Where did you leave my friend?" Henessey then demanded. "In the cell where I found him, O Honored One," Xangrl had reported, with a front face of frankness and humility. But being young and inexperienced, he had not been wary enough to keep his rear face quite hidden; Henessey had just a glimpse of the furtive, rat-like eyes. However, he was unable to discover just what it was that Xangrl was concealing.

It had been even worse when he had sent Xangrl with a message to the High Webbed One. With one word, that official could free both Dave and Eunice, no matter where they were; and, surely, he would give every consideration to the request of a Webnate. So Henessey had supposed, when he sent Xangrl with the appeal. But the servant, returning a long time later, had reported, "The High Webbed One, may his cycles be many! will do nothing, O Reverenced Master!" This time Xangrl had kept his rear face concealed, too carefully concealed; and answered all questions even more vaguely than before. "Bet the scoundrel never even saw the Big Chief," Henessey reflected. "He's plumb scared, or maybe he just doesn't give a hoot."

But there was not a thing that Henessey could do. There was no one else to take his message; and he himself couldn't any more have crossed the maze of cables to the High Webbed One than he could have walked a circus tightrope.

"Still, it's mighty funny about Dave and Eunice," he kept telling himself. "I'm sure Dave would have come back, if he could. At least, he'd have whistled to say all was well. But no more word than if he'd dropped into a black pit. By God, hope he hasn't dropped into a black pit!"

As Henessey drearily pondered, the ceiling light gradually changed from yellow to yellow-green, indicating the approach of night. And all at once the hive awakened. With a whirring, grating and buzzing of renewed activity. Thousands of eight-limbed creatures began to crawl and sidle in all directions, moving backwards and upside down amid the webbed labyrinths; and wide wall-flaps, after a time, were flung open to admit the air and starlight. Henessey meanwhile had drawn his pistol, with which once or twice he warned off some striped or spotted monster. "It's my salvation," he thought, "not one of those brutes has any guts.

Nevertheless, the incessant waiting, the uncertainty, the monotony were preying upon Henessey's nerves. He was even thinner than before; the very thought of the Yxion plant was enough to give him nausea, though it remained his only food; and the boredom would turn him crazy If something, yes, almost anything, didn't happen pretty soon. There were times when he had been sorely tempted to come down from the web, though he would never be able to fight his way back again. But his natural caution had triumphed—that is, until today. Now, more seriously than ever before, he was weighing the idea of descending as soon as night was over, and looking for Dave and Eunice. "Maybe I'll end up by being the late Earle W. Henessey," he reflected, bleakly. "But might as well take a chance. I'm not living as it is now."

He had all but determined to make the audacious, the reckless move. And then, just as the night began, destiny—or, rather, the Ugwugs—unexpectedly intervened.

The web-creatures had no sooner begun their nightly crawling, pilfering and battling when Henessey became aware of an unusual commotion. From far below, he heard screeches, shrieks and yells. The cries, spasmodic at first, swiftly gathered strength, until within a few minutes they were almost continuous. As they grew in volume, they seemed to proceed from ever-nearer sources, as if the shouts and screams had been taken up by successive rings of throats, each higher on the web than the one before. At the same time, the web itself began to sway; and the movement grew, then waned, then grew again, until the hive's very stability seemed to have been upset.

"What in perdition is it?" Henessey muttered aloud. "An earthquake?"

Now the noises continued, with howls, roars and bellowings that grew constantly nearer. Looking through the peephole, Henessey saw the Ugwugs, moving about in wild agitation. All were traveling in one direction—down! A momentary thought came to Henessey of the proverbial rats deserting the sinking ship. The dread flashed over him that the entire hive would collapse. And then, while he quivered and clutched uncertainly at the cables of his shaking platform, he at last made out one clear word. "Rantangle! Rantangle!"

A shriek intervened—a shriek as of mortal agony. Then the yells, "Rantangle! Rantangle! Rantangle!" broke again upon his ears.

"Let's see, what can it be—" he pondered. And then suddenly he remembered. A rantangle was some sort of a celebration—no, not a celebration, a riot, when those fiends of Ugwugs turned against the Lil-bro. Well, he personally had never thought much of the bird-people; still, he didn't approve of such roughhouse tactics—as a matter of fact, he was rather sorry for them.

"Rantangle! Rantangle! Rantangle!" the cries were borne to him again. And he thought he detected a note of glee—impish, unholy glee, mingled with a howling fury as of wild beasts let loose. And from somewhere far below, deeper and more continuous than those shouts of "Rantangle! Rantangle! Rantangle!" he could distinguish a shrieking, a wailing, a low, distant ululation as of a sorrowing multitude.

Xangrl, awakening with a start, echoed the cry, "Rantangle! Rantangle! Rantangle!" swung himself over the edge of the web; and was gone.

One by one all the neighboring webs were being deserted. Suddenly Henessey felt all alone—more alone than ever before in this hive. At the same time, he was swept by terror—terror he knew not what of, as if he had caught the contagion of fear that pulsated in a multitude of breasts. And he felt himself caught by the herd impulse—like that of a man swept into a mob rushing to a fire. He felt. a powerful prompting to go down, to join the multitude still screaming, "Ran tangle! Rantangle! Rantangle!"

He crept to the edge of the shaking web, and held on fearfully. Here, surely, was his chance. No one would notice now if he did leave. He might even be able to steal back unobserved. But when he thought of letting himself down on the long rope-ladders and latticed meshes through the unmeasured immensities, he felt his heart fluttering. He had never been anything of a steeplejack; he could picture too clearly what it would mean to lose his balance and plunge, plunge through the fathomless gulf.

"Rantangle! Rantangle! Rantangle!" the shouts still rose, amid crashes, groans, wailings and demoniac cries such as Henessey had never heard before. And then, during a momentary lull in the din, while he still hesitated, another sound burst over him. Though evidently dimmed by distance, it was so shrill, so distinct, so unexpected that he clutched at the web amazed and bewildered, and for a moment was in danger of tumbling off.

The sound was repeated—three swift short strident blasts. The call of a police whistle!

"Glory be to God!" Henessey muttered, as he recalled Dave's code. "S. O. S!"

CHAPTER TWENTY-FOUR

AS HENESSEY FUMBLED for, his whistle, the three swift short blasts were repeated again.

The seconds before he could flick the instrument to his lips seemed to hold endless duration. "What the devil shall I answer?" he asked himself, dazedly. And he remembered the code signal for "I'm coming!"

Even as his two longs and two shorts shrieked through the air, three shorts broke over him again from far below.

"It's Dave!" he thought. "Yes, sure enough it's Dave." And, then swiftly he added, "Still, by George! It could be Eunice! Most likely, though, she never had a chance to learn the code. Why in the name of sense didn't we think of some identifying signal?"

Ten seconds went by; and then, from far below, an answering two longs and two shorts. It had been agreed that signals might be acknowledged by being answered in kind.

"Must be a mile off, judging from the time it took," Henessey reflected. "After all, guess it's nearly a mile to the bottom."

The three swift shorts were repeated, began once more, and were drowned out by renewed cries of "Rantangle! Rantangle! Rantangle!"

"Well, here goes," Henessey told himself, as he made sure his knapsack was tightly strapped on; gave a loving tap at his pistol;. and then, with a shudder, placed one foot on a ladder leading down from the web-platform. "Better hurry to poor old Dave's rescue, though God only knows what I can do!"

He was thankful now that he had lost so much weight; it made the descent that much less precarious. Still, he was in a constant sweat of terror as he clung to the swaying meshes and cables, which rocked much more violently than usual. He knew now what had caused that shaking which he had mistaken for an earthquake; it was the unusual tugging produced by the simultaneous down-rushing of a multitude of Ugwugs. Lucky that the flimsy strands had held at all!

"Rantangle! Rantangle! Rantangle!" a demon's chorus still bawled from far beneath, amid continued shrieks, howls and wailings. And from time to time, though at rarer intervals, the three short whistle blasts still urged Henessey on. "I'm coming! I'm coming!" he would answer with the code signals. But before long he began to fear that he was not coming fast enough.

Though he was making reckless speed, he seemed to draw little nearer to the hive-floor, which was hidden by innumerable loops, mats and whorls of the swinging deserted yellow-green web, weirder and more terrifying beneath the phosphorescence of night than in the plain gray drabness of day. He had never in his life been so near to praying as when he descended swinging rope staircases, swung across bridges so narrow that one misstep would have hurled him into the abyss, and crawled down precipitous web-walls to which he clung with both hands while his feet sought a doubtful hold. He had never known that it was possible for so many muscles to ache all at once, nor that a man could keep on for so long after he had begun to puff and gasp. Actually, as a hasty glance at his watch later told him, the descent had taken less than an hour; but he would have Sworn it had lasted several times as long.

"I'll be late! Too late to help poor Dave!" he kept repeating, while, surprising himself at the chances he was taking, he went down and down.

Finally, through a break in the webs, he had a glimpse of the floor, perhaps four hundred yards beneath. The tumult of shouts and cries, which never entirely died down, had gradually grown louder and more savage. He saw some creatures, doubtless bird-people, scurrying through an open space, followed by a mob of Ugwugs, who made greater speed than he would have thought possible for such heavy, thick-set creatures. Within a few seconds, both pursued and pursuers had streaked out of view; and then, after another few seconds, shrieks of pain and howls of glee came from the direction in which they had vanished.

A new S. O. S. hastened Henessey's steps. And after another nerve-wracking fifteen minutes, he stood on the floor of the hive, reeling just a little and with a giddiness in the head, but thankful to remain alive.

Almost the first thing that caught his eyes, as he stood trying to get his bearings, was one of the Lil-bro, who lay on the floor upon his back, his eyes closed, his feet sticking stiffly in the air, a little like a slaughtered fowl.

"Merciful Lord!" Henessey swore softly to himself, as he noticed the deep yellow gashes about the dead creature's throat. "This isn't a riot! It's murder!"

Three short whistle blasts, louder than before, shrilled through the air.

"I'm coming! I'm coming!" he signaled back. And then, after four or five seconds, while he stood staring about him uncertainly, there came the response, which was repeated several times: one short and one long.

"Let's see, let's see," Henessey reflected. "That means, 'Hurry! Straight ahead! ' Doggone that Dave, he must be getting in deeper and deeper water... Guess he heard me gradually coming nearer; that's why he signaled, 'Straight ahead! '"

Anxiously he covered a hundred paces, in the same general direction as when he was slanting his way down the web. Coming out around a great tangle of meshes, suddenly he found himself opposite a pair of Ugwugs. One glance, and he knew the danger. Their heads, in their eagerness, shot toward him like projectiles; their front faces, which they made no effort to control, were contorted with a gloating ferocity.

"Rantangle! Rantangle! Rantangle!" they shrieked and started for Henessey.

It was his salvation that one of the bird-people fluttered into view, providing a diversion that enabled Henessey to slip away. He could hear the screams of the unfortunate creature behind him as he raced to safety—or rather, comparative safety.

"Jesus!" he muttered to himself, wiping a cold sweat from his brow. "It's pretty clear they don't know I'm a Webnate!" And then, after a minute, "Now I begin to see what Dave's up against!"

The whistle blasts were repeated: three shorts, and three shorts, and again three shorts.

"Well, might as well all die together, he told himself. "Don't see what in blazes I can do against such an outfit.

Five minutes later, after a comparative lull in the roars and shouts, a commotion broke out just ahead of Henessey, so violent that the webs above him trembled as if in a gale, and the floor beneath him seemed to quake. The thudding of many feet and the clamoring of many voices merged in one overwhelming uproar as a multitude rumbled toward Henessey. He had barely time to hide in a little pocket of the web crouching with his chin against his knees and his hands clasped together beneath his legs, when the procession began to storm past.

It was composed mostly of Ugwugs. There were not quite so many as he had supposed—not more than forty or fifty—but their phosphorescent greenish eyes glowed with gleeful fierceness, their arms waved with exultant fury, and their long distendable necks shot back and forth as if snapping at invisible prey. In the midst of this mob, five or six Lil-bro walked—or rather, were prodded along, pricked by their captors' horns and slapped by their whip-like hands. Their heads drooped, and their eyes were blank with despondency; their scales were spotted With gashes, from each of which a yellow blood was oozing. But their screams were almost drowned out by the cries, "Rantangle! Rantangle! Rantangle...! Down with the Lil-bro! Down with them! Down with them...! Kill the dirty Lil-bro! Kill the black-hearted Lil-bro! They've made all our troubles...! Kill them! Kill them! Kill them!"

Within plain view of Henessey's hideout, the Ugwugs paused; lashed their captives to stout web-strands; and began circling about them in a sort of rude, jubilant dance.

Henessey remained just long enough to see the Ugwugs begin taking turns in butting the prisoners. He heard the howls of agony of the lacerated victims; heard the persecutors' shrieks of mirth; and longed devoutly for a machinegun to turn upon the Ugwugs. But after a minute, seeing the beasts' concentration upon the Lil-bro, he was able to steal forth, clasping his pistol in one hand and crouching close to the floor.

As he slunk away, the cries still dinned in his ears. "Rantangle! Rantangle! Rantangle...! Down with the Lil-bro!

Kill the Lil-bro! Kill the devils! They've made all our troubles…
Kill them! Kill them! Kill them!"

He was not sure if he was going in the right direction; there
were moments when he thought he was lost. "Ought to have a
dog's hearing," he ruminated, "so as to trace those signals."
Only at rare intervals, when for a moment the storming of the
mob died down, did he hear the whistle at all. And then he
could only make out the repeated three short blasts. They
seemed nearer, but it was hard to be sure, since the sounds were
muffled by the racket of those ungodly Ugwugs.

At last he paused, leaning for support against a fencelike
tangle of webs. He was tired, so tired that he wanted nothing
better than to throw himself down and rest. His head ached, and
he felt giddy; his heart was pumping fiercely, and his panting
breath testified to his forced speed. For several minutes he
stood hesitating, not knowing which way to go. Then shrill and
clear, above the subsiding commotion of the mob, he heard the
signal. One short and one long, then a pause. One short and
one long, and another pause. One short and one long…

"Hurry! Straight ahead!" he once more interpreted, muttering
into his beard. "Dave sure can't be far off now!"

As he shot forward, a fresh tumult—a fury of angry voices—
arose from a new direction; or, rather, seemed to come from
several directions all at once. He crouched close to a thick
webbed wall, and slid forward. And then, as he turned at a sharp
angle, eager to proceed yet ready to dash back at any suspicious
sign, he stopped short with a gasp. His eyes had been caught by
something as unexpected, as bewilderingly strange as a new
planet. A light!

It was not merely the ordinary yellow-green glow of the web-
structure. It was a sharp, sticking point of white light, which
stabbed in his direction, then went off, then stabbed again
through a lattice-like veil of webs.

"Dave!" he shouted, at the top of his voice. "Dave! Dave!"
And, forgetting caution, he spurted ahead, around the latticed
web-wall.

As he did so, an answering cry shrieked to his ears; broke hysterically upon him—in a woman's voice.

"Saints above!" he muttered; then clutched with one hand at his furiously palpitating breast; and yelled his reply. "Eunice! Eunice!"

Staggering out on the further side of the wall, he saw more than he had expected, Eunice was there, surely enough—wild-looking, bedraggled and disheveled, her long golden-yellow hair flying loose about her slender tall form. Her back was to one of the great branching roof-supporting pillars; at her side, huddling close in terror, were half a dozen Lil-bro. In her left hand she held a whistle; in her right, a flashlight, which she switched on and off intermittently, so keeping at bay an Ugwug rabble, which encircled her at twenty or thirty yards. Even as Henessey rushed into sight, she was turning the rays upon a black-and-red monster, who had been sneaking up on one side, but catching the flashlight full in his eyes, howled with pain and staggered as if blinded.

"Eunice! Eunice!" Henessey repeated, in a cracking voice.

He did not know if she had heard him; for the moans, groans and mutterings of the mob made a noise like the menace of stormy waters. "Rantangle! Rantangle! Rantangle!"

But she threw her arms toward him, pitched forward, and would have fallen if two Lil-bro had not seized her.

At the same time several Ugwugs, taking advantage of the confusion started toward her with still louder vociferations. "Rantangle! Rantangle! Rantangle!

Henessey's next act was faster than reason. Grasping his pistol, he plunged forward with a leonine bellow. He was staking his life, he later realized, upon the chance that all the hive knew of the pistol's deadliness. But evidently all the hive did know; or else Henessey's appearance, as he dashed toward Eunice, waving his gun and shouting. like a savage, was so redoubtable that the Ugwugs were intimidated. Snarling and hissing, they shrank back; and within a few seconds Henessey was at Eunice's side.

She had recovered from the moment's collapse, but faced him heavily panting, clutching her heaving bosom with one hand, her face white and tear-stained, and her lips drawn wide in agonized amazement.

"I—I thought it was Dave," she gasped.

"I—I thought so too," he blurted out. "But good Lord, Eunice I'm glad to've found you! I'll help you—we'll get free together from those devils!

She sparkled the flashlight at a blue-black beast stealing up from the left. At the same time, Henessey waved his pistol at the mob, which retreated to about a hundred feet, where they waited in a circle, grimly certain of their prey.

"Where—where's Dave?" she demanded, in a broken voice.

"Don't you—don't you know?"

"I—I only saw him once," she walled, struggling to keep back the tears. "They—they took him away. I don't know what in the world's happened to him."

"Wish I could tell you. Haven't seen him for weeks. But just you trust Dave to find a way," Henessey consoled, voicing a confidence he did not feel. "He'll pull through somehow."

"I—I hope so," she answered, with a sobbing half-gasp. "I—I was so sure that was him now!"

"Rantangle! Rantangle! Rantangle!" roared the mob, with a threatening forward surge, which was only checked by Henessey's pistol waving.

At this the Lil-bro pressed closer than ever about Henessey and Eunice. They were fluttering as if in a gale; their eyes glared with terror.

"The poor creatures!" explained Eunice. "My flashlight is all that saved them from those horrible beasts. They rushed to me just in the nick of time. They trusted me because—well, because some of them knew Dave."

For the first time, Henessey glanced at the bird-people. One was a slightly undergrown thing covered with yellowish brown scales; a second was full-sized and had steel-gray scales, and a large crescent scar on its milky brow and left cheek. And a third was immense for a Lil-bro; and had a gray-brown wrinkled face that appeared very old. Henessey did not know that these were Dave's friends Tintle, Glarr and Go-glabbo; but he did feel their confidence in Eunice and himself. And somehow, a little to his own surprise, he had a fellow feeling for these creatures, and wished to rescue them.

"Rantangle! Rantangle! Rantangle!" the rabble shrilled again and again. But the pistol and the flashlight still kept them at bay.

"How—how do you happen to be here?" Henessey asked, when for a moment the enemy seemed a little less menacing.

"I—I really hardly know," she answered, talking by spurts and gasps, "I was working below—in the sub-web—when those awful Ugwugs broke in, crying 'Rantangle! Rantangle! Rantangle!' They drove some of the Lil-bro up to the hive-floor and me among them; and did terrible things to those poor creatures. They blamed them—oh, I don't know just what for— kept saying some of the Ugwugs had gone out on a raid last night, and didn't come back, and it was all the Lil-bro's fault. I thought of the flashlight just in time—how I'd turned it on once simply in fun, and an Ugwug screamed as if I'd hit him. They wouldn't come near so long as I shot the rays in their eyes, but they wouldn't go away, either. I backed against this, column, so that they couldn't get me from behind, and I've been fighting them ever since—oh it seems hours and hours. I knew the flash-light couldn't hold out forever—in fact, it's getting dimmer already. That's why I sent the S. O. S. I thought maybe Dave— or you, of course—would hear, and come before the batteries gave out. Why, I wanted to go down on my knees and pray to be heard. So you can guess how thankful, how very thankful I was to hear your answer.

"Well, I'm sure glad I came," mumbled Henessey. "What has me worried now, though, is how we'll get out of this mess."

Suddenly he rushed forward, waving his, pistol and shouting. But though the Ugwugs in front of him retreated, others began to press forward from the rear.

"That's just the horror of it," he reported, as he shot back to Eunice's side. "You can't make any more impression on that pack than on a cloud. Why, if we left the shelter of this column for even one minute, what was left of us wouldn't be worth one snap of your fingers."

"Don't I know?" she moaned. "Oh, if Dave would only hear!"

She put the whistle to her lips, and blew three short swift blasts; and then, after a few seconds, three more blasts. But though they both repeated the call time after time, there was no response.

"Rantangle! Rantangle! Rantangle!" the old monotonous cry dinned forth. But now it had a new note, of rising exultation, evil desire, and glee; the eyes of the nearest Ugwugs glowed ghoulishly from their phosphorescent greenish depths. At the same time the Lil-bro, as if their keen senses could feel the sinister vibrations in the air, whined and whimpered, and pressed ever closer to their protectors. With shaking fingers, Glarr and Go-glabbo were pointing upward.

While some subconscious monitor flashed them a warning, Henessey and Eunice stared into the confusion of webs above. An impenetrable tangle stretched at a height of about fifty feet, connecting with the intricately branching columns. And suddenly the whole tangle began to shake—to shake ominously, without visible cause. Or, rather, at first without visible cause. After a minute, while the watchers still gazed in a fascination of horror, a long tentacled arm flashed out of the web. And something dark and heavy—a rock as large as a baseball—came crashing down, and narrowly missed a Lil-bro's head.

Immediately there followed another, another, and another still, until all of the little group were dodging missiles. Against such a peril, the flashlight and the pistol alike were useless.

"Away! Come! Let's get away!" Henessey yelled.

With Eunice at his side and the Lil-bro surrounding them, he darted into the open, away from the sheltering pillar.

The Ugwugs screamed in triumph. "Rantangle! Rantangle! Rantangle!" they squeaked and gibbered. And while Henessey vainly motioned them off with his pistol and Eunice's flashlight cast its last sputtering rays, the web-creatures began slowly to narrow their circle, in the manner of besiegers who have the enemy bottled up, and need only close in at their leisure in order to make the kill.

CHAPTER TWENTY-FIVE

"TONIGHT, O SMARDL, we will go to the nearest colony of the free Lil-bro. We will put you down near the hives, and you will make friends of the people who are such unsuspicious fools as to think well of all of whom they have learned no evil. On the tenth night we will return, along with many of our brothers; and you will bring the Lil-bro to the edge of the woods, where we hide, that we may capture them. Having trust in you, they will be easy victims."

"They will be easy victims," acknowledged Dave, as he listened to his instructions for the twentieth time. He was now in the charge of two burly Ugwugs, a purple-spotted tawny brute known as Thgal, and a mahogany-brown beast with a double-length horn, whose name was Zrach. Both were members of the Division of Wild Life, though the only wild life of interest to them was that of the Lil-bro, whom they were anxious to make less wild.

Within Dave's mind one question kept knocking: how, without risking all, could he pretend and yet avoid compliance?

It was as if Zrach had read his thoughts. "By the High Webs!" he swore, butting his monstrous horn tentatively at Dave, while his front eyes flashed with a menacing blaze. "You must listen, and obey to the last syllable! A cycle or two ago, there was a Lil-bro that did not obey, but thought to get away into the woods. When we caught him, we tied him to the web, and killed him bit by bit by tearing the flesh off his body, so that many sleeps had passed before he died in slow agony."

"There was another," reported Thgal, clawing the air with his tentacled hands, who committed the crime of warning his people. We buried him alive in the Ninth Sub-Web, where, unless he still gasps miserably in the dark and cold, you would find the traitor's remains."

"No one, in a hundred cycles, has ever gotten away!" warned Zrach, with a snort, and a flare of his greenish eyes. "In all the woods there is no place where we could not smell him out. Word is sent to every Ugwug hive in the district, of which there are many, all zealous to punish the crime of treason."

"I will commit no treason," Dave assured them. And this, he told himself, was the solemn truth; the only treason would be to betray the Lil-bro.

"The last sun goes to its sleep," Zrach remarked, when after a time the yellow-green glow of night was overspreading the web "Come! We leave!"

The next thing Dave knew, he had been lifted to the creature's back, and was held, face to the ceiling, in six powerful arms, just as when carried by Oesle. An acrid animal smell a little like that of raw leather, tormented his nostrils; his muscles were cramped, and he was jerked about like a bag of beans; but he was powerless in the mighty grip. Accompanied by Thgal, who took turns in carrying their charge, Zrach lumbered to the edge of the hive; passed out through one of the numerous wall-flaps; and trotted into the wilderness.

Dave could not judge their direction, for they twisted and wound, at times jogging on narrow trails through underbrush in whose darkness they could see like cats; then coming out into open spaces that afforded glimpses of the strange constellations and even stranger red, white and blue banded moons. They seemed to be on their way a long long while: although actually, as he afterwards reckoned, the Journey could not have lasted much more than two hours. But finally they came out into a partially open space on the wooded plain, and Dave noticed something familiar about his surroundings.

Twinkling in the starlight, and shimmering faintly red, white and blue by the rays of the colored moons, was the long oval of a lake, and the longer loop of a river. And between him and the river Dave saw a cluster of beehive structures which fluttered gently, and glistened so that one might have thought them all of pearl and silver. With a sob of emotion, he recognized the very Lil-bro colony at which he and his companions had been received so warmly.

But his masters, not suspecting that he had ever been here before carried him to a tongue of the woods not far behind the beehive structures. Releasing him, so that he stood stamping his feet and trying to restore the circulation to his cramped limbs. Zrach pointed to a tree that rose with storm-stripped upper limbs twisted so as to form a rude cross.

"We will wait here on the tenth night—we and our comrades. When one third of the night is gone, we will be here, hiding in the darkness behind that tree. By the honor of the High Webbed One, may his cycles be many! do you understand?"

"I understand. I am to lead the Lil-bro here, so that you may fall upon them."

"Then the good spirits of the web be with you! We go!"

"We go!" echoed Thgal. "We must be back in the hive before the red sun is in the sky." And then, thrusting his head almost into Dave's face, with a warning sparkle of the greenish eyes, "if you fail us, by my father's scales! you will regret the day you first drew breath!"

A moment later, Dave was alone.

After a much needed nap on a leafy bed and a breakfast of some mealy roots and succulent stalks, Dave felt greatly refreshed.

"By glory! There is some way! There must be!" he kept telling himself. "I'll simply have to fool those fiends!" But when he thought of Eunice, and how all his efforts on her behalf had been balked, so that now he seemed further than ever from rescuing her or aiding her in any way at all, he was overcome with a chilling sadness.

The red sun rose, its great crimson-fringed mass suffusing the world in a ruddy light. Several hours later, the white sun had its fiery dawn above the serrate far-off western ranges; and in a little more than another hour, the blue luminary followed. And not until then did life revive in the beehive structures.

Once more the dozens of scintillant four-winged creatures came forth, flashing and flickering in the light of the triple suns with their metal-like colored bodies, emerald and ruby and gold, amber and purple and canary and they flew, in flights like the hummingbirds, leaping and diving in air, pirouetting, somersaulting, chasing one another in spirals, now hovering high above the plain With wings furiously beating, now sweeping to rest in long graceful curves, and now, after scarcely a moment's pause, looping again skyward in their never-ending round of fun.

For a few minutes Dave, lying concealed in a clump of shrubbery, listened to the singing of these gay elves, and watched them in wonder and enjoyment and yet with just a touch of bitterness. So these were the prey that the Ugwugs wanted to enslave! These joyous, vibrant beings, with their beauty of form and grace of movement and their freedom and sheer zest and glory of life, were wanted by the Ugwugs as prisoners and drudges! These children of a superior race were to have their wings clipped, their spirits broken, and the fire drained from their eyes! And all for what were they to be beaten and scorned? All for the sake of those monsters, the Ugwugs!

Dave clenched his fists, and once more vowed that never, no matter how terrible the penalty, would he betray these bright and lovely creatures.

Then, encouraged by his own resolve, he stepped into the open.

Instantly, it seemed, he was surrounded by a merrily crying, fluttering flock that hovered above him and settled on the ground all about him like boys and girls before some unexpected welcome guest. "Look! He's back! He's back! The Wingless One is back! The Two-Eyed One is back!" they called to one another, in their trilling musical voices. And not many minutes had passed before the entire community had settled around him.

"I am glad to be here," he said. And everyone screamed with glee, astonished and overjoyed that he could speak their language.

"Where are your friends? Your friends? Where are they?" twenty voices demanded all at once.

He sighed, and gestured vaguely with one hand. "With the Ugwugs."

Little squeaks and grunts of horror answered him, followed by a long dismal wailing, in which all the Lil-bro seemed to join.

Even before this sound had died down, Dave's gaze was attracted to a new arrival, who, with creased careworn face and pearly opaque wings veined with rich green and crimson, stood out instantly from all his fellows.

"Lo-klantho! Lo-klantho! Lo-klantho!" cried the others in their bell-like voices, as they wheeled and swung about their leader.

"Lo-klantho!" Dave repeated, and pressed forward eagerly.

"Welcome back, Wingless One!" the leader greeted him. "My people surprise me with good tidings. They say you now speak our language."

"I speak it but poorly," Dave deprecated. "Such words as I know, I learned from other Lil-bro, among the Ugwugs."

"Ugwugs?" Lo-klantho repeated, scowling mightily, and spitting out the word as if it were some morsel that he loathed. "If you were caught by the Ugwugs, how did you escape? It has not come to my ears that anyone ever escaped for long from the Ugwugs."

"That, Lo-klantho, is what I would speak with you about." Dave glanced doubtfully at the shimmering, fluttering, chattering flock. "It is not a thing I can talk of in a crowd."

With a swift flapping of his forward wings, Lo-klantho brought his followers to attention.

"My people," he said, pointing toward the lake, "if you will take flight yonder, I will see you a little later."

Instantly, with a great whirring of wings, all the flock except Lo-klantho were in the air. A minute later, they made but a spangled galaxy twinkling and glittering in the red white and blue sunlight.

Lo-klantho pointed to a little nook amid the blue-green shrubbery; and there, seated with his wings folded and his legs crossed on a bed of a mossy purple plant, he listened to Dave's story.

Squatted opposite his hearer, Dave told of the capture of his comrades and himself by the Ugwugs, and of all that had since happened, including his forced enlistment as a decoy.

"Since I report all this frankly," he ended, "you will know that I never meant to obey the Ugwugs. You will know that I would sooner die than betray you."

Lo-klantho's grave, pale face was furrowed with deep thinking. It was a moment before he answered.

"Wingless One," he responded, slowly, "I believe that you meant no betrayal. Yours are clear, good eyes, and no blackness hides behind them. Nevertheless, this is a grim, unhappy event."

"But why should it be?" argued Dave. "I will warn you of the Ugwugs' coming. You will know when they come, and where. None of your people will be caught."

"For more than three cycles," replied Lo-klantho, his aged countenance more deeply wrinkled than ever, "the Ugwugs have caught none of our tribe, though other colonies have been less fortunate. We have had some bad times at night, when we have rushed away in great alarm. But they have been too slow and stupid to catch any of us. Not being able to fly, they cannot get us even with their nets except by trickery. That is why they wished a decoy. That too is why, if you fail them, their anger will be more terrible than a great wind in a forest."

"I do not fear their anger."

"If your wits are not less than dust, you will indeed fear it. You will be a bugruth—a marked man. None such ever escapes from the Ugwugs. They trail him down, no matter where he be. All other Ugwug hives join in the hunt. They track him with their sense of smell, which is their only well-developed sense. There is no escape. And that is why, Wingless One. That is why we cannot let you sacrifice yourself."

"I will not sacrifice myself, Lo-klantho. I've found my way out of worse webs than that," Dave insisted, although he did feel a passing chill at the old Lil-bro's deadly earnestness. "One thing certain is that we won't let any of you folks be caught by those monsters."

"May the Shining Ones forbid! Still, we must not abandon you to their cruel hands. We might make the Ugwugs think they had almost caught us, so that they might still believe you tried to help them."

Dave shook his head. "No, no, that's not right. You'd have to take too many chances. And afterwards, if I didn't come back to them, the Ugwugs would know just where I stood."

Lo-klantho meditatively plucked at a strand of the purple mossy plant.

"The Ugwugs," he ruminated, "have been the one shadow across the lives of us Lil-bro. My people think little about them, but all my cycles have been dark with worry lest they capture us in a surprise raid. It is strange, they look upon us as upon the small things wriggling in the soil. Yet who built their civilization—that is, all that they have of a civilization? Their very language was taken from us, though they speak it in a coarse, corrupted form. All their arts, such as they know of them, were borrowed from us. True, they weave webs, by some marvelous instinct, out of their own bodies; but we taught them how to make the stone for the columns and ribs of their hives, and how to weld it together with an invisible mortar. Their original hives, even the largest, before we became their slaves, were of a ruder, less durable construction. We also, as you know, supply all their workers; while they, bloated with their own fumes, pass their time in sleeping, scheming and fighting. That, no doubt, is why they deem themselves the highest things created by the Radiant Lord of All on all the planets of the universe.

"One thing I cannot understand," reflected Dave, "is why, if the Ugwugs need you so much, they treat you so badly—beat you, kick you, and work you to death, and even so, I've been told, hunt you to death in brutal raids."

"Yes, rantangles," Lo-klantho took up, his head drooping sadly. "But the Ugwugs are not consistent beasts. They pride themselves on their reason, but if any of them shows signs of logic he is hounded out of the hive. They do not see that it makes no sense to be in dire need of us Lil-bro, and then kill us in rantangles. They are ruled by their passions. Being used to dangling sidewise or face down on their webs, they see things twisted or upside down; and If any one by chance sees things straight, it looks to them as If he sees them crooked. Unhappily, they were not made to see things as they are."

"Yet they have two pairs of eyes," Dave pointed out.

"What! Do you not know? Their rear eyes, which express their true feelings, are so shortsighted as to be almost useless. That is because they are so much in the habit of looking at small things close at hand. It is said, though I do not know if this is true, that they are gradually losing the vision of their front eyes too."

"Well, did you notice that they cannot stand much light?"

"That is true. Their eyes, being lidless, cannot protect themselves like ours. And having been used to the dimness of the hives for many generations, they are poisoned by bright light. Thanks be to the Shining Ones for that! since We need not fear their raids by day... But hadn't we better talk about this threatened night raid?"

"Well, we've got nearly ten days to plan against it. You just give me time to think it over, Lo-Klantho, and I'll figure out something, so that your people won't be in any danger."

"Also, so that you may save yourself, Wingless One."

"Also, so that I may save myself." And then in English, beneath his breath, "And go back and get Eunice out of that villainous hive!"

"Well, think about it, Wingless One, think about it!" counseled Lo-klantho. "As I love the three suns, I cannot see what you will do. I cannot see. You do not know how strong, how terrible the Ugwugs can be."

With a sudden lift of his four wings, he arose. But his flight, as he sped off toward the soaring cloud of his fellows, seemed to lack the other Lil-bro's animation, vibrancy and joy of life.

CHAPTER TWENTY-SIX

IT WAS ONE THING, as Dave soon learned, to promise to balk the attack; it was quite another thing to carry out the promise. The days went by, four of them, five of them, six of them, seven of them; but Dave seemed no nearer than ever to forming a plan. Meanwhile he passed his time among the Lil-bro; he conferred frequently with Lo-klantho and his advisers; he slept in one of their shimmering beehive dwellings; he rambled by day through the fields and woods while gathering edible roots, herbs, gums and berries. (Now that he could speak the language and explain his need for food, he had overcome the people's objections to his taking of plant life, which they would otherwise have considered impious).

Fearing to create panic, the leader had not notified his people of the approaching peril. He had, however, confided in three sages, the Knowing Ones, who, like Lo-klantho, had the grave, wrinkled faces of seers.

Ran-dultro, the first of the trio, was small even for a Lil-bro; but his flaming large front eyes burned so brightly that Dave could hardly bear to gaze into them. "With such vermin as the Ugwugs, it is unreasonable to take chances," he advised. "We have lived in fear too long already. Let us end our terror; let us go elsewhere—yes, the whole community of us, and with no further foolish delay!"

Or-lippin, the second, was a large Lil-bro with a wizened sagacious face. "I am not quite of Ran-dultro's mind," he counseled. "I think it unnecessary to give up our good homes.

But let us be gone the whole night when the Ugwugs arrive. We will hide in the woods till dawn, and thus avoid the danger."

Per-ducco, the third Knowing One, was a slim creature whose head was so large that Dave almost lost sight of the rest of his body. He agreed with Or-lippin that his people need not leave their homes for more than one night; but he recommended that they dig deep trenches and cover them with leaves and branches, so that the unwary Ugwugs might fall in and be killed.

Lo-klantho listened solemnly to all these recommendations.

"We have not time to dig trenches before the Ugwugs get here," he objected, dealing first with Per-ducco's proposal. "Besides, they may be many—more than we can catch. The remainder, out of vengeance, may destroy our homes and lay waste our beautiful country, even if they cannot capture us. As for going away, forever or even for a night—that must not be considered, since it would leave the Wingless One at the mercy of the Ugwugs."

"Oh, please just forget me!" Dave demurred.

With an angry flare, Lo-klantho turned upon him.

"What is that, my friend?" he demanded, his normally mellow voice harsh with resentment. "You ask that we do as the Ugwugs?—put ourselves first? No, O Wingless One, we Lil-bro have suffered danger and misfortune, but we have not lost all moral sense. How would we have one night's sound sleep again if we knew we had abandoned our protector?"

"Why can the Wingless One not come away with us?" asked Ran-dultro.

"I cannot come," answered Dave, "because my two comrades are in the Ugwug hive, and I must save them."

The Knowing Ones nodded, accepting this reason as sufficient.

"Then we come back to my original plan," decided Lo-klantho. "We will take a few of our people into our confidence, and they will hide in the woods where the Ugwugs are expected. They will be near enough to be seen, but will flyaway just as the monsters approach with their nets.! Thus the Ugwugs will believe the Wingless One has done his best, and will not punish him."

"No, no, no, that still doesn't sound right," Dave dissented. "I don't think you should take such a risk to protect me." In imagination he could hear the screams of the caught Lil-bro and could see them as they were whipped, pummeled: bruised, and transformed from shimmering, joyous children of the sunlight to wingless droop-necked slaves of the hive. No, they must at all costs be shielded from this doom!

But how? Not for a week did an idea come to Dave. And then one day he was examining the spaceship the *Shooting Star,* which still lay in the woods where it had fallen. He was inspecting the broken compartment, and had concluded that the damage was no greater than one or two men could repair by a few days' hard labor. But suddenly another thought flashed over him. His eyes chanced to catch a sun-reflecting sparkle from the great searchlight at the vessel's prow; and he hastened to examine the instrument, and found that it had not been damaged.

"By heck!" he cried aloud, shaking his own hands in self-congratulation. "The very thing!"

He remembered how carefully he had selected the light. It was a powerful affair, capable of shooting a penetrating beam as much as ten thousand yards. Furthermore, it had a less concentrated alternate ray, which, in order to provide for the contingencies of space travel, could focus on nearer objects— could fling a blaze like daylight at spots a hundred or two hundred yards away. It was powered by the latest Ward-McCutcheon batteries, which—like those in the flashlights— were so sealed and insulated that they would lose none of their strength if not used for centuries. And it hung on a swinging removable pivot, which not only enabled it to be turned in most directions, but permitted it to be detached for transference to the ship's stem, top or underside.

It required but a few minutes' work with a screwdriver to unfasten the light. "Thank God that I thought of it in time!"

Dave muttered to himself as he labored. Mounted directly across from the Ugwugs' hiding-place, it would reveal them so clearly that none of the Lil-bro would be in danger. And the Ugwugs, knowing that the bird-people were cleverer than they and had made many inventions, would suppose that this was some new Lil-bro contrivance, and would not hold Dave responsible.

The instrument was so heavy that Dave had to take it apart; the various portions—lens, silver reflector, bulb, batteries, etc.—had to be carried off separately and reassembled in the woods near the settlement. The Lil-bro, who could not imagine what Dave was about, looked on in wonder, fluttering and laughing about him like children. Only Lo-klantho and the Knowing Ones, to whom he had confided his purpose, revealed any misgivings.

"True, your light-machine, O Wingless One, may show us the Ugwugs," reasoned the leader. "And thus our people may escape their claws. But for how long? The light will cause the Ugwugs pain, and the pain will anger them, and they will return with more of their people to spread terror among us."

"With my light-machine, I will be able to see them all," promised Dave.

"I like not such a strange invention," objected Or-lippin. "It is like a tool of the Evil Ones. What if the light should not shine when we need it?"

"What if it shine not bright enough?" asked Ran-dultro.

"With your own eyes you will see," promised Dave. And when at last the searchlight was mounted on a little rise of brushy land, in such a position that its operator might conceal himself amid the bushes, he made a test in the presence of Lo-klantho and the Knowing Ones. It was in the early morning, when only the red sun shone in the sky and most of the colony was still asleep. And though even the one sun considerably dimmed the light, a blinding white brilliance shot out toward the Ugwugs' expected hideout.

For a moment the watchers were silent.

"It is good. Very good," concluded Lo-klantho. "As surely as I take pride in my wings, this is a wonder-light. We will see the Ugwugs clearly. Unless my people are slower than the little things that creep on the ground, none of them will be caught. But I still think we should not use it. The Ugwugs are distrustful animals, and will suspect the Wingless One, and it will not go well with him."

"Have faith! All will be well with me!" Dave reassured them, with apparent confidence, although he knew that he was taking dire chances. But he was as far as were the Lil-bro from foreseeing the results.

*   *   *

Like a general planning a campaign, Lo-klantho prepared against the attack. Just before the crucial night, he took a few of his followers partly into his confidence, stationing one as a sentinel at each of the houses, with instructions to awaken the people in case of need. He selected four or five of the most fleet-winged, and bade them wait near the point of the Ugwugs' expected arrival; and he carefully calculated the distances, so that they might avoid the web-creatures' nets, and yet give the impression that Dave had done his best as a decoy. And having arranged all this, Lo-klantho decided that the three Knowing Ones and himself should hide in the woods just behind the searchlight, so as to be ready for any emergency.

Dave himself was sanguine. He did not doubt that the searchlight would succeed; and he beat down his misgivings as to what might happen should the Ugwugs suspect the part he had played. "If that time comes—which it probably won't—it'll be just one knot more to untangle," he told himself. "Good Lord, I ought to be an expert at knots by now!"

No sooner had the blue sun gone down behind the eastern ridges than the watchers took their stations. Although the Ugwugs were not to come until a third of the night was over—in other words, not for nearly two hours—Dave and Lo-klantho had decided to take no chances on their earlier approach. In a straight line, as Dave now realized, the distance to the Ugwug hive was not many miles, although he and his comrades had taken a long while to reach it by a roundabout route. The attackers, leaving at sunset, might easily arrive in less than two hours.

The night was darker than usual, since neither of the moons was in the sky. A heavy wind was blowing, rising at times in gusts that raced through the treetops with a screeching challenge. Dave, as he lay in the brush with one hand upon the searchlight switch, wished fervently for calmer weather, for the noise of the elements might drown the sounds of the approaching Ugwugs. He shivered just a little as time dragged endlessly on; from behind him the gentle breathing of Lo-klantho and the Knowing Ones come to his ears between pauses in the wind; ahead of him, beyond a meadow little more than a hundred yards across, a dark tongue of the woods was dominated by a storm-stripped tree with upper limbs twisted so as to form a rude cross. And beneath the trees there was a fringe of ragged thin bushes, in which the chosen Lil-bro stood, ready to fly at the first danger sign.

The wind, as the night wore on, whooped and hooted with ever greater fury. Between the gusts, now and then, the low whirring calls of night-flocks sounded, varied by flutelike notes, and muffled distant howls. Dave shifted uneasily, and shook off a small slimy thing that started to crawl up his sleeve. "Isn't it about time?" he whispered to Lo-klantho.

"More than time."

"Maybe those beasts won't come after all."

"That is better fortune than we can hope for, Wingless One. In all my cycles, I have never heard of the Ugwugs missing a chance for a raid."

"Maybe the wind will keep them away—"

But Lo-klantho broke him short. "Come, come, better not talk now, though our tones be lower than it rustling leaf's."

The squally wind that broke over them a moment later, with swirling, twisting blasts, would in any case have ended the conversation.

It seemed to Dave that another endless period went by. He had had no sleep for twenty-eight hours, and despite all his efforts, he was becoming drowsy. And then all at once, when he was almost fading into unconsciousness in the pleasant half-belief that the Ugwugs would not come after all, things began to happen so fast that he afterwards found it hard to put them together in their true order.

From across the meadow, in the direction of the woods, a scream broke forth. In the first startled second, Dave thought it only the shrieking of the wind. But instantly it was repeated— shrill, agonized, terror-stricken, the cry of some creature in mortal torment.

Automatically, even as the meaning of that sound penetrated to his brain, Dave turned the switch. And pain stabbed his eyeballs as a sun-like brilliance shot across the meadow and flooded the edge of the woods. Yet the pain was lost in horror as the scene stood blindingly revealed.

He did not even hear the cries of despair and alarm from his rear and all about him. His eyes, his whole being were concentrated on the dread sight that shot up within the circle of the searchlight rays.

Struggling on the ground, its wings, legs and arms entangled in what looked like a magnified spider-web, one of the Lil-bro was caught like a trapped fly. Several others, newly risen into the air, were zigzagging away with panicky speed. Two Ugwugs, each with their six arms tugging fiercely, were holding the net in which the Lil-bro was enmeshed. Lo-klantho had miscalculated the distance! The Ugwugs, unheard because of the noise of the wind, had crept nearer than anyone had thought possible!

Amid that same noise, Dave did not hear the yells of the two Ugwugs as he caught them in the searchlight blaze. He did not hear the howls and wailings of the other Ugwugs—a score of them altogether—as he rapidly swung the light on its pivot and illuminated them all in its powerful beams. But even as he was wondering how to rescue the luckless Lil-bro, who was threshing wildly about in the net, he witnessed a series of events so strange that it was long before he could quite believe in their reality.

Each of the Ugwugs, as the flaming light fell upon him, threw his two front hands before his forward eyes; while the two middle hands shielded the rear eyes. This was only as Dave had expected, since the lidless orbs were unable to endure much light. But he had not foreseen the sequel.

The first two Ugwugs—the captors of the Lil-bro—loosed their hold on the net, and began to stagger away, with drunken, blind movements as of creatures that have lost their sense of balance. Neither had gone more than a dozen paces before both seemed to stumble over some invisible obstacle, and pitched to the ground, where they lay writhing, with convulsive movements that gradually died down to faint squirmings and eventually ceased.

At the same time other Ugwugs, struck by the blaze of light, were likewise reeling away, stumbling, and collapsing among the weeds and bushes.

Meanwhile a great buzzing and whirring diverted Dave's attention. Lo-klantho and the three Knowing Ones had risen into the air; and seeing the retreat of the attackers, rushed screaming to aid their entangled brother. Simultaneously, the alarm having spread to the beehive houses, shrieks and howls arose in all directions even above the commotion of the wind; and the people, rudely awakened, spurted skyward through the roof openings.

For several minutes Dave swept the searchlight back and forth in a wide are, to make sure that no Ugwugs had escaped. And then, protected by the light, he started across the meadow. A little cautiously, he approached the first Ugwug, which lay motionless on its back, its six arms dangling limply in air. Suspecting that it might be shamming, he seized a long stick, and prodded it. But it gave no response—not even when he rapped it on the sensitive lips and nose. And it was the same with the other Ugwugs. In various ungainly attitudes they lay sprawled near the borders of the woods, the whole twenty of them, lifeless as boards. The light, to which they were unadapted, had penetrated their systems as a poison, blinding them, shocking their nerves, upsetting their delicate internal balance, and killing them almost instantly.

CHAPTER TWENTY-SEVEN

UNTIL THE RED SUN ROSE in a crimson dawn, Dave clung to his post by the searchlight. He was still just a little afraid that some of the Ugwugs would revive; or that some, having escaped the deadly rays, were still prowling in the woods. But in the ruddy morning light, he saw them lying in all manner of grotesque postures, motionless where they had fallen. And only then did he really rejoice.

Of the Lil-bro there was not a sign. The captured one, he knew, had been rescued by Lo-klantho and the Knowing Ones; and had flown off, immensely frightened, but otherwise little the worse for his fearful experience. Apparently the entire community were hiding in the wilderness until they knew the danger was over.

Exhausted, Dave threw himself down on a sun-warmed patch among fern-leafed purple-blue creepers; and knowing that no Ugwug would attack by day, instantly fell asleep. His rest lasted longer than he had expected; when he awoke, both the white sun and the blue were some distance above the horizon. Even so, he might have slept for hours longer had it not been for a whirring of wings just above.

Still dazed, he peered into the seamed face of Lo-klantho, who was circling and hovering almost within touching distance.

Even before the old Lil-bro spoke, Dave was struck by the uneasiness, the distress on his features.

"Wingless One," he said, his voice clear and musical as usual, but infinitely troubled, "we are in a sorry pass."

"Sorry pass?" demanded Dave, not sure if he had heard correctly. "How can that be?" And, rising, he pointed to the lifeless shapes of the Ugwugs, around which predatory insects were buzzing, while beaked six-winged creatures wheeled above like vultures. "Aren't those brutes killed dead enough?"

"Yes, truly, Wingless One," Lo-klantho agreed, as he settled down at Dave's side. "As surely as my father and my father's father detested the Ugwugs, those creatures will never trouble us again. But alas! the other Ugwugs are still alive. When their brothers do not return, they will come to see what has happened. They will come tonight. There will be many of them, and they will take vile vengeance."

"Never mind," consoled Dave. "I'll strike the whole lot of them with my searchlight, just as I struck the first batch."

Lo-klantho took a rapid pace or two back and forth, and plucked absently at a pink-tasselled weed that grew on a waxy stem.

"Do not be too confident, Wingless One. Last night you hit the raiders because you knew where they would be, and where to turn your light. How can you know where the next ones will come? They may set on you from behind, where your light will be of no help."

Dave remained silent.

"Meanwhile my people will not stay by night in their homes," the leader went on. "But if the Ugwugs do not find them, they may destroy the homes out of vengeance, and lay the land waste. And that is not even the worst. They will not be content until they have taken life. Every night they will prowl about the countryside, until they have caught some of our people, and killed them in ways that I shiver to think about. While any Ugwugs remain alive, there is no escape for us."

Dave looked thoughtful, but not discouraged.

"Listen, Lo-klantho," he imparted, picking his words in the slow, precise way of one who unfolds a secret. "There's something that occurred to me as soon as I found that my light would kill the Ugwugs. If it put an end to the few prowlers last night, it could put an end to many more. In fact, it could work havoc in the main hive—if we could get it there."

"The main hive?" Lo-klantho echoed; and let out a little shriek. "What are you thinking of, Wingless One? Have your brains all poured out of your head, that you would venture back to the main hive—and at a time like this, when the Ugwugs are all aroused against you?"

"But if I could turn the light through an open flap of the hive, it would be the Ugwugs' disaster, not ours. Don't you see, Lo-klantho, don't you see?" Dave urged, on a rising wave of enthusiasm. "This might be your salvation!"

"I see," answered Lo-klantho, slowly, "that you are brave, and would take foolish risks. But though I love my people, I would not have you take such risks for us."

"It is not only for you, Lo-klantho. It is for my two comrades. My two comrades, who are in the claws of the Ugwugs. I would not hesitate—no, not even as long as it takes me to say this—if I knew how to reach the hive, and bring the searchlight there."

"As for that, Wingless One," Lo-klantho reflected, "we could help, if it seemed wise. We could lead you to the hive, though we try to keep away from such an evil place, whose smell hurts us like a blow. Some of our people could take hold of your light, and fly it to the hive. But they would have to take care, lest they be caught by the Ugwugs."

"If they kept in the air," Dave argued, "how could they be caught, seeing that the Ugwugs have no wings?"

"I know, Wingless One, I know. That sounds like wisdom, but we Lil-bro would be mad with excitement, and any accident can happen to excited people. I would not ask anyone to take such a risk, except in a very great cause."

"And is this not a very great cause? Tell me, when have you had such a chance before to strike back at the Ugwugs?"

"Never—not if this really be what it seems. It is a weighty matter, Wingless One. I must discuss it with the Knowing Ones. I will hear what they say, and let you know our answer."

"Better decide pretty fast!" Dave threw out, as his companion again took to the air. "I'd like to get at those devils before they come back tonight!"

Hours went by, many hours, and Lo-klantho did not return. Dave, as he rambled through the woods, caught an occasional distant glimpse of the leader, who was standing in a little hollow of an ancient grove, in earnest discussion with the Knowing Ones. Meanwhile few of the other Lil-bro—such was their awe of the Ugwugs, dead or alive—returned to their homes except in flitting, frightened flights; and none would approach the corpses of the monsters.

The red sun had left the sky, its white companion had just followed, and the sunset of the blue orb was but an hour away, when Lo-klantho came wheeling back, followed by six or eight followers.

"Wingless One," he reported, beginning breathlessly even before his feet had touched the ground, "it is decided! Our debate was long and hard; Ran-dultro believed the hazard too great to be taken, and for a while Or-lippin agreed with him. But Per-ducco held that if there was any hope of deliverance from the Ugwugs, though it were but a chance in a thousand, that hope should not be lost. After a time I too came to his way of thinking, and Or-lippin also was persuaded, though Ran-dultro still vowed it was wrong to endanger even one of our people. But since two of the Knowing Ones and I are of one mind, it will be as you say, o Wingless One! Six of the strongest and bravest of our people have volunteered. They will lead you to the Ugwug hive, and carry your light there through the air!"

"Thank God!" Dave muttered in English, though he wished that the Lil-bro had cut short their debate, so as to give him a chance to attack by day.

Their preparations, though simple, kept them busy almost until sunset. Dave had already procured some stout hempen ropes from the spaceship; and these he attached to the searchlight in such a way that it could be seized from above by the six Lil-bro. He himself, to lighten the burden, carried some of the batteries in his knapsack.

"For God's sake, don't drop that light!" Dave cautioned. "And put it down very gently when the time comes!"

"We will not drop it. We will put it down very gently," the six carriers chanted in chorus.

"May the Shining One be with you!" prayed Lo-klantha. "May he guard you, and bring you all back safely."

Stooped in solemn meditation, he stood watching as Dave started away in the pale uncanny twilight of the blue sun, his shoulders hunched beneath his pack, the six searchlight-bearers flying above and calling out directions while circling back and forth with their big glittering burden.

CHAPTER TWENTY-EIGHT

DARKNESS EXCEPT FOR the light of the stars and three brilliant planets. Through wooded gulches, over ridges, into groves and brushy tangles, across meadows and along streams in which he was continually splashing, Dave made his way beneath the guidance of the Lil-bro, who, with their four eyes, could see like owls, and flew above crying constant instructions.

Scratched, torn, bruised, muddy, and wet with perspiration, he kept on for more than two hours—so at least he judged, though he had no way of measuring time. But some inner urgency kept pushing him on. After all this delay, he argued with himself, an hour or two could not matter. Yet that unexplained force still whipped him forward. "Hurry, hurry, hurry!" The reason, he tried to convince himself, was his own impatience to see Eunice, to get her out of that devil's den. And yet somehow that cry persisted. "Hurry, hurry, hurry, hurry!"

Finally low excited calls from the Lil-bro sounded another warning. From the crest of a little ridge, he saw a many-peaked glowing yellow-green edifice rising, mountainous in the distance, with wide, open flaps revealing the intricately webbed interior— almost beautiful, seen thus from outside.

Most of the remaining distance lay across an undulating plain, on which he could make better speed; while the six Lil-bro, swinging above with their burden, urged him to greater effort.

But he needed no coaxing. "Hurry, hurry, hurry!" that mysterious voice within him repeated and still repeated.

At first it was so faint and far-away that he could not be sure. But he thought—would almost have sworn—that there were three short whistle blasts.

His heart pounding fiercely, he pushed on. Surely, he had but imagined! And then he stopped short, and listened. The sound was repeated: three short blasts, and a pause, and again three short blasts, remote but unmistakable. S. O. S!

"Do you hear? Hear that?" he shrieked to the Lil-bro. But they fluttered low, and answered in babbling surprise. And all at once he remembered that they were deaf to the whistle tones.

"That's them! By Jove, it's Eunice—or maybe Earle! They're in trouble—bad trouble!" he told himself; and pressed forward in a panic.

As he panted on his way, sometimes stumbling over stumps or stones in his heedless hurry, the signals were repeated...repeated at regular intervals...repeated so often that Dave realized that there were two whistles. "The good Lord help them!" he thought. "They're in some awful mess, and calling me!"

Gradually the hive drew nearer, with the outlines of fantastic luminous sierras against the unfamiliar constellations. The detested hive-odors were borne to Dave in fetid whiffs: the vinegar-like sour smell, and the stench as of a menagerie. And then, as he came still nearer, new sounds dinned upon him: at first a vague indistinguishable distant roaring, which gradually resolved itself into a combination of howling, shrieking and wailing, and rose and fell in irregular waves, and gave the impression of a multitude shouting. But all the time, cutting through this din at intervals of a few seconds, the whistle signal recurred: three shorts and a pause three shorts and a pause...three shorts and a pause three shorts...

Almost with his last energies, Dave strained forward. Even so, a long time seemed to go by—a cruelly long time—before the hive-walls rose sheer above him. And only then, when a mere hundred yards separated him from his goal, could he make out any clear words amid the commotion. "Rantangle! Rantangle! Rantangle...! Rantangle! Rantangle! Rantangle!"

Suddenly he understood. Frantically he waved to the Lil-bro to put the searchlight down near a large open flap.

They meanwhile were swinging about in such excitement that he feared they would drop their precious freight. Awed at their nearness to their deadly foe, they rose and fell rose and fell wheeled about aimlessly, approached the hive and receded: as if trying hard to fit their courage to the demands upon it.

Momentarily Dave's eyes were distracted to the hive. From somewhere within the tangle of webs on the floor, a savage bawling burst out, and a number of figures swept into sight and disappeared: Ugwugs, all of them, their squat, heavy bodies moved to some unusual exertion, while behind the rearmost a small two-armed shape hung with its head bumping against the floor.

At this Dave's comrades let out a long-drawn shriek. At the same time, from within, the whistle blasts burst forth once more: three shorts and a pause three shorts and a pause...three shorts and a pause to be lost amid a storm of voices, "Rantangle! Rantangle! Rantangle!"

The sight of their slain fellow may have been what goaded the Lil-bro to a fury overcoming their terror. As of one will, they flew low in obedience to Dave's directions, and let their burden gently down at the hive entrance. But they acted swiftly, and once the searchlight had touched the ground, they dropped the ropes as if these were poisoned, and whizzed skyward with the speed of creatures pursued. And then, after a moment, one of them came streaking back, and called to Dave, who was already struggling with the searchlight, "Make speed, O Wingless

One! Make speed! We will wait for you in the air! May the Shining One bless you!"

Dave, as he struggled to install the searchlight on its swinging pivot and adjust the batteries, knew how precious was every second. If the Ugwugs were to see him now—if they were to attack—all would be lost.

Again the S. O. S., coming at shorter, more urgent intervals. Again that savage "Rantangle! Rantangle! Rantangle," accompanied by yells, shouts, screeches, bellowings of glee, and howls of terror. Then all at once Dave saw two pairs of phosphorescent greenish eyes staring at him from behind a web ladder. Two squat blue-black bodies started toward him. Two horns were aimed at him on long projecting heads, while bear-like growls came from two throats.

The distance, a good city block at first, narrowed to half, a quarter as the monsters bore down upon their prey. But with a final furious wrench, Dave thrust the last battery into place, and pulled the switch.

A blaze of light...two agonized screams...and both monsters began staggering away; then simultaneously pitched over, and lay quivering and helpless.

Attracted by the commotion, half a dozen Ugwugs instantly rushed forward; and within a few seconds all had been disposed of.

Then, following his pre-arranged plan, Dave began to turn the long penetrating rays about the hive in great sweeps and curves. Particularly, he shot them level with the floor, where they stabbed through the green-yellow translucency of the webs as through glass. Immediately the cries of "Rantangle! Rantangle! Rantangle!" ceased, to be succeeded by a bellowing confusion of noises, as of a stampede of cattle. A mad rush of Ugwugs burst into view—pushing and crowding, scrambling over one another, beating against one another in their panic to escape. Upon them all Dave turned the purging beams. And all howled and collapsed.

Then he flashed the rays into the webs above, so as to catch any monster who had sought refuge on high. And a series of screams was followed after several seconds by heavy thumps.

A minute later, as he switched the rays back to the floor level, he heard a sound unlike that of the Ugwugs. Once more the whistle call! But not the dread three shorts!

Three longs and a short. Then a pause. And again three longs and a short. The code signal "I'm coming!"

He had scarcely had time to flick his own whistle to his lips when, from behind a confusion of webs, two figures shot forward. He had no eyes at all for the man; but tottered like a drunkard and could barely hold his balance as his arms opened to receive the woman's reeling, throbbing, hysterical form.

*　　*　　*

"You'll never know, Dave, how desperate we were. They had us surrounded. They were closing in. In another few minutes—"

"In another few minutes," Henessey took the story out of Eunice's lips, while they all stood at the hive entrance and Dave still shot the searchlight rays up and down and right and left, "you'd have been just in time to write our epitaphs."

"I tell you, dear, it was a miracle from heaven," Eunice went on, "when we saw that light and the Ugwugs yelled and began dropping all around us. We knew at once, of course it was the *Shooting Star's* searchlight—it couldn't have been anything else. And oh, it was just like seeing God's hand reaching out for us. With the light to guide us, we couldn't help finding you."

Unashamedly Eunice wiped a tear from her wet, red face; while Dave, operating the searchlight with one hand, reached over gently with the other, and patted her on the shoulder.

Even as he did so, his attention was diverted by a series of cries; and Go-glabbo, Tintle and Glarr, who in their panic had been racing in circles, came running out of the depths of the hive; rushed to him with screams of relief; and clung to him as to a life raft.

"Thank heaven, thank heaven some of them did escape," said Eunice, as she tried to soothe the fluttering, torn, bruised creatures. "I thought those Ugwugs were going to kill them all."

"What do you think, old fellow? Those devils supposed we were Lil-bro too," Henessey reported. "That's why they wanted to kill us, making their rantangle because some of their crazy hunters went out last night and forget to come back."

"I'll be hanged! Now I see!" burst out Dave, as a dull distant thud announced that one more Ugwug had fallen out of the web. "Then I'm the cause of the rantangle! Yes, folks, I'm the cause! I started it all last night by killing twenty Ugwugs. When they didn't show up in the hive this morning, the Lil-bro got the blame!"

"We always get the blame," murmured Glarr, who was huddling close to Eunice. "No matter what happens, we always get the blame."

A distant rumbling and roaring from within the hive was gradually dying down. "Hope we've about wiped out those crawling horrors," Dave remarked. "Still, I'm not for taking any chance. How about going in to clean up the hive?"

The others looked at him dumbly.

"I'd have done it right away," he went on, "if the darned searchlight wasn't so heavy. Besides, I had to stay outside so that none of those rogues could work his way behind me. Here, Earle, lend me a hand."

Aided by Henessey and the three Lil-bro, Dave bore the searchlight inside the hive, where from time to time he put it down upon its pivot, and switched its rays in every direction. On each occasion, he was rewarded by a series of growls followed by thuds and thumps, and knew that new victims, concealed amid the mazes of the web, had fallen to their doom.

Meanwhile all the little party felt like spectators in a sacked city. Eunice shuddered, and kept close to Dave, trying not to see the ugly shapes sprawled all about them in fantastic attitudes of death, some crushed and shapeless, some twisted into knots, some flat on their backs with their six arms clutching at the air like overturned dead beetles, some lying on their sides with their heads protruding on their distendable necks, but all with greenish eyes that stared blankly, as if in wonder and surprise. Now, for the first time, their rear and forward faces had precisely the same expressions. The young and the old, the commoners and the Webnates were mingled indiscriminately in that vast mausoleum; but nowhere did the intruders see a live Ugwug.

Now and then, however, some Lil-bro did come rushing to join the group from some hiding-place amid the maze of webs—some poor terrified creature fortunate enough to have concealed itself from the mobs. Eventually these rescued ones numbered twenty-five—apparently all that had escaped the fury of the worst "rantangle" in many cycles.

Not until they had crossed the mile-long reaches of the hive did they start back to the entrance. They made the return trip in a silence that seemed weird and unnatural, the great webs swinging above them bare and deserted, their spirals and ladders and intricate whorls ripped and broken in scores of places where their former occupants had torn them in falling. Meanwhile the rays continued to cut with sword stabs through the dim, faintly glowing distances. And in the eyes of the Lil-bro, an even stranger light began to shine—the glitter of a gradually growing realization, the awareness of a freedom they had never expected to regain.

CHAPTER TWENTY-NINE

AS THE BLUE SUN surmounted the western sierras, the Lil-bro flashed and shimmered in the light, dipping, soaring, looping and pirouetting in buoyant scores. But they did not sing as usual; an excitement an uneasiness was evident as their eyes turned repeatedly toward the rolling northwestern ridges.

An hour or two went by; then, with shrill joyous cries, the whole flock began speeding northwest. Six flying dots, with a sparkling mote suspended beneath them,. had risen above the maze of hills; and those six dots, which would have been no more than dust-specks to human eyes, were instantly recognized as half a dozen fellow Lil-bro, who were carrying the big light of the Wingless One.

"The Wingless One! He comes! Our brothers! They come!" shouted the foremost of the flying host, as he spurted ahead with the speed of an airliner. And then, after a moment. "There are three Wingless Ones! And a crowd of our people! A crowd of our people, all without wings!"

Five minutes later, Lo-klantho was fluttering above the trail where Dave trudged beside Eunice, Henessey and the wingless Lil-bro. He let out a series of excited squawks; loud

ly greeted his freed kinsfolk; and told them they would be welcome to remain among his people forever. And they, some weeping and some laughing but all with jubilant cries, accepted the invitation. Among them, with happy shouts, Lo-klantho recognized two of his own tribesmen, who had been kidnapped four or five cycles before.

Then, turning to Dave, Lo-klantho learned of all the night's happenings, and of the destruction of the Ugwugs. Nevertheless, though he rejoiced, he did not seem satisfied.

"It is a great and noble deed, O Wingless One," he commended, as he half flew and half hopped at Dave's side. It is such a feat as we Lil-bro have long dreamed of. It will go down in the memory of our people for thousands of cycles; mothers will tell it to their nestlings before they learn to use their wings. Even so—though this, unhappily, you could not foresee—it has made our problem harder than ever."

"How is that possible—"Dave started to demand. But Lo-klantho mournfully cut him short.

"If we knew that you had killed the last Ugwug in the hive, then truly we could be glad. But out of so many thousands, surely some escaped into the woods. It is these, no matter how few, that we must fear."

"Why must we fear a few: even if they did escape?"

After hiding from the light by day in dark hollows and caves and their own web-huts, they will find their way to other Ugwug hives. All Ugwugs being bitterly vengeful, the other hive-dwellers will come in great numbers to destroy us. There will be no escape. Several big Ugwug hives are not much further off than the one you attacked—at least near enough for their inhabitants to reach us and return in the course of a night."

"But how can they know just who slew their brothers?"

Lo-klantho uttered a low displeased croak. "Wingless One, you do not use your wits. Are we not the nearest Lil-bro? Will they not learn that the twenty lost hunters were slain near our village? Are the twenty dead Ugwugs not even now lying where they fell? No matter what speed we make to bury them, their kinsmen's keen noses will smell them out."

"Well, in that case," snorted Dave, his eyes flashing challenge, what's to stop me from killing them all with my searchlight?"

"If you knew just when they would come, Wingless One, you might indeed slay them. But this time they may strike from behind Yon cannot turn your big light everywhere all at once."

Gloomily Dave nodded.

"I'll tell you what," he offered. "Just lead me to their hives, and I'll wipe them out, the way I did the first one!"

"I admire your courage, Wingless One," approved Lo-klantho, shaking his head sadly. "But it is not that simple. This time you were favored by the Shining One—you caught the Ugwugs in the middle of a rantangle, when their minds were on nothing else. Even the guards had left their posts."

"You bet they had," affirmed Henessey, who had just come up along with Eunice. "Why, I saw some of those so-called Guardians of the Hive right in the thick of the ran

tangle, murdering the very Lil-bro they were supposed to protect."

"The Guardians of the Hive were egging the others on," added Eunice.

"You see, Wingless One," pointed out Lo-klantho, "the conditions were unusual. In some other hive, you would not even have the chance to put your light in place. You would be caught, and die in torment. No! as I consider you a friend and a brother, I would not let you take that risk!"

He fell into silence, his head drooped in meditation.

But when he looked up, his eyes flamed with a momentary light. "Have you heard of the island of Laro?" he asked.

"Laro?"

The name struck an echo in Dave's mind, but it was a few seconds before he could identify it.

"Why, yes," he at last recalled. "Go-glabbo did mention it. Isn't it—isn't it a country where there are no Ugwugs?"

"Yes, indeed, Wingless One! The only country where there are no Ugwugs. It is a large island in the middle of the wide salt waters, as far to the sunrise as we can fly between the rising of the red sun and the setting of the blue. Not being able to fly or swim, the Ugwugs have never reached it."

"Don't they make any craft to cross over?" Henessey asked.

"They make nothing except webs. And that is the protection that the Shining One has given us. There are many Lil-bro on that island, but room for many more. Our people have often talked of going there."

"And why haven't you gone?" asked Eunice.

Lo-klantho wrinkled his seamed old face until it looked more aged than ever.

"My friend, have you never known what it is to love your home? My people love theirs, where their fathers have lived for more cycles than we have scales on our bodies. Hence few have really wanted to go. I have always foreseen, however, the time when we would leave for Laro."

"And can your people fly that far?"

"Their wings, thanks be to the Shining One! are strong. They can fly that far."

Lo-klantho paused; narrowed his tired old eyes, which had lost their fire; and lowered his voice.

"However, we would not desert you, O Wingless Ones. Nor would we forsake our comrades, whom you have rescued. Yet they cannot fly across the wide salt waters to the island of Laro. And we cannot carry them that far. Nor can we remain here to be slain. So I know not what is to be done."

For several minutes, all trooped on in thoughtful silence. Then, with a triumphant clap, Dave brought his hands together. "By Jove, I have it!"

"Have what, Wingless One? A way for us all to leave together?"

"Well, no, though we might manage that in the space ship— if we had to. But I tell you, it goes against the grain to run away from those Ugwugs. Would you and your people not sooner stay here, Lo-klantho?"

"It would be a mercy from the Shining One. But that, my friends, cannot be," testified the leader, with wings that drooped sadly.

"Sure, the old boy's right. It's nothing but a pipe dream," concurred Henessey, on the side.

"Well, maybe it's a pipe dream, but I'm going to try!" asserted Dave, sharply taking up the challenge. And then, to Lo-klantho, "Can you and your people sleep in the trees a few nights more, nesting where no Ugwugs can catch you?"

"It would be hard, O Wingless One. Nevertheless, we can do it. But why must we suffer this torment—"

As if not hearing the uncompleted question, Dave had started off abruptly. "Come on, old fellow!" he shot out at Henessey. "Lend me a hand! There's work to do!"

*　　*　　*

The blue sun and the white and the red arose and set seven times while the two men, assisted by Eunice and many of the Lil-bro, labored with scarcely more than the minimum time for eating and sleeping. Their first task was performed inside the *Shooting Star,* where they dismantled the miles of wiring that had been part of the ship's lighting, heating, and communications system. The wires, under Dave's directions, were taken to the vicinity of the Lil-bro settlement, and were made to encircle it completely, running low through the bushes, and hidden in the weeds and shrubs in a way that it was almost impossible to detect. Next Dave robbed the *Shooting Star* of the hundreds of high-power light bulbs contained in the various compartments, and supplemented this supply with the thousands of reserve bulbs meant for replacement and emergency purposes. And when at last these globes were all in place, he set the vessel's atomic engines to vibrating, turning the power into electrical energy by means of generators provided for that purpose by the ship's builders.

"Wingless Ones, what are you doing?" demanded Lo-klantho repeatedly. "I fear you waste our time. It is hard to nest in the woods. Soon my people will tire, and come down, and then the Ugwugs will get them."

"Soon the Ugwugs will get them!" echoed the Knowing Ones, dolefully.

"Never fear, they will not get them," Dave reassured his hearers. But though hundreds of the bird-people fluttered about his head, trilling and chirping and busily asking questions, he refused to answer any query before the eighth day.

Then he summoned the entire community to a cluster of trees near the settlement, not far from where the *Shooting Star* had fallen.

"My people cry out, the Wingless Ones keep us here, and tell us not what for, and any night the Ugwugs may come," complained Lo-klantho. "Why must you keep us here, O Wingless One?"

Hardly had he finished when a sudden simultaneous exclamation, a cry as of multitudes of startled wild-fowl, broke out from the Lil-bro. In the bushes, and from the limbs of trees, and all around the settlement in a great circle, thousands of electric orbs had burst into brilliance at unbroken intervals of only a few feet, dominated by the dazzling eye of the searchlight.

"By glory, I'll give you credit, Dave," conceded Henessey, while the pandemonium of the bird-folk still rang in their ears. "It works! It really works!"

"What have you done, Wingless One?" demanded Lo-klantho.

"Oh, nothing much, except to surround this whole place with wires, arranged so that anyone pushing against any of them even. slightly at any point will automatically set off a switch, turning on the lights in the whole circle."

The flame of half incredulous joy brightened on the old Lil-bro's furrowed face.

"But how long will it work, my friends?" he asked a little doubtfully.

"The atom power will last long. And before it's exhausted we'll dam the stream down there,"—he pointed toward the cascading river—"and harness water-power to give us electricity forever. Do you not see, Lo-klantho, what that will mean?"

Joy had given place to exultation on the leader's weather-beaten countenance.

"Yes, truly, my friends, I see! I see that when the Ugwugs come at night, they will push against the wire, which they cannot make out in the dark, and then it will be light everywhere—and there will be no more Ugwugs!"

"And then it will be light everywhere—and there will be no more Ugwugs!" a flutelike chorus triumphantly took up the call.

"O our blessed friends," acknowledged Lo-klantho, half inarticulate with tears of happiness, "the Shining One has sent you from the sky to save us forever from the Ugwugs!"

As soon as they could escape from the rejoicing crowd, the earth-trio hastened back to the *Shooting Star*. And there Dave stood with one arm about a moist-eyed young woman, and one hand grasping that of the other man. "From now on it will be a better life," he foretold. And as they saw the myriad-ridged world all gorgeous-hued in the splendor of the three suns,

Henessey warmly returned Dave's clasp, the girl looked up at her lover with brimming trustful eyes, and a rush of emotion almost choked the three.

Meanwhile, with a flight like the hummingbird's, multitudes of flashing and gleaming creatures dipped and soared and pirouetted and chased one another and sang their songs of everlasting gladness in the rich changeful light of the triple suns.

THE END

If you've enjoyed this book, you will not want to miss these terrific titles…

ARMCHAIR SCI-FI & HORROR DOUBLE NOVELS, $12.95 each

D-121   **THE GENIUS BEASTS** by Frederik Pohl
            THIS WORLD IS TABOO by Murray Leinster

D-122   **THE COSMIC LOOTERS** by Edmond Hamilton
            WANDL THE INVADER by Ray Cummings

D-123   **ROBOT MEN OF BUBBLE CITY** by Rog Phillips
            DRAGON ARMY by William Morrison

D-124   **LAND BEYOND THE LENS** by S. J. Byrne
            DIPLOMAT-AT-ARMS by Keith Laumer

D-125   **VOYAGE OF THE ASTEROID, THE** by Laurence Manning
            REVOLT OF THE OUTWORLDS by Milton Lesser

D-126   **OUTLAW IN THE SKY** by Chester S. Geier
            LEGACY FROM MARS by Raymond Z. Gallun

D-127   **THE GREAT FLYING SAUCER INVASION** by Geoff St. Reynard
            THE BIG TIME by Fritz Leiber

D-128   **MIRAGE FOR PLANET X** by Stanley Mullen
            POLICE YOUR PLANET by Lester del Rey

D-129   **THE BRAIN SINNERS** by Alan E. Nourse
            DEATH FROM THE SKIES by A. Hyatt Verrill

D-139   **CRY CHAOS** by Dwight V. Swain
            THE DOOR THROUGH SPACE By Marion Zimmer Bradley

ARMCHAIR SCIENCE FICTION CLASSICS, $12.95 each

C-55   **UNDER THE TRIPLE SUNS**
         by Stanton A. Coblentz

C-56   **STONE FROM THE GREEN STAR**
         by Jack Williamson

C-57   **ALIEN MINDS**
         by E. Everett Evans

ARMCHAIR MASTERS OF SCIENCE FICTION SERIES, $16.95 each

G-13   **SCIENCE FICTION GEMS, Vol. Seven**
         Jack Vance and others

G-14   **HORROR GEMS, Vol. Seven**
         Robert Bloch and others